THE HAITIAN CHRONICLES BY DOUGLAS TURNER WARD

PLAY I: THE RISE OF TOUSSAINT L'OUVERTURE

PLAY II: THE FALL OF TOUSSAINT L'OUVERTURE

PLAY III: DESSALINES

Contents

THE NEGRO ENSEMBLE COMPANY
5

PREFACE BY GUS EDWARDS
7

PLAY I: THE RISE OF TOUSSAINT L'OUVERTURE
19

ACT ONE
23

ACT TWO
97

ACT THREE
149

PLAY II: THE FALL OF TOUSSAINT L'OUVERTURE
183

ACT ONE
187

ACT TWO
227

ACT THREE
257

ACT FOUR
277

PLAY III: DESSALINES
321

ACT ONE
323

ACT TWO
347

AFTERWORD
371

THE NEGRO ENSEMBLE COMPANY

Since Gus Edward's Preface to *Play 1: The Rise of Toussaint L'Ouverture* includes biographical information about me, I am using this space to highlight The Negro Ensemble Company's work and impact on world culture and especially on giving me the space and encouragement to create *The Haitian Chronicles*.

The Negro Ensemble Company was founded in 1967 by Douglas Turner Ward, Robert Hooks, Gerald Krone and a host of supporting players. Since opening its doors on Second Avenue and St. Marks Place in New York City, this legendary ensemble has introduced and honed the skills of such artists as Mary Alice, Ethel Ayler, Angela Bassett, Graham Brown, Rosco Lee Brown, Norman Bush. Adolph Caesar, L. Scott Caldwell, Godfrey Cambridge, Rosalind Cash, Marilyn Coleman, Todd Davis, David Downing, Bebe Drake, Judyann Elder, Giancarlo Esposito, Lawrence Fishburne, Frances Foster, Arthur French, Carl Gordon, Moses Gunn, Sherman Hemsley, Dean Irby, Samuel L. Jackson, Bill Jay, David Keith, Gil Lewis, Tony Major, Lon Meyers, Barbara Montgomery, Garrett Morris, Denise Nicholas, Ron O'Neal, Rosco Orman, Shauneille Perry, Phylicia Rashad, LaTanya Richardson, Esther Rolle, Roxie

Roker, Richard Roundtree, Clarice Taylor, Glenn Turman, Seret Scott, Michelle Shea, Cotter Smith, Joyce Sylvester, Denzel Washington, Charles Weldon, Samm-Art Williams, Hattie Winston, Lynn Whitfield, Allie Woods, and the list goes on.

A few of the classic plays produced by the NEC include: *A Soldier's Play* by Charles Fuller (Pulitzer Prize), *Ceremonies in Dark Old Men* by Lonne Elder III (Drama Desk Award), *HOME* by Samm-Art Williams (2 Tony Award Nominations), *The Sty of the Blind Pig* by Phillip Hayes Dean (Dramatist Guild Award and Drama Desk Award), *Daughters of the Mock* by Judi Ann Mason, *Nevis Mountain Dew* by Steve Carter (OBIE Award), *First Breeze of Summer* by Leslie Lee (OBIE Award and Tony Nomination), *Zooman and the Sign* by Charles Fuller (OBIE Award and Tony Nomination), *The River Niger* by Joseph Walker (Tony Award, OBIE Award and Drama Desk Award), *The Great MacDaddy* by Paul Carter Harrison (OBIE Award), *Dream on Monkey Mountain* by Derek Walcott (OBIE Award), and *Happy Ending/ Day of Absence* by Douglas Turner Ward (OBIE Award, Drama Desk Award, and Outer Circle Critics Award).

PREFACE
BY
GUS EDWARDS

Some years ago, when Doug Ward asked me to read his long gestating, long in development work *The Haitian Chronicles* I'm not exactly sure what I expected. I knew that Doug had been a Jack-of-all-trades theatre practitioner who at various times during his tenure as Artistic Director of The Negro Ensemble Company (The NEC), a company he had co-founded in 1967 with actor Robert Hooks and theatrical manager Gerald Krone, had functioned as an actor, producer, director, playwright, dramaturg and inspirational guiding light for any number of young aspiring black or African American theatre hopefuls. But as he always explained to anyone who was interested, he was a writer first, last and foremost. He must've said that to me more than a dozen times in the early years when we first became acquainted and began to know each other.

"As soon as I learned my ABC's it seems that I fell in love with words as a means of expression and ultimately words as art, I guess. This led to me becoming an avid reader. I began to devour books wherever I found them." *

This love of words led him into a career in Journalism, sports writing primarily, after which he moved on to becoming an editor for the left-wing newspaper *The Daily Worker*. This was in 1953. Ward was 23 and politically quite active.

"My politicization began with the realization of my relationship as a black person to the dominant white society. How it was designed to suppress all black attempts at self-worth, self-sufficiency and self-pride. I had already read enough black history to realize that there was nothing natural about the role blacks were assigned to play in the American Society of the time. It angered me and stirred me up and made me want to do something about it. So, I became active in all sorts of political groups."

This political activism brought him to New York where together with his friends Lorraine Hansberry and Lonne Elder he became a member of the Progressive Party campaigning for Henry Wallace, a Third-Party candidate for the presidency running against Truman in 1948. Ward, despite his youth, was so politically active that he started attracting attention to himself from the opposition.

"I had just reached eighteen and couldn't even vote. But here I was a regional leader in New York politics for young progressives in that election campaign. That was for three years or so. There I was on the street corners in Harlem leading and fighting for political candidates I couldn't even vote for."

It was during this time that he began to explore the idea of writing in a dramatic form. It began with short satirical sketches.

"I wrote them just to lighten up the heavy political raps. It wasn't anything serious, just some stuff for fun. Then I wrote *The Star of Liberty*, a short play about Nat Turner that was performed before an audience of five thousand. The response to *The Star of Liberty* at this particular rally is the thing that set my course. Now I knew that I not only wanted to be a sportswriter but I wanted to write creatively as well."

But before he could explore this new avenue of interest Ward ran afoul of the Selective Service Bureau who accused him of dodging the draft and had him arrested.

"This came as a result of my political activity as a Left-Wing activist youth leader. This was the time of anti-communism preceding Joe McCarthy. I was 19 or 20 and eligible for the draft.

I registered with the Draft Board in New Orleans then moved to New York. I was a kid and the last thing I had in mind was stuff like what was happening with my status at the Draft Board. I was moving around a lot. Hardly stationary. So, I wasn't keeping up with any damn Draft Board. So, they would be sending forms to my parents' home in New Orleans and my father would be trying to find out where I was so he could send them to me. Anyway, this all led to the fact that they ultimately sent me an induction notice which I didn't know about. In fact, my father had to physically come to New York to deliver it. When he did, I filled out the paper and sent it back to them. Then right after I turned 21, they came and arrested me claiming that I was evading the draft. It was ridiculous.

"If I was trying to evade the draft why would I fill out the forms giving them my New York address where they could find and arrest me? The truth is they did it to take me out of circulation due to my outspoken activities against the Korean War and also to get me away from the organization."

Ward was sentenced to three years in prison. The case was appealed and he was told to go back to New Orleans to await the outcome of his appeal. While awaiting the outcome, Ward wrote his first full length play, *The Trial of Willie McGee*, based on the infamous true case of a black man (Willie McGee) who was executed in 1951 for supposedly raping a white woman. The case became a flashpoint for the burgeoning Civil Rights movement and was covered in various newspapers around the country. And it was from these reports and his imagination that Ward wrote his play. This was how he described it:

"It was a magnum opus of a play, four acts in a script that ran damn near 6 hours. I knew nothing about dramatic construction or the practicality of presenting it. It was a subject that I seized upon and I became passionately involved in writing it. I mean, I was 21 years old, so I was writing not so much out of my imagination but out of the fabric and texture and the lived experience of being part of the community. In other words, it was true to what I knew and saw. And I had managed to put it down with a fair amount of accuracy."

Right after this his case was reviewed by the United States Supreme Court, which ruled in Ward's favor.

"The whole thing was a setup right from the start and the Justices at the Supreme Court saw right through it and dismissed the Selective Service's case out of hand."

So, he was free once again to pursue his life's goals without the shadow of the Draft Board hovering over him. He returned to New York and with his friends Hansberry and Elder did a reading of his Willie McGee play at the Hotel Theresa in Harlem.

This reading is credited with inspiring both Lorraine and Lonne, who had been aspiring poets, to become playwrights themselves and ultimately contributing *A Raisin in the Sun* and *Ceremonies in Dark Old Men* to the canon of American and African American theatre. So already Ward was functioning as an inspirational leader as well as an artistic one.

I knew all this about Doug Ward and much more when he gave me *The Chronicles* to read, yet I didn't know what to expect.

I had both seen and read all of his previously produced works; namely: *Happy Ending, Day of Absence, Brotherhood, The Redeemer* and *The Reckoning*. And except for *The Reckoning*, all were short plays written in a comedic or satirical vein.

Now he had decided to write not one or two but three plays on the subject of the Haitian Revolution with the possibility of a fourth waiting in the wings. What would these works be like? I had no idea. I guess I sort of imagined that they would be intelligently constructed dramatizations of the events and individuals who were the primary architects of the revolution. What I got when I sat down to read the works was a whole different plate of fish. A dish I wasn't prepared for at all. A large, slashing, epic sized spectacle that would smash, deconstruct, reorganize and completely reconstruct my idea of theatre and its possibilities henceforth both as literature and as a performing art.

The Chronicles is comprised of three plays but it's *Play I: The Rise of Toussaint L'Ouverture* that sets the tone and template for all the ones to follow. Even the single character play *Dessalines*, because, in spite of the size of its cast and mode of its narrative, it still requires the same expanded view and close attention to details and surrender to its sweeping sense of scale and rhetoric that the other works require and demand.

Preface

The first thing one has to do when approaching this work is to cast aside all notion of theatre as we have previously known and experienced it. Because, with *The Rise of Toussaint L'Ouverture* we're breaking new ground, exploring virgin territory in a way the stage space is being configured and utilized. It is being utilized not just as a confined terrain where individuals (members of the dramatis personae) meet and interact. But as a world representing islands in the Caribbean, battlefields, ballrooms, bedrooms, decks and holds of ships, prison cells, the French Court and a whole host of other locations and locales. That alone should clue us to the scope and ambition of the work. It begins with a description of the set.

"A vast stage dominated by a gigantic WHEEL that is equipped with devices which can swivel, opening and closing to suggest the changes of locales and also providing a dramatic metaphor for the entire dramatization."

Also, within the context of this first play we are introduced to a vast array of characters who put in an appearance, disappear only to return again sometimes in a different guise or attitude with each appearance stripping away the façade and revealing more about that character and his or her role in the revolution. But by far the most fascinating is the development of the title character, Toussaint L'Ouverture, a dark-skinned man of small physical stature (according to some historians) who, through his political and military genius grew into recorded legend as a colossus who stood 10 feet tall, fathered 16 children and spearheaded the only slave revolt that led to the founding of a republic. He was known as the slave who defeated Napoleon and was sometimes himself called "The Black Napoleon."

"I was born a slave but nature gave me the soul of a free man."

Within the course of this first play we witness his growth from shrewd voice of reason to full-fledged revolutionary. The play ends in Act 3 with Toussaint standing center stage while a voice intones:

"There stands this Spartacus, the Black whose coming Reynal prophesied—whose destiny it is to avenge the outrage perpetuated against his race. This savior of constituted authority and protector of Blacks and Whites alike."

When was the last time we have witnessed that kind of theatrical embrace? For me personally, almost never. Sometimes in the opera but hardly ever on the so-called "legitimate stage," even when viewing productions of Shakespeare's classics. They're always reduced and herded into narrow confines, including when productions are presented outdoors where there should supposedly be no limitations or barriers . . .

Now, for a very long time I have held the opinion that American Theatre, the American Stage, has lacked large scale ambitions due to the fact that it is and has been hobbled and hamstrung by an emphasis and overemphasis on economic concerns. Hobbled in a way that tampers down imagination and emasculates expanded ambition.

How many times have I heard Artistic Directors iterate and reiterate that based on budgetary restrictions they cannot consider plays with nine or more characters no matter the excellence of the work. And seen the playwrights, understanding this reality and wanting to see their works produced, turn out plays that fit snugly into this tunnel like requirement.

Thus, the proliferation of two-character and single character plays. Some of which are quite excellent but nonetheless small in ambition and execution. I remember once sitting with some fellow playwrights lamenting this state of things and going through Tennessee Williams' *A Streetcar Named Desire* and eliminating all the characters not directly related to the main thrust and action of the drama and commenting on how impoverished the work would be. But sadly, these are the times and conditions we're generally forced to live with and accept. Even in *A Raisin in the Sun*, with its few characters, I have seen productions where the moving men in the last scene were eliminated due to budgetary considerations. Curiously and ironically, one of those moving men was played by Douglas Turner Ward in the original Broadway production . . .

My contention here being that with this kind of reduction, this narrow concern with practicalities and economics have had a deleterious effect on the theatrical imagination and ambition of its creators and practitioners. So much so that the American stage is the poorer for it . . . It has been said many times that you can't write a masterpiece on the head of a pin, and I fully agree. And that's why I applaud and enthusiastically support the imaginative bravery Doug Ward, who had been producing theatre with limited resources for so many years, displays in ignoring all of the producing realities and commonsensical concerns that must've entered his mind while conceiving and working on this trilogy. How many times must he have said to himself: "This isn't possible? This is insane. This can't or will not be done. This just doesn't make sense economically. This just isn't practical." I have no idea. I'm just guessing, I'm just speculating. But when it became time to weigh the practical against the imaginative, imagination and ambition won and we're all the richer for it artistically speaking.

 Ward said, "After the first play, I was satisfied in realizing my own intentions and was content that the work existed even though at that early stage I knew the fact of it being produced was remote. Why? Because of the sheer scope of it. That one play (*The Rise of Toussaint*, etc.) is just so goddamned massive that it would require I don't know how much money and resources to produce. I figured that when I was finished with the whole thing that perhaps I could get them published in book form."

 He is right because thus far the works have not been produced. Some organizations have considered it but the sheer size and daring of the first play, a play with 80 or so speaking parts and an innumerable number of set pieces including life sized marionettes, has discouraged their intentions and I understand that. It is a work of overwhelming ambition that hurtles forward into our consciousness without even a sidelong glance at the realities of the marketplace. Ward had a story to tell. A big story. The story of the most successful slave revolt in the Americas. A revolution that eliminated slavery and established The Republic of Haiti. It is an enormous story with many issues, ideas, philosophies and ramifications that resonates from then even to now. It involves questions about the human condition that have haunted civilized man since time immemorial. To tackle such large-scale ideas and incidents on anything less than the largest canvas possible to my mind, would've been timid and cowardly on Ward's part. It would've also been insulting to both the subject matter and to the history that surrounds it. And this is as it should be.

Large subjects require large ambition and a large talent or talents to fulfill that ambition. And this is what one encounters with *The Rise of Toussaint*. A work that is writ large in every way. From the hurtling force of its narrative, to the many, many characters brought to life via sharp biting language and gnarly confrontations. At every point this is a work that challenges, threatens, and makes enormous demands on the producing entity, the artists involved, the critics attempting to assess its value and its audience attempting to deal with it on any level. This is a work that insists on being viewed and more important experienced on its own terms as well as its own large-scale ambitions.

I use the word "experience" deliberately because this is a work not meant to be viewed from a dispassionate perspective but attended and experienced up close and from within. This is a work that confronts us, embraces us, pushes us away, attacks us, then pulls us back to its bosom before pushing us out again. I remember putting the script down halfway through the first act in order to get some emotional and intellectual respite from all that was being hurled at me. All the activity, the sensations, the splendors and the cruelties, the harsh logic and pragmatic rationales, the atrocities and the tenderness combined in ways I have never seen or experienced before on a stage. And this is just from reading it as a literary work. It is also difficult, unyielding, and continuously unrelenting.

It begins with the sound of drums, screams and the sight of two naked Mulatto men (race and color distinctions are crucially important in the context of the work) being cruelly stretched to death; then it moves to a man addressing the audience in arrogant and obscene terms. And then beat by beat and moment to moment scenes of both a visual and auditory nature begin to overtake the stage and our senses. They come at us without warning or preparation, requiring us to mentally and emotionally adjust to each new assault in a matter of seconds and sometimes even less. The stage comes alive with any number of women and men doing a multiplicity of things, working, fighting, eating, arguing, making love, and sometimes just standing still meditating on the state of their lives and the fate of the times in which they live. The women are frequently seen in various states of elegant and provocative outfits functioning as they did in the historical time of the play or in their other role as classical chorus voices, setting the context of the events and keeping the narrative moving in a forward motion.

To create this enlightening and sometime monstrous work for the stage Ward had to draw on, assemble and utilize every bit of stage convention known to western dramaturgy including Direct address, Choral embellishments, Choreography, Dramatic dialogue scenes, Prayerful incantations, Chants, Music and sometimes just pregnant eloquent silence. And all this he has had to corral into one organized style that doesn't clash and then collapse in on itself. He often described himself as Brechtian in his theatrical outlook and aesthetic. Even going so far as to name his theatre company The Negro Ensemble and modeling it after Brecht's Berliner Ensemble. But with this work he transcends the Brechtian style and creates something more formally classical in order to tell this story of war, revolution and all its terrible consequences.

So that in the final analysis the work, stylistically speaking, is a hybrid of any number of theatrical conventions and cinematic ones as well including Eisenstein's constructivist montage technique but reconfiguring it for the stage in ingenious ways. So, despite its references to classical Greek and African theatrical traditions this is a modernist perhaps even post-modernist work in its final realization. But it does reflect Brecht's theory and practice of "Epic theatre" to explore theatre as a forum for political ideas. This is as it should be coming from a man who is both a politically aware and astute observer as well as activist and lifelong theatrical artisan.

As one goes through the play one encounters a multiplicity of thoughts, images, ideas, notations and broadsides addressing the origins of slavery in the Americas, racial division and divides, violence in extremis, shifting of political alliances along with multiple betrayals as political boundaries are crossed, re-crossed and then double crossed by the French, British and Spanish.

Yet there is also humor and sly social commentary blended into this mix of sweeping classical styled drama and down and dirty in your face assault. And sexuality, something we rarely find in Western drama, is powerfully, potently present at nearly every turn. The erotic force that can and will often command and control the behavior of powerful men is dealt with here in unapologetic and unflinching terms. And finally, there is religion, that force that has and continues to both unite and separate men into warring groups and tribes is also an integral part and principal player in this dramatic panorama; particularly Christianity with all of its convenient contradictions that allow men to commit beautiful and terrible acts in its name. That, contrasted with Voodoo as practiced in Haiti and the Caribbean at that time, makes for a very heady mix in the body politic of the events portrayed . . .

Next, we have to deal with the language of the play. It is a mix of stylized dialogue, Caribbean patois, French and Spanish words and phrases and British styled declamations, along with exotic, rhythmic chants and incantations. But then there is also poetry and blank verse added into the mix. And if there is any truth to the idea that all accomplished writers develop idiosyncratic styles in which to serve their narrative purposes this is it. Doug Ward has created the linguistic means with which to bring his large-scale human drama vividly alive. It is not unlike watching a painter, Impressionist or Pointillist or whatever discovering the brush strokes that will render his flat two-dimensional image into a three-dimensional world pulsing with life.

That the play is a political as well as historical work has been said before. Doug Ward is a political creature, which is why many years ago he changed his name from Roosevelt Ward to Douglas Turner Ward, creating a combination of two admired black leaders. Frederick Douglass, the black intellectual freedom fighter and Nat Turner, the messianic rebel leader who fought American slavery with a major revolt. So, it requires no great leap of imagination to see why he was attracted to the Revolution in Haiti (1791—1804) as the subject of the greatest literary endeavor of his life. And for 20 years and more he read, researched and wrote what would become his most ambitious and complete theatrical undertaking ... And referring back to his quote during his Willie McGee period, he has come a long way from not knowing anything about dramatic construction. Twenty years and more of attending to all aspects of theatrical presentations at The NEC prepared him for tackling this most ambitious literary/theatrical undertaking. Yes, a lot has changed but one thing remained constant and deepened over those same years and that was/is his political fervor and passion for putting it all on stage.

As of the moment, sadly, *The Haitian Chronicles* remains unproduced. But as a reading experience I find it comes vividly to life in a flowing, uninterrupted manner no amount of sophisticated stage machinery can provide, that only the theatre of the mind can produce ... One can go on ad infinitum about the oddities and innovations contained in this work but it is best to let you the reader discover its multiple riches for yourself. You have been provided with at least something of a guide and perhaps a warning about what this remarkable work contains. Now the rest is in your hands.

GUS EDWARDS is a playwright and academic who has had his plays produced in the US and abroad. He has published many books and was a professor of theatre and film at Arizona State University from 1988 to 2010. He is currently a member of their Emeritus College.

The following plays by Gus Edwards were produced by the Negro Ensemble Company: *The Offering, Black Body Blues, Weep Not for Me, Manhattan Made Me, Louie and Ophelia, Lifetimes on the Streets,* **and** *Old Phantoms.*

*All quotes are taken from audio taped interviews with Douglas Turner Ward conducted by Gus Edward

PLAY I: THE RISE OF TOUSSAINT L'OUVERTURE

Play I: The Rise of Toussaint L'Ouverture

CENTRAL CHARACTERS

ACT ONE

BOUKMAN	BIASSOU
PLANTERS	JEANNOT
CHRISTOPHE	TOUSSAINT
WOMEN'S CHORUS	BEAUVAIS
VINCENT OGE	RIGAUD
CHAVANNES JACQUE	PINCHINAT
OGE MIRABEAU	BLANCHELANDE
FRENCH OFFICIALS	ROUME
BLACK SLAVES	ST. LEGER
JEAN-FRANÇOIS	MIRABECK

ACT TWO

DAUGNY	GALBAUD
SONTHONAX	POLVEREL
OFFICIALS	WOMEN'S CHORUS
BIASSOU	LAVEAUX
JEAN-FRANÇOIS	BOUKMAN
TOUSSAINT	MACAYA
CHRISTOPHE	PIERROT
DESSALINES	MOISE

ACT THREE

TOUSSAINT	VAUBLANC
SONTHONAX	WOMEN'S CHORUS
LAVEAUX	BOUKMAN
RIGAUD	AGE
BEAUVAIS	RIGAUD
PINCHINAT	BEAUVAIS
REY	PINCHINAT
BOURDON	

ACT ONE

(AS curtain rises, steady drumming is heard. In the darkness, a piercing, bloodcurdling scream rings out. Lights slowly illuminate a vast stage dominated by a gigantic WHEEL. Extending from the WHEEL are platforms spreading out like tentacle-arms from the outer rim. These arms, positioned at upper and lower levels, provide playing space for actors. The top area of the WHEEL, ascended from the floor, also provides playing space. The WHEEL is equipped with devices which can swivel its inner ring-center— opening or closing the space to suggest changes of locales, supplying onstage entrances, exits and other possibilities.

In addition to being a variegated playing area, the WHEEL also represents a dramatic metaphor.

Upstage, left to right, a huge transparent floor to ceiling scrim covers the entire back area. It serves also as backdrop for visualizations.

The form of the play is epical—multileveled, multifaceted, moving freely in and out of time, shifting rapidly in locale, dramatizing crucial events and significant individuals, incorporating actual facts and fashioning imaginary episodes. The canvas is broad, the style is eclectic, all inclusive. The unifying concept is the inexorable progression of the historical narrative.

The drama highlights important personalities while also focusing upon the masses. The form of the play, necessarily episodic, must allow for the leisurely unfolding of scenes so as not to slight the subtle development of characters and the nuances which give events their importance.

AS lights illuminate the Stage, two completely nude MULATTO MEN imprisoned within the ringcenter of the WHEEL are being stretched gruesomely to their deaths. One cries and screams, the other, despite his pain, is mute.

Atop the WHEEL, a drummer, completely uninvolved with what transpires below, pounds steadily.

ONLOOKERS move back and forth across the stage. WHITES vilely curse the victims and even defile them.

A short, ugly, frock-coated BLACK MAN, with a madras scarf tied around his head, crosses, stops momentarily, then moves on.

*A huge YOUNG BLACK MAN approaches
and curses the dying men before being prodded
on by another BLACK who obviously wields
authority over him.*

*A young city-dressed BLACK MAN crosses
without pausing.*

*Many other BLACKS pass, looking on impassively,
their demeanor masking whatever thoughts
they entertain.*

*A smaller number of MULATTOS cannot suppress
flashes of overt sympathy for their unfortunate
brothers-in-skin.*

*When the parade of PASSERSBY has ended, only
a huge, fierce-looking BLACK MAN remains
onstage, gazing emotionlessly for a long time at the
two dying men. Finally, HE turns to the audience.)*

BOUKMAN

Gruesome, huh? . . . Dumb! Might even be heroic if it wasn't so dumb! French education went to this—(*Pointing*)—**bastard's head. Stupid fuck thought he could scare pissy whites with talk—"We're coming to get you, at so-and-so-hour, on such-and-such a day—GIVE UP!" . . . Hah, musta thought he'd get a hug of welcome!—ami-de-noired like his aristocratic friends done him in Paris! . . . He forgot these pootbrains ici are not called 'PETITS' blancs for nothing. Takes more than threats to stop 'em from enjoying a magnifique crap . . .**

*(HE stalks out as the YOUNG BLACK MAN, seen
crossing earlier, enters in waiter's garb and swivels
the tortured duo out of sight.*

The drumming continues as the scene is transformed into a drinking-Hall-Inn-Hangout where WHITES are talking raucously and drinking heroically.

A stunning collection of Black-to-Mulatto-to-Octoroon WOMEN are entertaining; OTHERS are draped about their WHITE PARAMOURS.

The YOUNG BLACK WAITER weaves in and out, seemingly oblivious to conversations at the tables which merge into a buzzing, unintelligible roar.

Suddenly, a VOICE penetrates the din.)

PLANTER

I say MERDE on the king!

PLANTER A

Watch out that you don't get guillotined you drunken ass!

PLANTER

What good is my head when our balls are crushed?!

PLANTER B

If your nuts are crushed, what do you pump Cecile with?

PLANTER C

Let me have her! Whatever you poke her avec can't satisfy her! How much? ...

(Turns to CECILE)

Switch to me Cecile, cheri – leap to a garcon whose balls are not crushed, but très ronde and grande!

(Laughter rings out)

PLANTER

Idiots! This is no time for jokes. Riots spread through the streets of Paris! Filthy peasants and the stinking rabble of the gutters agitate—yet here we sit still obsequious to bloodsucking Royalists!

PLANTER C

Oh, but how glorious we sit! No one could suffer more contentedly amidst such ecstasy!

(HE crushes his WOMAN tightly around the buttocks!)

PLANTER A

We "sit" because we are faithful subjects of France!

PLANTER

And where has that loyalty gotten us? Strangled by the Exclusives' Regulations! Governed by outsiders!

PLANTER A

We are ALL nothing if but Frenchmen, Msieur!

PLANTER

France forbids us to buy from anyone but France—to sell to no one but France! She takes all and gives nothing in return!

PLANTER A

She blesses us with our citizenship and protects us with her power!

PLANTER

She will soon have no power avec the King and his nobles squandering the wealth we produce!

PLANTER B

Is it revolution you preach, mon ami?

PLANTER

IF it is revolutionary to demand justice for San Domingo—YES!

PLANTER C

You jackanapes wouldn't prattle about 'revolution' if we hadn't backed the Americans against England! . . . Take care that you don't get "justice" choked around your treasonous neck!

PLANTER

IF Louis don't get his tête chopped off before mine.

PLANTER A

SACRE BLEU! I WILL NOT PUT UP WITH MORE OF THIS!

> (HE grabs for his knife. OTHERS leap to restrain him. Suddenly, their attention is diverted to the long table, now mounted by the WOMEN conducting a torrid, provocative DANCE. The MEN observe raptly as antagonisms dissipate. One by one, their own MISTRESSES join the performances, heightening the sensual atmosphere.
>
> The luscious WOMEN strip to scanty attire while the MEN gaze in utter silence. The WOMEN proceed to take it all off—the MEN at dick-

hardening attention. Abruptly, the WOMEN break contact and focus upon the THEATER AUDIENCE, as the MEN are left in a freeze.

Accompanied by DRUMS, the WOMEN address the AUDIENCE, supporting their commentary with body movements.

The recitation is shared among the WOMEN individually and chorally—some stanzas delivered by the entire group, some dispersed among the participants. While some orate, others supply physicalizations. Crucial verses are declaimed by the entire group, climaxed by a final phrase uttered by a single member—and vice versa.)

WOMEN'S CHORUS

In 1492, Chris Columbus on his way back to
Espanyol was told to visit the Isle of Gold
Better known to Natives as Ahyti, Land
of Mountains
No gold did Chris discover on his stopover
But what he saw he liked just fine
So much so he christened it Hispaniola
So grateful was Chris for Native kindness
He beckoned his countrymen to hurry and lay eyes
upon this Isle of Paradise
"The most beautiful site in the world"

Compañeros took him up on the invitation
And long after Chris departed
Had better reasons to like it too
Presto, the fabled ore was spied underground and
Toute Suite they started to mine

Conscripting the Indian population to conduct the
risky Occupation to their decimation

A depletion so complete until after
forty-three years
Only four hundred of one hundred thousand
Indians still survived to weep

Soon there were none

A good priest by the name of Las Casas
Appalled by the disappearance of potential
converts to the Lord Implored the King of Spain
to ship him some sturdier Africans to keep alive
God's purpose

Marvelous!

His Majesty sympathetic to the plan
Thus slavery in the Americas began

With Blacks taking up the slack
Business prospered IN Hispaniola
Fresh sharks raced to the killing
British and French colors they wore
Buccaneers fought up and down the Spanish Main
Until France won a permanent claim

Women were shipped to cohabitate
Vixens from prison cells
Sluts from gutters as well
Hussies with tongues as vile as their morals
And pee-boxes as poxed as the Devil's porridge
Yet, when women are few
Even tainted pussy outranks high morals

"However more—Since these damaged goods have bodies As corrupt as their manners, it were better to send no more Women than the sort we are getting. They serve only to infect the colony, destroy health and cause so much worry as to drive the men to an early grave."

The screwing was satisfactory
But syphilis was much too drastic
If the Colony hoped to survive
A less crippling kind of fucking need be devised

MON DIEU!

The Answer was Crystal clear
With slaves multiplying throughout the land
Ebony wenches could be had upon demand
Without a moment's hesitation
Dusky thighs were pried open and healthy cunts penetrated So wonderful was the intercoursing
Congressions increased to epidemic proportions
Not content with humping black mothers
White fathers were soon pumping their own
Creole Daughters

Spilling sperm so prodigiously until their offspring came to be divided into one hundred twenty-eight gradations of color

NEGRE TO SACATRA TO GRIFFE TO
MARABOU TO MULATRE TO QUARTERON
TO METIS TO MAMELOUC TO QUARTERONNE
TO SANG-MELE TO TIERCERON

Appetite for café-au-lait caresses grew so ravenous until our Envious White sisters had laws passed making it illegal for We mongrel bitches to

appear publicly in silk frocks or
Without headrags tied around our flowing locks.
If so defied, streetguards were ordered to strip us
bare until We stood exposed in naked modesty.
The law never got off the ground

We put nary a foot in town
Avec our shapely forms not IN evidence
Streets took on a ghostly appearance
Our absence was so unattractive
Business plunged to the edge of disaster
Prompting the law to be abandoned with alacrity

In matters of State our influence was unesteemed
Mais between the sheets our presence
reigned supreme
Since proof of the pudding is in the fucking
The census of seventeen-seventy-four registered
Seven thousand mulatresses
FIVE THOUSAND listed as White men's mistresses

More politely . . . Cunt-cu-bines

*(Immediately, lights pinpoint a
MALE MULATTO.)*

WOMEN'S CHORUS (CONT'D)

As for our Brothers of Color . . .

*(As the MALE MULATTO begins to speak, the
WOMEN resume dressing, while remaining in
silhouette.)*

MALE MULATTO

Barred from public office
Not allowed to be priest, doctor, teacher
or apothecary
Forced to serve in the Marechaussee hunting
Maroons and Arresting niggers
Keeping roads safe by risking our own damn necks
When our policeman's task is terminated
Three more years in the Military await us
Special seats in churches, theaters and
public conveyances
Banned from riding in private carriages
Required to dismount from a horse before
entering town
Must not be addressed as Mister
Can be insulted or beaten
Without hitting back
Our property trespassed, our thresholds
transgressed
Our wives and daughters seduced and accosted
Without a hint of protest expressed
Lift your hand against a blanc and risk getting it
Cut off by law

(Lights crossfade upon the WOMEN)

WOMEN'S CHORUS

With fathers busy fucking the daughters
The only ambition undenied the sons
Was the right to pile up the money
AN oversight les Papas now find
anything but funny

(Lights expand to include PLANTERS talking angrily without halt, even after the WOMEN rejoin them.)

PLANTER 1

When property is auctioned, they bid it up until the price is exorbitant. We can't afford it or find ourselves ruined if we try!

PLANTER 2

Mais oui, the bastards lend us money and keep us in debt while we carouse in Paris!

PLANTER 3

Stop producing niggers! We've lusted into our own destruction!

PLANTER 2

A mulatto cur will soon sit at the table his black mother once served!

PLANTER 3

Banish half-breeds to the mountains! Make them give up their property—and their slaves. They hate Blacks but they still have mothers and brothers among the wretches—while we won't even allow White-blood Affranchis to claim our name!

PLANTER 1

They don't need our patrimony. In Paris, "Les Amis ou Noirs" fanatics insist that Affranchis be made our equals!

PLANTER 2

Sacra Bleu! What Blanc would betray his own color?!

PLANTER 3

Flog-whip the traitors like niggers!

PLANTER 4

(Jumping upon a bench)

Mes amis! For one hundred years we have submitted to France's prohibitions—proud to consider ourselves loyal Frenchmen—but in seeking to place half-breed cochons on equal footing with Whites, France goes too far! We must set up our own Colonial government in San Domingo and demand representation in Paris! IF the King and Clergy reject us, we will appeal to the Third Estate!

(Lights pinpoint MIRABEAU replying to this plea as if in direct response to the request.)

MIRABEAU

You claim eighteen delegates in the States General according to your Island's population—among whom you have listed Mulattoes, Free Blacks and even slaves—all denied participation in your new Colonial Assembly... Msieurs, these Mulattoes and Free Blacks of property are taxpayers, are they not?...

Shouldn't they qualify for a ballot?... As for slaves, do you consider them men?... IF you class them men, should you not grant them rights?... IF you do not consider them men and still count them officially should we here in France not ourselves count the population of our mules and horses towards increasing our own representation...? I, Mirabeau, rule that you should be allocated six, not eighteen, deputies.

(Lights fade on MIRABEAU and a spot again pinpoints the MALE MULATTO.)

MALE MULATTO

Forbidden to wear swords, sabers or even dress in
European clothes
Must have special permission to
purchase ammunition
Banned from congregating in public meetings
Even for weddings, feasts or dances
Barred from playing European games.
Denied the right to eat with a White
Even in the privacy of our own domicile

(Lights crossfade to PLANTERS at the Inn; a COURIER rushing in shouting.)

COURIER

THE BASTILLE HAS FALLEN! THE KING'S TROOPS HAVE BEEN ROUTED! THE BASTILLE HAS FALLEN! THE BASTILLE HAS FALLEN!

RICH COLON

The Bastille has fallen?

WOMEN'S CHORUS

(To AUDIENCE)

The rich Colon dreams of self-rule—

PETIT BLANC

The Bastille has fallen?

WOMEN'S CHORUS

The Petit Blanc yearns for a better share
of the spoils—

ROYALIST

The Bastille has fallen?

WOMEN'S CHORUS

The Royalist seeks to maintain the status quo—

RICH COLON

Vive l'Indépendance!

(Repeat)

PETIT BLANC

Long live the Revolution!

(Repeat)

ROYALIST

Vive le Roi!

WOMEN'S CHORUS

The Colon dreams of self-rule
The Petit Blanc wants a better share of the spoils
Royalists seek to maintain the status quo

(Repeat)

(Lights pinpoint a FRENCH NATIONAL ASSEMBLY REPRESENTATIVE)

REPRESENTATIVE

"We Representatives of the French people, constituted as a National Assembly, recognize and declare that men are born free and remain forever equal in rights . . ."

(MALE MULATTO (LACOMBE) appears Downstage accompanied by a few other MULATTOES.)

LACOMBE

In the name of all Mulattoes, I, Lacombe, demand total social and political rights for my people—in accordance with the decree of the National Assembly of France!

(The COLON, PETIT BLANC and ROYALIST unite in attacking LACOMBE.)

TRIO

DOWN WITH THE NATIONAL ASSEMBLY!

(Repeat)

(LACOMBE is struck down)

PETIT BLANC

**Bastards, never equals!
You must swear to respect Whites!**

MULATTO

We will never swear our own enslavement! Jamais!

(Carrying LACOMBE in their arms, the MULATTOES are driven offstage by the BLANCS who shout; "DOWN WITH THE NATIONAL ASSEMBLY, DOWN WITH, ETC...."

Spotlight returns to pinpoint NATIONAL ASSEMBLY REPRESENTATIVES.)

REPRESENTATIVE

Upon learning of the unrest in San Domingo, we representatives of the National Assembly declare that it was never our intention to include the Colonies within the Constitution framed for the Mother Country—or to subject the Colonies to laws incompatible with their local regulations. The National Assembly would never institute new practices directly affecting the Colonies without seeking the prior advice or participation of those Colonies.

> *(Lights capture WHITES reacting to this news with a boisterous victory celebration at the Inn. They toast and cheer as the WOMEN CHORUS dances.)*

PLANTER

WE WILL NEVER CONFER POLITICAL RIGHTS UPON A BASTARD DEGENERATE RACE!!!

> *(Cheers of assent resound around the hall. The prancing CHORUS moves Downstage and comments to the AUDIENCE.)*

WOMEN'S CHORUS

With Mulattoes IN place
Back beneath the White man's boot
Blancs could renew their quarreling

Toots

The Colon dreamed of self-rule
Petit Blancs wanted a better share of the spoils
Royalists yearned for return to the status quo
The North was jealous of the South and West
The South and West were envious of the North

The Rich thought the Poor were a pack of Boors
The Poor cursed the Rich as a gaggle of Shits
Royalist pined for all stood against the Wall
Mulattoes licked their wounds plotting leur enemies doom

(Lights blackout the entire stage and without break SCENE shifts to VINCENT OGE and CHAVANNES [The two Mulatto victims seen at the beginning of the play.] OGE is composing a letter, reading it aloud while penning it.

CHAVANNES paces behind him impatiently. JACQUES OGE, VINCENT'S BROTHER is also present, stacking heavy boxes.)

OGE

I, Vincent Oge as protector of Mulatto rights, insist upon the immediate observance of the March eighth decree of the National Assembly of France conferring equal rights upon Mulattoes—

CHAVANNES

(Breaking in heatedly)

Why, Vincent?! ... These canailles respect no rights! They scrub their asses on decrees favoring us!

OGE

They can no longer ignore us, Chavannes.

CHAVANNES

Oui—'cause they slaughter us!

OGE

(Still composing)

Now they are busy at each other's throats.

JACQUES

And nos paysans are united as never before!

CHAVANNES

Then call our people to revolt! Maintenant, Vincent! With Governor Peynier's troops pinned down at Port au Prince! The Blancs don't know that you have landed with arms from America!

OGE

(Interrupting his writing momentarily)

Spoken like a true soldier, Chavannes—but not like the statesmen we must become... We must prove to the world that we are more compassionate than Blancs.

CHAVANNES

Diable avec la compassion!... Notre frère, Lacombe, hanged! Old Blanc ami, Beaudierre—hauled from his jail cell and strung up, too! Nothing but musketshot will convince these merdes!

OGE

In Paris, Chavannes—Mirabeau, Abbé Grégoire, Condorcet, Robespierre and other amis—deliver fatal blows to colonial propagandist of the Massiac Club. Support for us increases throughout the world—Msieur Clarkson in London, American sympathizers in Charleston—

CHAVANNES

What good is foreign backing ici on this soil?!... Before surrendering to us, colons will cease quarreling among themselves!

OGE

Once convinced that we have no intentions of destroying the source of San Domingo's prosperity—our plantations—sensible Blancs will overcome their aversion to our skin-color and join in opposition against royalist foes and petit blanc rabble.

CHAVANNES

Threaten them all with slaves and they'll come to their senses quicker!

OGE

AS slave owners ourselves, that wouldn't be wise, Chavannes.

CHAVANNES

What if they reject your appeal?

OGE

We proceed as otherwise planned—as you wish, we convince them with arms. See that our men are positioned at the outskirts of Le Cap. There—we will await their answers.

(A loud volley of gunfire crackles as the Scene fades and BOUKMAN enters addressing the AUDIENCE.)

BOUKMAN

He got it, a red-hot powder... While the silly fop along with two or three hundred other half-breed imbeciles, preened and promenaded outside Le Cap, a thousand colon soldiers snuck up on them. Mulattoes won the first skirmish, but—in a second go-round, Pissoirs attacked with twice as many men. The Breeds didn't stand a chance. Beaten in battle, they soon had to scatter.

Vincent Oge, his brother Jacques, and Chavannes fled across the Spanish border, and fastly, got tossed back to the French ... So much for Spanish sympathy ...

Blanc Colons gave them all a showy two months trial—enough time for Peoples-of-Color to get trampled the length and breadth of San Domingo, avec Petits Blancs doing most of the stomping. When the trial fini—thirteen half-breeds sentenced to ship galleys for life, twenty-one hoisted up hanging gallows dispatched to After-life.

Vincent and Chavannes—received special tribute ...

>   *(A VOICE intones their sentences to the staccato accompaniment of military drums)*

VOICE

They are to be taken to the Place d'Armes, to the opposite side of the street from where White criminals are executed—and while still alive have their arms,

>   *(OGE and CHAVANNES as they were when the play began are swiveled into view)*

VOICE (CONT'D)

legs and ribs broken—then placed by executioners upon wheels—

... with their faces turned toward heaven—there to remain as long as it pleases God to preserve life; after which their heads are to be severed from their bodies and exposed upon stakes.

BOUKMAN

..."Their lives snuffed out on the opposite side of the street from where Whites are executed..." Poor idiots—even in death they were to be denied "equality"... As their yellow limbs stretch outta they sockets, Chavannes, a soldier who fought recent side Blancs in America, didn't even whimper... Vincent Oge, cock-o-the-walk, man-bout-town in Paris for too much life—broke down. What the sniveling jack couldn't know is that he was accomplishing more in death than he could even dream in life.

(Uproarious VOICES are heard as lights pinpoint an ORATOR)

Barbarous! Shocking! Obscene!

ASSEMBLY ORATOR

(Shouting above the noise)

The martyrdom of this fine representative of the colored race exposes to the entire world the depravity of a system which will stoop to the limits of degradation to keep unfortunate men of a different color in bondage!... This is triumphant evidence of the monstrous character of the rulers of San Domingo!... Vincent Oge was not a Parisian, but he spent many years here in the company of civilized men! As his friends can attest, no finer, more compassionate man could be found. His only crime was burning ambition to improve the lot of his brothers and sisters who for hundreds of years have suffered oppression from the same monsters—detestable liberticides, vicious brutes, at whose hands Oge has now perished after undergoing cruelties which would shock even medieval torturers of old!... France is outraged at this barbarous crime. I demand that we, the representatives of the people, communicate the sentiments of our outraged citizenry by bestowing upon Oge's brethren the rights which have been so stubbornly denied them by his executioners. The rights of all men are at stake here in this Assembly!

(REWBELL, Assemblyman, jumps up pinpointed in light)

REWBELL

I, Assemblyman Rewbell, move that every Mulatto in San Domingo born of free parents be hereby enfranchised!

(Tumultuous "AYES!" are heard greeting his motion; immediately followed by Lights shifting to SAN DOMINGO where CROWDS shout in equally rebellious rage.)

CROWD

Monstrous! Barbarous! Outrageous! Down with France! À La Bas avec the National Assembly! San Domingo Whites unite! Mulattoes to the gallows! Mulattoes to the gallows! Mulattoes to the gallows ....

(Repeat last phrase)

(Lights flash to a MULATTO rousing his unseen COMPATRIOTS)

MULATTO

Defend yourself! Flee to the West! We'll make our stand where we are strongest!

(Repeat last phrase)

(Lights flash to a ROYALIST OFFICIAL)

ROYALIST

The Planters are in revolt! Save the colony for the King! The Colony must be saved for the King!

(Repeat last phrase)

(Lights flash to PLANTER ASSEMBLYMAN)

ASSEMBLYMAN

France has abandoned us! Secede! We will assemble at Le Cap on the twenty-fifth of August, this year of our Lord, seventeen ninety-one, and declare our Independence! On to Le Cap! The Colonial Assembly will rule San Domingo alone!

> *(Before HE has completed his dialogue a CHORUS OF BLACK WOMEN file On-stage stealthily; OTHER BLACKS follow behind as a low but intensely throbbing drumming is heard.)*
>
> *(Singing)*

CHORUS

> **Eh! Eh! Bomba! Heu! Heu!
> Canga, bafio te**
>
> **Changa, moune de le!
> Canga, do ki la!
> Canga, do ki la!
> Canga, li!**
>
> *(The CHORUS is repeated over and over as the MALE BLACKS murmur in low but distinct tones.)*

BLACK MALES

Eight hundred plantations of sugar—three thousand plantations of coffee—thirty-four hundred plantations of indigo—seventy-two million pounds of raw sugar—seventy-one million pounds of coffee—seven million pounds of cotton—twenty-three thousand hogsheads of molasses and rum and cocoa—Half of Europe supplied—San Domingo, the richest Colony in the world—

> *(The WOMEN'S CHORUS takes up the oral narration as the MALES shift to singing Canga stanzas.)*

WOMEN'S CHORUS

Stately Senegalese, copper-colored Fulahs,
Smelly Angolese, pointyteeth Mondongoes,
cheeky Bambaras proud Aradas, angry Congolese,
kingly Nagoseses, stubborn Nunes, chattering
Aradras, melancholy
Iboes, lean-limbed Quimbas, regal Dahomeans
and many More
Transported from Africa
To the Paradise of Cotton, Sugar, Coffee and Indigo

First a trickle
Then a flood
To occupy the Isle of San Domingo

For every soul who took root

Another gave up the ghost
Of one million transported in one hundred years
Only half survived
The death-rate high as the birth-rate

No matter—there's plenty more where the
Others came From

For we who fail to die—
Four yards of cloth apiece, a woolen shirt, a hat,
Eighteen pounds of salt per month to produce the
cotton, Sugar, coffee and indigo

Packed into shacks twenty inch by twenty-five
inch by twelve inch by fifteen inch, cubicled into
three- or four-room Stalls, the only
Window the open door, the trodden earth
the only floor
Where mama papa and baby huddle in a crowd

Stretch out your ration to last a week or else you're
out of Luck for more
Whip crack rise before sunrise
Stay from dawn to sunset

Rest as long as it takes to swallow a bite
Sleep and trudge off into night
Four hours sleep and off again—

Never mind that hand sliced off in the machine or
Sleepdrugged, plunge into scalding
Sugarvat syrup
Hum and sing you'll stop it from happening
You want to eat? Don't ask me! Raise
crops on the day
We set aside
But never manage to provide
Most of all don't step out of line
Because—
We've got the whip, the rigoise and the lianes

(all displayed)

(Suddenly, lights flash, spot methods of punishment all over the Stage. A combination of lifesize BLACK MANNIKINS and REAL BLACK ACTORS are utilized to detail the full brutality of treatment. The WOMEN'S CHORUS bark out the orders, but a WHITE FIGURE carries them out.)

[Alternatively: projections can be utilized.]

WOMEN'S CHORUS (CONT'D)

Treat him to the four-post—(tied to four posts upon the ground)
Delight him with the ladder—(tied to ladder)
Comfort him with the hammock—(suspended by four limbs)
Caress her with the collar—(heavy collar around the neck)
Soothe 'im with hot sealing wax—(poured into wounds)
Spice him with brine and pepper—(poured into wounds)
Invite him to a barbecue feast—(roasted)
Bum powder in the arse of a nigger—(just what it says)

(Narrative picks up momentum)

Heat in the furnace—Roast in the flames—
Sweeten the pot—(tossed into boiling sugar water)
Give a diving lesson—(drowned)
Barrel-ride 'em down a mountain
Jerk to a warm climax—(fire the balls)
Make a dick cum clean—(cutting it off)
Sign of the cross 'im—(crucify)

**Stickaniggeronapike—(beheaded and staved)
—EAT SHIT!**

(ALL BLACKS *suddenly freeze upon shouting out this excremental directive; a VOICE intones.*)

VOICE

Let any fair-minded and well-informed person compare the deplorable state of Negroes in Africa with the mild and pleasant life of those in the Colonies—guaranteed against need, supplied with comforts unknown to most of the peasants of Europe; nursed in times of sickness at a cost and care unavailable in the most famous hospitals of England; protected and respected in the infirmity of their old age; at peace in respect to the future of their children, relatives and friends; subject to work and labor matching the strength of each individual—such is the unvarnished picture of the lot of our Negroes.

(*The FREEZE breaks with the BLACKS resuming a low singing of "CANGA TE" as drums pound . . . More BLACKS stream Onstage as lights dim and the mood darkens ominously—eerily.*

The BLACKS slowly begin a ritual dance which gradually builds to a peak, accompanied by the thunderous rumblings of troubled elements—and crashing thunder.

Pulsating chants rise as VOODOO GODS are intoned—OGUN, BADAGRIS, MADAME ERZULIE, DAMBALLAH, QUEDO, etc. . . . Torches illuminate the ceremony . . . Bowls of food and large gourds of liquid are placed before an altar. A YOUNG NUDE MAN dances through flames, followed by a YOUNG NAKED WOMAN who does likewise.

Clearing a pathway through the CROWD by shaking a loud rattle, a PAPALOI leads a pig to the altar. Behind him, a MAMALOI carries a white chicken. The pig is expertly severed with a razorsharp machete and the blood captured in gourds which pass from hand to hand, the blood quaffed by MEMBERS OF THE CROWD.

Suddenly, a FAMILIAR FIGURE appears, chanting in Creole, building his intonations to a mesmerizing climax. It is BOUKMAN, our omnipotent NARRATOR. At the end of his chanting, drums cease abruptly. BOUKMAN mounts the WHEEL and wings his messianic oratory over the ASSEMBLED CROWD into the ears of the Audience.)

BOUKMAN

God who created the sun that gives us light!... God, Mon Dieu, who uplifts waves and rules storms—though hidden in clouds... watches over us!... Damballah speak!... And command us to wake up from deep slumber!

Like dummies we stood by, we stood by, we looked on, we looked on—in silence! We looked on in silence as the White man fought the White man! We looked on in silence as the White man band together to fight Mulattoes who fought back in return. We looked on in silence as they all fight against each other. And as they fought against each other, we were the forgotten ones! Forgotten Black Slaves!—Forgotten beasts toiling in leurs fields and in leurs mills!—Forgotten canailles cutting their cane!—Forgotten worms cropping their cotton and rooting up leur indigo!—Producing, multiplying wealth, making them ALL RICH!

Years ago, the grande French LeRoi of the Whites order them to excuse us hungry slaves one day a week from our labor so that we might cultivate food to stay alive! Instead of obeying their King, they drove us harder—drove us harder until we toppled over like cane stalks struck down by machetes!

The White Man's God infect him with crimes! Our God calls upon us to do good deeds!

>   (CROWD *repeats:* "*To do good deeds!*")

... Yea though our God is merciful, he commands us to revenge our wrongs!

>   (CROWD *repeats thrice:* "*Revenge our wrongs ....*" *etc.*)

Le temps arrivay to cast off the evil petro of the Diable Blancs! To cast aside the God idol of the Whites—their God who sit above gloating, gloating above over our suffering, gloating over our suffering—causing us to weep! Causing us to weep!

Eradicate, banish his image, erase out his image, destroy his image and heed the voice of liberty!

>   (CROWD *repeats thrice:* "*Heed the voice of liberty ....*" *etc.*)

Maintenant in the still see-lence of La Nuit—White men hurry on their way to Le Cap to foment evil! But tonight, Damballah speaks, Damballah speaks—calling upon Slaves to shatter their chains! To shed their chains and revolt against tyranny.

On every plantation Slaves wait the signal, wait the signal—to seek Vengeance, to seek Vengeance! To scourge this Island of the Diable Blances!

To seek Vengeance! To scourge this Island of the Diable Blancs! To scourge this Island of the Diable Blancs and make San Domingo free!

> (CROWD continues to repeat: "Make San Domingo free ....")

We are the mighty descendants of the tribes of Guinea!

> (CROWD: "GUINEA ...", etc.)

We are the mighty descendants of the tribes of Guinea! The mighty warriors of Ogun! ...

> (CROWD: "OGUN! OGUN! OGUN! OGUN! ....")

If you seek liberty—I, Boukman, head-drover of the Turpin plantation. Chief Houngan of all Blacks will lead you to Freedom! ... On to the Turpin plantation—MY MASTER—FIRST!

> (With a mighty roar, accompanied by rapid, thunderous drumming, the BLACKS race Offstage, torches and machetes aloft, singing "CANGA TE", now also delivered in English: "We swear to destroy Whites and ALL that they possess. Let us die if we do not keep this vow." ... The WHEEL swivels and the now-silent SLAVES reappear at the Turpin-Flaville plantation. A SLEEP-DRUGGED WHITE MAN, staggers toward them, still in nightclothes.)

TURPIN

What's the matter? Get back to your quarters you black dogs! Get back chiens before I whip you all! ... What's gotten into you?

(HE snaps his whip and the SLAVES, burdened by the subservience of years, pause indecisively.)

TURPIN (CONT'D)

Get back swines before I set the dogs on you! Put out those fires! Have you gone mad! I'll have you broken on the wheel!

(HE strikes one of them with the lash. The OTHER SLAVES continue to hesitate. As TURPIN draws back his whip again and hurls it forward, BOUKMAN steps in and swings his machete down. The whip plunges to the floor— TURPIN's hand along with it, severed clearly from the wrist in a single stroke.

TURPIN stares dumbly at his handless limb and the SLAVES gaze on also in stunned silence. Then, exultant cries erupting, THEY descend upon TURPIN, machetes flashing up and down, cleaving into the hated flesh as TURPIN sinks to the ground in crimson gushes. SLAVES are finally exorcising fear forevermore and their bloodchilling howls convey their certainty.

With TURPIN done, the Stage is peopled with SLAVES wreaking their marauding fury upon all MASTERS. Vivid, vicious brutalities, sparing neither WOMEN or CHILDREN, abound.)

Play I: The Rise of Toussaint L'Ouverture

NOTE:

(Utilizing lifesize marionettes, the Stage (and Audience) is rife with simulations of SLAVE-vengeance—including beheadings, pikings, crucifixions, bodies sawed in half, rapes [lifesize sex-dolls possibly can finally be put to good? use]; the WHEEL itself should be employed as a torture device. The ferocity of the rampage is also depicted with raging flames appearing behind the Upstage Scrim, indicating SLAVES torching everything in their paths.

When the scene has peaked and subsided, BOUKMAN moves slowly toward the Audience, surveying the destruction; then, fixing attention upon the Audience, HE addresses them calmly.)

BOUKMAN

Forgotten, huh...???... Oui, the Blancs thought they had trouble enough with yellow Mongrels—they never figured on Black Curs snapping at they haunches! When they woke up, we'd already chawed through their juicy flanks spitting out bleached splinters... Some blanc cocksuckers still couldn't even believe it when machetes sliced through their fat necks ...

My only regret is that I got myself killed ...

Some say I fell in battle—others say I was captured. What they all agree is that my cheeky tête was chopped off and stuck high above Le Cap city as a warning ... Unfortunately, ...the lesson didn't stick—'cause other incorrigible niggers insisted on finishing what I had begun. No Mackendall this time ...

Huh...? Oh, yes—years ago, a one-armed nigger Maroon, Mackendall, schemed to take over San Domingo by poisoning all Whites—sprinkle loads of African killing powder in Le Cap's reservoir de l'eau and any Blanc who survive that would be bumped off by their own chérie servants—wit a lil fatal-sauce in the kitchen stew, a bit of goodbye-powder in the drinking gourd . . .

A pretty good scheme. But Mackendall made une mistake—a last one! Busting with overconfidence the night before carrying out the plan, he decided to celebrate ahead of time—get some fun sneaking into a plantation dance to frolic, stuff himself with a bellyful of liquor and a dickfull of putain. What he didn't bargain is that one jealous nigger slave, resentful that his woman already been sharing her snapping delight with Mackendall—that this slave bugger would betray him to the Whites.

End a Mackendall, adieu revolt . . .

Not this time! Now, when I give my signal, the only liquor drunk and the only pussy fucked was what could be snatched from Massa and Missia as they was being fastly dispatched to judgment!

I wasn't missed a bit. Others took my place. Like JEAN-FRANÇOIS—

> *(A handsome BLACK enters, dressed resplendently in an elegant gray uniform, plumed cockaded hat, footspurs and huge cavalry sword.)*

BOUKMAN (CONT'D)

—Msieur Papillon's ex-slave. A Maroon chief holed up in the mountains ten years or so after he escaped . . . Biassou—

(BIASSOU enters; a short squat, ugly Man, also dazzlingly uniformed—of no help to his appearance—a bottle perpetually in hand, swilled as perpetually.)

BOUKMAN (CONT'D)

—former slave of the Fathers of Charity, priests who ran a farm and had a reputation for dealing with nègres better than most . . .Jeannot—

(JEANNOT enters bearing a pennant standard, painted with the body of a naked White Baby impaled on a stave; as huge and fierce as the flag emblem suggests.)

BOUKMAN (CONT'D)

—ex-property of Msieur Bullet, a master who treated niggers so bad they thought they had been mistakenly transported to Satan's Dominion instead of San Domingo.

Soon after the revolt, Jean-François, Biassou and Jeannot each built his own army and kept the Blancs so busy, they couldn't stop crapping in they britches, trembling over the evil black pestilence fate bedeviled them with.

All except one Blanc clan—the Bayou de Libertat family of the Breda plantation . . . One week before the uprising, manager de Libertat, taking a little trip, ordered his trusty slave animal-tender, sometimes coachman, Old Toussaint, to keep an eye on things—especially on Madame de Libertat.

With negres rampaging, Old Toussaint saw to it that the Breda slaves stayed in check. And true to his word, he took loving care of Madame Libertat—no, not in the smut way you thinking—

but truly protecting her, making sure no darkie ravisher got a sweaty paw on her.

With everything around burned down, the Breda plantation stayed calm. Apres one month, Old Toussaint packed up Madame de Libertat's belongings suddenly—bundled her and her children into a coach side his own family, and drove them all to Le Cap.

Madame safe there, he then took his own wife and children across the Spanish border to security.

—then he crossed back into San Domingo, hiked on foot to the Gallifet plantation where Jean-François and Biassou was camped out and volunteered service to the revolt.

There's a lot of contrary opinion about why Old Toussaint waited so long. His admirers claim that he was secretly directing the revolt ALL along—I don't know where the fuck that leave me—detractors, wanting to cut him down a revolution peg or two, claim he dawdled because he first wanted to see which way the wind would blow . . . The only thing I know is that he wasn't ici at the start, but he still got there plenty time enough . . . My own guess is that after having lived a not-too bad but more-than-shitty long life, Old Toussaint was not to be rushed into anything—not even a revolt. Also, it was common knowledge that he was not in the habit of wasting his forty-five some years blabbing what was on his mind—especially avec so much of it was dangerous.

> (TOUSSAINT *appears, book in hand, reciting as if HE is committing its contents to memory.*)

TOUSSAINT

"Natural liberty is the right which nature has given to everyone to dispose of according to his own will . . . The slave, an instrument in the hands of wickedness, is lower than the dogs

… Only a courageous chief is wanted … Where is he, that great man whom nature owes to her vexed, oppressed and tormented children? Where is he …? He will appear no doubt. Everywhere people will bless the name of this hero who will have reestablished the rights of the human race. Everywhere people will lift trophies in his honor … Only a courageous chief is wanted … only a courageous chief is wanted … "

(*TOUSSAINT exits*)

BOUKMAN

… from some old Spanish or French priest called Abbé Raynal … We slaves looked up to Old Toussaint for his book learning, but what we liked much more was his knowledge of animals and plants. He was no Voodoo Houngan like me—In fact, being a dedicated Catholic, he didn't like us witch doctors for shit. But he knew as much about herbs and plants as the best Papaloi or Mamaloi, and his animal-tending skill made him the best and only kinda human doctor we slaves had at all.

That's what Generalissimo Biassou appointed HIM—Docteur to the Troops. Biassou wasn't impressed with Old Toussaint's "courageous leader" crap, figuring that he himself already fitted that description—but he did need a doctor. More significant—Toussaint mastered another book called Caesar's Commentaries, instructions about military matters. That was more to Biassou's liking—It made Old Toussaint a very valuable man in dealing with the issue now at hand. The only one who didn't agree was Jeannot. Any fool who kept his White mistress from getting what she had 'coming' was not a man to Jeannot's taste.

(*JEANNOT stands at the WHEEL where a WHITE PRISONER is strung up. HE takes out a glint-edged machete and calmly proceeds to slit the PRISONER's throat, then catches the gushing blood in his cupped hands and drinks it. HE turns to his BUG-EYED SOLDIERS looking on aghast.)*

JEANNOT

Ah, mes amis, how sweet—how bien this White blood is! Come and drink—take deep swallows. Let us swear revenge against our oppressors. Come drink!

(Fearful of their CHIEFTAIN's wrath, a few MEN obey quickly; a FEW comply more out of terror than desire; ONE SOLDIER, unable to overcome his aversion, shakes his head rapidly. JEANNOT is angered.)

JEANNOT (CONT'D)

Drink! Drink the blood, chien! Then we'll chew the heart and liver to make us invincible against Blancs. Drink!

(The SOLDIER, though frightened, continues to shake his head vigorously. JEANNOT, machete raised, pounces upon him and hacks him to death.)

JEANNOT (CONT'D)

Canaille! Slave, keep your master company as he journey to his ancestors! Cochon!

(JEAN-FRANÇOIS suddenly appears, followed by BIASSOU, TOUSSAINT, TWO WHITE PRIESTS and SOLDIERS.)

JEAN-FRANÇOIS

JEANNOT?! WHAT ARE YOU DOING?!

JEANNOT

Preparing this dog to join his master!

(TOUSSAINT and the PRIESTS rush to the DEAD SOLDIER as JEAN-FRANÇOIS crosses to the DEAD WHITE PRISONER. BIASSOU drinks from his bottle; the SOLDIERS stand around.)

JEAN-FRANÇOIS

Jeannot?! Why have you killed this man? He is a prisoner!

JEANNOT

I keep no prisoners.

JEAN-FRANÇOIS

It is custom of war!

JEANNOT

White man's custom!

JEAN-FRANÇOIS

We obey rules of war. We are not brigands!

JEANNOT

Shit on your rules! Jeannot have no rules for Blancs—his rule is death! Master Bullet's rule!—Rule scarred into Jeannot's back. ... You wasn't particular about rules when we hacked Blancs to ribbons, JEAN-FRANÇOIS. Have old White-loving Toussaint sold you on his White man's God?

TOUSSAINT

We are fighting for freedom, Jeannot? All Blancs are not our enemies!

JEANNOT

"Friends" are those greeting they maker!

TOUSSAINT

These priests—

JEANNOT

They masquerade! Where was your priests when Master Bullet beat us to death?

TOUSSAINT

They uphold our cause!

JEANNOT

Muskets and machetes uphold our cause! . . . Too late! We need no White man's Fathers!

TOUSSAINT

To butcher helpless prisoners is cruel enough, but to slaughter your own men, Jeannot—you degrade yourself and us avec barbarity unworthy of heathens!

JEANNOT

You lecture me, Old Toussaint?! You dare criticize JEANNOT?! . . . Biassou?—You hear? Do old Toussaint speak for you? You are his Chief—or is he now the General and you the docteur? . . . Avec his Blanc books and White man's liver—have old Toussaint jelly your courage too, Biassou? . . . Where was old Toussaint when we trounced Whites?—Burying his head up his Blanc missis' petticoat, that's where! . . . Have he infect disease on you avec his love for Whites?! Made you see the light, Biassou? . . . Not me! No one tell Jeannot how to treat Blancs! By my oath to Ogun and Damballah, I will roast their carcasses and ship they spirits to the hell they fear!

JEAN-FRANÇOIS

Seize him!

> (SOLDIERS *quickly surround* JEANNOT, *pinioned by the arms,* JEANNOT *is restrained, his* MEN *held at bay.* JEAN-FRANÇOIS *and* BIASSOU *confer at a distance. Eventually,* TOUSSAINT *is beckoned to join them.* JEANNOT *screams.*)

JEANNOT

HOW DARE YOU PUT HANDS ON ME! I AM JEANNOT! LIBERATOR OF OUR PEOPLE! I FIGHT BLANCS LIKE A TIGRE! YOU WOULD ALL BE MORTS IF IT WAS NOT FOR ME, JEAN-FRANÇOIS!

JEAN-FRANÇOIS

> (*Moving to* JEANNOT)

We can afford you no more, Jeannot. Your mission is fini.

> (*Turns to* SOLDIERS)

JEAN-FRANÇOIS (CONT'D)

Shoot him.

> (HE *turns his back on* JEANNOT *and walks away.* JEANNOT *rages as* HE *is wrestled towards the* WHEEL, *struggling mightily*)

JEANNOT

YOU CANNOT DO THIS! I AM JEANNOT, GRAND JUDGE OF THE ARMY OF BLACKS! YOU CANNOT KILL ME! I AM INVINCIBLE! YOU CANNOT KILL ME ....

(The SLAIN WHITE PRISONER is cut down and JEANNOT, still hurling defiant curses, is strung up in his place. SOLDIERS march to firing-squad positions. THEY take aim and a volley of shots finally silences the screaming JEANNOT. . . A PRIEST, treading cautiously as if the fierce REBEL might still be alive, benedicts the executed demon. EVERYONE exits, even JEANNOT's MEN who abandon him to death without looking back. The slumped, suspended corpse of the terrifying CHIEFTAN remains spotlighted on Stage before lights dim. While so, BOUKMAN walks up to the hanging corpse, surveying him longly . . . Finally, HE turns to the Audience.)

BOUKMAN

Poor Jeannot . . . no one need ever again be frightened or embarrassed by his bloodthirsty presence . . . It's a pity there was nobody to rid the Whites of their butchers de coeur . . . They kept right on piking and staving in the North . . . However, in the West—

(Lights rise upon a collection of WHITES conferring with the MULATTO LEADERS— RIGAUD, BEAUVAIS, and PINCHINAT.)

WHITE OFFICIAL

We bring you words of peace. With your victory at La Croix de Bouquets let hostilities cease. All factions among us extend this offer. We come to bargain in the spirit of justice and peace, to accord you authentic recognition of your rights. To ask you to recognize in us Whites your friends and brothers . . . This endangered Colony invites you—nay, begs you to unite in order to overcome our joint afflictions.

May this day on which the torch of reason give enlightenment to us all be forever remembered. Let it be a day of forgetfulness for all errors and a pardon for all injuries. Henceforth, let us be rivals only in our zeal for bettering the public's welfare . . . We accept entirely without reservations the pact that you propose to us.

WHITE AIDE

(Reading a Proclamation)

On this day, October nineteenth, seventeen ninety-one, the Provincial Assembly of the West Province is to be dissolved immediately. Deputies to the Colonial Assembly are to be recalled. Two Battalions of Mulattoes shall be recruited for the National Guard. The memory of the Mulatto Patriot, Oge, is to be rehabilitated. All terms of this agreement shall be presented to the National Assembly in Paris for ratification and approval of the King.

> *(The Proclamation's end is greeted with MUSIC for a Te Deum Mass. The Ceremony is briefly illustrated with EVERYONE participating. When the Ceremony concludes, the MULATTOES are left alone Onstage.)*

BEAUVAIS

So!—At last we feast at the table of equality.

RIGAUD

AN invitation prompted by a few bayonets! . . . Do you suppose the "torch of reason" would have flamed so brightly if it hadn't been ignited by arms? Enlightenment always sprouts with haste in the mouth of cannons.

PINCHINAT

Not just cannons, mes amis. Don't forget a few salvos of thunderous oratorical bombardment.

RIGAUD

"Concede what we request—if not, civil war!" ... Your tongue was as stiff as your quick-rising dick, Pinchinat.

PINCHINAT

Both are unerring in aim and unsurpassed in pricking their targets, Rigaud. Age merely improves my skill.

Come, let us now sign the pact in ink instead of the blood we were primed to extract ....

> (THEY *exit as a jubilant mixed-*CROWD *of* WHITES *and* MULATTOES *march Onstage, circling around arm-in-arm, shouting "*UNITY, FIDELITY*"* ... *The* MULATTO LEADERS *return at the tail end of the March, linked in arms with the* WHITE LEADERS .. *The mixed-*CROWD *exit, leaving* RIGAUD, BEAUVAIS, PINCHINAT *and another* MULATTO OFFICER, PÉTION, *to remain Onstage with* THREE WHITE LEADERS.)

WHITE OFFICIAL A

An historic occasion, mes amis. I hope that this Province will serve as a model for our entire troubled Island. However, Msieurs, er, er, ... what of the slaves in your battalions ...? Now that peace reigns, what are your plans for them?

RIGAUD

They will return to the plantations.

WHITE OFFICIAL B

Excuse moi, General Rigaud—for being apprehensive, sir . . . but with the uprising continuing in the North, do you think our own slaves here in the West will return docilely to their plantations?

BEAUVAIS

The slaves of the North rebelled against unforgivable treatment, Msieur. They sought to be treated like men, not beasts.

RIGAUD

Here in the West our own slaves have no fear about being treated fairly. They will lay down their weapons and work obediently.

WHITE OFFICIAL A

And your crack regiment, the—?

PÉTION

The "Swiss."

WHITE OFFICIAL A

Yes—"The Swiss." They are not plantation slaves, but ex-fugitives, are they not?

RIGAUD

Yes—former Maroons.

WHITE OFFICIAL A

Will men of such stubborn temperament be content to return to plantations?

RIGAUD

Why should they not?

WHITE OFFICIAL A

After such courage at La Croix de Bouquets, humbling scores of Whites in combat, are you certain they will be able to readjust—to the necessary constraints of bondage, no matter how lightly enforced?

BEAUVAIS

Treat with them honorably and you remove all cause for their brigandage.

CARADEU

Nevertheless, after so many years of fugitive independence, they have become accustomed to a bandit form of liberty. Their awesome prowess at La Croix de Bouquets has given them a greater taste of glory. I for one, doubt that they will be easily contented.

PÉTION

Why not just free them?

WHITE OFFICIAL A

I think that we would all agree that such a course would not be appropriate, Msieur Pétion. IT would set an abominable precedent. For no slave would thereafter need dream of liberty. He would need only to seek a conflict—a few Whites to humble and automatically be rewarded with freedom.

PÉTION

Why couldn't those same admirable battlefield qualities of the Swiss not make them stable models for fellow Blacks in times of peace?

WHITE OFFICIAL B

Msieur Pétion, we in the West this day are toasting the advent of peace—yet we dare not forget the majority of the Colony is still beset with strife. As long as this conflict continues, the fragility of our own unity is constantly jeopardized.

PÉTION

What are you suggesting, Msieur?

CARADEU

That we fashion a solution which would eliminate the Swiss' influence upon our other slaves.

PÉTION

(Sarcastically)

Why not just pike them?!

WHITE OFFICIAL A

Non, non, non, mon ami! IT is not our intention to penalize such valiant warriors. No, msieurs, we merely seek a solution which would isolate the Swiss from their brethren—

CARADEU

Seriously enough, Msieur Pétion, your own proposal—would best resolve our quandary. It has great merit. We should indeed free the Swiss—and transport them away from the Colony.

PÉTION

??? Out of San Domingo?

WHITE OFFICIAL B

We have found the perfect place, Msieurs—an unoccupied but fertile spot off the Spanish Coast of Mexico—without inhabitants for hundreds of miles inland. It is virgin territory. The Swiss would be able to live without interference. From Port au Prince here, it's a three-month voyage by ship.

PÉTION

(Bitterly)

A safe distance to quarantine them!

WHITE OFFICIAL A

Msieur Pétion—the Swiss . . . are men whose rebellious nature certifies their desire to live independently . . . Is it not reasonable to expect that they would prefer liberty far removed from this colony rather than resume the precarious life of mountain bandits?

CARADEU

Msieurs, I urge you to approve commissioning a vessel to transplant the Swiss out of San Domingo!

PÉTION

I oppose it!

BEAUVAIS

So do I!

PINCHINAT

Mes amis—mes frères . . . No solution which requires men being uprooted from their native habitat is praiseworthy . . . I suspect we all would prefer the travails of mountain bandits amidst familiar surroundings to traipsing as free men upon alien terrain

... However, in this particular instance, our White Compatriots present us with rather unassailable arguments ... The Swiss will not be comfortable for us. I abhor the proposal—after all, these warriors have done us admirable service and should not be cast adrift—but commonsense recognizes the practicality of the recommendation ... Unless we can offer better alternatives, it seems that this unique solution best resolves our dilemma ... Have you alternatives to propose, General Rigaud?

RIGAUD

... Non.

PINCHINAT

Pétion ... ? Beauvais ... ?

PÉTION

Non.

BEAUVAIS

Non.

PINCHINAT

Do you join me then, mes amis, in agreeing that the Swiss be relocated as suggested?

RIGAUD

Oui.

(PÉTION nods assent; BEAUVAIS remains mute)

PINCHINAT

Then we are all in accord, mes amis. So be it—let it be done.

(Lights fade slowly and sadly on the scene. Before they are completely dark, they halt, remaining dim. The Stage is briefly vacant; then BOUKMAN emerges, moving Downstage where HE is solitarily illuminated.)

BOUKMAN

"The Swiss"—un nom from some old bodyguards of King Louis—had an interesting trip. Soon after leaving Port au Prince, their Blanc ship-Captain figuring that any deserted landing spot was as good as another, shortened his three-month trip to three days and dumped his passengers off at a cove in Jamaica Bay, a bit of a skip across the water from San Domingo. Before the Swiss could even set feet on the beach, the British Governor, informed about this unexpected increase in his darkie population—convinced that he already had more than enough niggers to cope with—rounded up the uninvited Swiss cargo and with a "no thanks" shipped it back to San Domingo.

The cargo put in at Le Cap where it was equally unwelcome; and was quick deported to Môle St Nicolas. Reaching the Môle, the Commander there ordered that the Swiss be sent back to Port au Prince . . . Whoever he told to "execute" the order, did just that . . . executed the load in de l'eau of Môle Bay and "washed" his hands of the whole affair . . . .

(The WHEEL is silhouetted dimly. One by one, we see FIGURES being forced to ascend it at gunpoint. At the top, after being prodded into facing Upstage, the VICTIMS are bludgeoned over their heads and pushed over the side. BOOKMAN continues his commentary.)

BOOKMAN (CONT'D)

For days the sky over Môle St. Nicolas harbor was soot-black with crows greedy searching for black bodies washed ashore.

The Swiss indeed rewarded in full. They bloated the bellies of hungry buzzards just as amply as they stocked the table for Mulattoes to feast at the banquet of equality . . .

But since Damballah never look too kind on thankless gluttony, the half-breed banquet didn't last very long . . . A mean, shit-eating Petit-Blanc named Pralotto—fed up with the unity nuptials, pounced on the Mulattoes and they aristocratic White grooms and drove them out of Port au Prince. After which Pralotto's mangy crew burned the town to the ground—massacring Breeds, rich Whites, women, children, pets and pussies—stuffing they own skinny bosoms with everything they could scavenge.

Once again Mulattoes were back licking they wounds and slicktalking Pinchinat sharpening his tongue—

VOICE OF PINCHINAT

"Fly mes amis and besiege Port au Prince. Avengers of perfidy and perjury, let us plunge our bleeding arms into the breast of these European monsters . . . .

(His voice trails off)

BOOKMAN

But for all his tongue-lash, things in the West stood standstill . . . .

Back North where only four months ago I first called down the vengeance of Ogun, Damballah and the loas of our ancestors, Jean-François, Biassou and one hundred thousand Black slaves was also running out of pissant!

Their armies stuck in a rut with little left to take in the countryside and unable to break into the barricade Blanc cities, Jean-François and Biassou didn't have a hunch of what to do next. So niggers and Whites took turns and flung proclamations at each other . . . .

> *(Lights pinpoint GOVERNOR BLANCHELANDE AND JEAN-FRANÇOIS casting threats at EACH OTHER at different locations.)*

BLANCHELANDE

As Governor of San Domingo, I order you to surrender and return to your plantations!—

JEAN-FRANÇOIS

IF you collect your belongings and vacate the Island, I promise not to harm you!—

> *(Alternating, THEY repeat their demands until fading out behind a Scene-in-Progress, with COMMISSIONERS ROUME, MIRBECK and ST. LEGER meeting with COMMANDER ROUVRAI, GOVERNOR BLANCHELANDE and OTHER COLONIAL OFFICIALS.)*

ROUME

Commissioners Mirbeck, St. Leger and I landed at Le Cap prepared to deal with one crisis—Msieurs, only to discover that an even more destructive conflict has erupted. Understandably, we are without instructions about the slave revolt.

OFFICIAL I

The way to restore order, Commissioner Roume, is for France to send thousands of troops to crush the Blacks!

MIRBECK

Unlikely, Msieur. But even so, before those troops arrive the situation could already be hopeless. No, we in San Domingo must rely upon ourselves.

BLANCHELANDE

Rebels will soon be begging to negotiate anyway.

OFFICIAL I

Negotiate with murderers?!—Jamais! The Black beasts must be annihilated!

ST. LEGER

Why have you not done this already, Msieur?

ROUVRAI

IF the Mulattoes had been placated as I advised, the Black revolt could have been avoided . . . Tell me, Commissioners, is the National Assembly deliberately trying to ruin San Domingo? First, you enact a decree favoring Mulattoes, then you rescind it. Now you restore it. You inflame passions on one side, then the other—constantly provoking discord and instability!

ROUME

That is irrelevant maintenant, Commander Rouvrai. Only the slave revolt must concern us. We must contact their leaders and warn them of the imminent arrival of French troops.

COLONIST I

You said this was unlikely, Commissioner?!

ROUME

Unlikely or not, Msieur—If Blacks believe it possible, it should have the desired effect. Blacks still swear loyalty to their King.

OFFICIAL I

It is we representatives of the King whom they rebelled against!

ROUME

Apparently, they make no distinction between local enemies of their grievance ici and you the King's colonial representatives. Let us hope that we Commissioners are viewed differently.

(Without break, the scene shifts to JEAN-FRANÇOIS, BIASSOU, TOUSSAINT and TWO WHITE PRIESTS.)

JEAN-FRANÇOIS

What does it say?

PRIEST

Amnesty.

JEAN-FRANÇOIS

Amnesty?

PRIEST

Freedom from punishment if we surrender.

BIASSOU

(Laughing heartily as HE swigs from his ever-present bottle.)

Freedom from punishment?! Ha! We are already "free from punishment!" It's they who are not free from being punished!

JEAN-FRANÇOIS

Who are these Commissioners?

PRIEST

Officials from Paris.

BIASSOU

HA, you see, Jean-François—the King's personal attention! Chopping off a few heads was all it took! . . . But what make these Commissioners different? Governor Blanchelande is also from the King.

TOUSSAINT

They represent new rulers of France.

JEAN-FRANÇOIS

Yet they ask the same as Governor Blanchelande, our surrender.

PRIEST

These Commissioners intend to negotiate sincerely. They know they confront military equals.

BIASSOU

SUPERIORS! We keep the chiens penned up like poodles!

JEAN-FRANÇOIS

Soldiers from France will not be poodles, Biassou. They will not be cowards.

BIASSOU

Afraid to take to the mountains again, Jean-François?

JEAN-FRANÇOIS

... Avec French troops hunting us, how long will it be before our people start looking back enviously about when they were slaves? ... No—we must talk to these Commissioners.

(Scene shifts to Le Cap)

COLONIST

(Enraged)

Treat with murderous scum?! I would rather see San Domingo reduced to ashes than make a single concession to savages!

MIRBECK

Refuse to treat with them and you may get your wish, Msieur.

COLONIST

These brigands have devastated our Land—indulged every loathsome depravity they can invent! Now you ask us to bargain with them? These are slaves—savages—still fresh from African jungles. They should be punished for their barbarity!

ROUME

It is unclear, Msieur, which side is guiltier of worse barbarity and which better earns the right to be called 'savage.' ... Envoys from the rebels inform me that their leaders seek an end to hostilities and are prepared to surrender if certain conditions are met.

(Scene shifts back to JEAN-FRANÇOIS, etc.)

JEAN-FRANÇOIS

(Dictating to a transcribing PRIEST)

Make it clear how difficult it will be dealing with our troops.

(TOUSSAINT offers his wording)

TOUSSAINT

"False principles will make the slaves very obstinate. They will claim they have been betrayed."

BIASSOU

With good reason!

JEAN-FRANÇOIS

(Ignoring BIASSOU and expanding upon TOUSSAINT's contribution.)

But if you grant freedom to those leaders whom we name, we will join with the soldiers of the King and track down slaves who refuse to surrender. This will not be easy, since intense feelings of defiance have been aroused. However, we pledge our full cooperation.

BIASSOU

(Continuing his bitter sarcasm)

If we hunt them down like Blancs tracked you, Jean-François, we'll never catch them!

JEAN-FRANÇOIS

(Ignoring the jeering interjection)

"We acknowledge having disrupted the life of this Colony, causing terrible pain and hardship to its citizens. When we asked Whites to evacuate the Colony, we were ignorant of the new law. Now that we are acquainted with this law and confident about the Mother Country enforcing it, we Blacks will gladly obey all future rulings.

In return for amnesty for four hundred leaders—we offer peace and tranquility to this rich Island which has been so sadly torn apart by strife and destruction...."

BIASSOU

Why four hundred, Jean-François?—, why so many? Which rascal will be lucky—and which man jack will have to reshackle hisself?... Four hundred is too much! A crowd like that will only draw attention to buggers left out. Reduce the liberty-list to just us ici! Then most everyone else will be in the same leaky barrel. Only a handful—just us—can be envied—and since everybody agree that we chiefs, because of our superior charm deserve special treatment—Then they all shuffle back into slavery, they'll all weep tears of joy at us specials being free!

JEAN-FRANÇOIS

(Still refusing to respond to BIASSOU'S taunts)

"To enhance our participation, it would be helpful to us, trusted slave leaders, to have the Governor deliver a proclamation promising to devote some attention to the slave's problems."

BIASSOU

Bravo! Bravo! We'll get them a new Code de Noir and salute it.

JEAN-FRANÇOIS

"We urge you to accept our proposals in good faith and await a speedy answer. Above all, we emphasize that liberty for the leaders we designate is an indispensable condition for the restoration of order and tranquility to the Colony."

BIASSOU

Above all else, liberty for us leaders!

> *(Focus shifts back to COLONIAL ASSEMBLY, with some lights remaining upon the BLACKS who simultaneously sign the document as it is read to the ASSEMBLY with TWO REBEL ENVOYS in attendance.)*

ASSEMBLY CHAIRMAN

(Tossing letter aside angrily)

GET OUT! GET OUT!

COMMISSIONERS

Messieurs, please—!

ASSEMBLY CHAIRMAN

Liberty?! . . . Not only will we not give them liberty but we will pardon only those curs who crawl back on their knees!

> *(Scene blacks out upon WHITES and focus remains on BLACKS responding as if already having received the reply.)*

BIASSOU

(Raging)

MERDES! MERDES! SHITS! I'm no slave! I am Biassou! Generalissimo of the Conquered Territories—Commander of forty thousand men! I will make them pay for addressing me with so little respect! Take all Blanc prisoners and shoot 'em!

(NO ONE moves)

BIASSOU (CONT'D)

I SAID, SHOOT THEM!

(SOLDIERS rush to obey; TOUSSAINT's gesture stops them. HE then faces BIASSOU, treading gently in the face of his anger.)

TOUSSAINT

No, General Biassou.

BIASSOU

Oui, oui, oui!!

TOUSSAINT

Shooting the prisoners will serve no purpose . . . Oui, the Blancs are disrespectful—stupides—victims of passion . . . .

BIASSOU

They'll get they passion drowned in leur sons' blood!

TOUSSAINT

The Blanc prisoners give us the upper hand . . . Shoot them and we lose our most valuable asset. It would turn the Commissioners against us—

BIASSOU

Commissioners?!—This insult is from the shitty Commissioners ...!

TOUSSAINT

No—the letter is from the Assemblymen alone. The Commissioners smuggle their own communiqué. Read it before acting...

BIASSOU

(After pausing for many beats fondling the missive)

... Old Toussaint—your precious Whites are safe for maintenant ... But beware, Docteur Toussaint Breda, that your sympathy for Blanc wolves don't get you infected with their Maladie ...

(Scene shifts back to ASSEMBLY)

COLONIST

(Addressing the COMMISSIONERS irately.)

You smuggle entreaties to the Blacks—conspiring against this Assembly!

ROUME

Will you let it sink in, Messieurs—that you are no longer dealing with slaves, but with one hundred thousand determined men, women and children who have fought you to a standstill and are still capable of destroying this Island and you along with it!

COLONIST

A hundred thousand beasts!

ST. LEGER

All the more reason why you should fear they never descend upon you! Conferring with them is the first step to avoiding that possibility!

ROUME

We have made excellent progress. Jean-François, chief of the Blacks, has agreed to meet with us personally—here in Le Cap, gentlemen, which attests to the sincerity of the Blacks and their confidence in us. I beg you to take advantage of this opportunity, Msieurs. If you harbor doubts about him or us, appoint your own observers to monitor our negotiations. Measure the Blacks up close then decide whether they should be dealt with further.

> *(During COMMISSIONER ROUME's dialogue, WHITES begin to take up positions to welcome JEAN-FRANÇOIS. Eventually,*
>
> *JEAN-FRANÇOIS enters with a COMPANY OF MEN. The two camps move towards each other, stopping to face across a space in between. Then JEAN-FRANÇOIS steps forward to bridge the gap. Suddenly, a WHITE MAN bolts out of nowhere, falling upon JEAN-FRANÇOIS, slashing HIM repeatedly across the face, cutting deeply. The WHITE MAN is BULLET, ex-Master of JEANNOT, the executed former slave-leader.)*

BULLET

Murderer! Scum! I wish you were my son-of-a-hyena, Jeannot—but you'll do just as well!

(JEAN-FRANÇOIS wards off the blows as best HE can. BULLET is finally dragged away by OTHER WHITES and JEAN-FRANÇOIS falls back among his SOLDIERS. The atmosphere is explosive. Just as tension promises to snap, ST. LEGER heads boldly towards JEAN-FRANÇOIS, calmly threading his way through the REBEL SOLDIERS, addressing the WOUNDED CHIEF.)

ST. LEGER

I apologize, Commander, for Msieur Bullet's disgraceful behavior. A warrior like you might shrug it off ... You suffered the blows, but the pain wounds me more. Accept my regrets, Commander. I pray that our discussion may proceed without this terrible outrage affecting a serious resolution of our mutual difficulties. However, I bow to whatever revenge you wish to extract.

JEAN-FRANÇOIS

(Deeply moved)

I bow to you, Msieur.

(Falls to his knees)

My prayers are answered. At last I have met a White man who shows human feeling towards a Black. I will ignore Msieur Bullet's transgression. By all means allow our discussion to proceed.

(HE rises and scene fades out; lights rising immediately upon the BLACKS with JEAN-FRANÇOIS having returned.)

BIASSOU

It's a trick! We give them four hundred prisoners—they give us rien, not even a promise!

JEAN-FRANÇOIS

They agree to release my wife and children from prison as evidence of their good faith.

BIASSOU

Fuck their faith! Pardon, Jean-François, but it is not a bargain. Four hundred Whites in exchange for one family. What about amnesty?!

JEAN-FRANCOIS

First, our French prisoners must be released as proof of our sincerity. Amnesty will follow.

BIASSOU

Why prove OUR sincerity. Our slate is clean, theirs is filthy avec betrayal! When could the weasels ever be trusted?!

JEAN-FRANÇOIS

St. Leger exhibited his humanity when Bullet attacked me.

BIASSOU

Bullet! The merde! I'd crack his neck! St. Leger ate crow because it was smarter than choking on musket shot!

Humanity, merde!—Blancs deal in trickery!

TOUSSAINT

Protect against it. Instead of four hundred prisoners, give them two hundred—half. If they favor treachery, they will have to think of prisoners still remaining in our possession.

BIASSOU

NON!

TOUSSAINT

Biassou, what does it matter how many prisoners? They are all a burden to keep!

BIASSOU

Shoot 'em and lighten the load!

TOUSSAINT

Two hundred hostages are good enough.

BIASSOU

(Weakening but still reluctant)

... Bien—c'est vrai—two hundred throats to slash is still enough for a blood-thirsty appetite ... Bravo, Toussaint—and since you are the only nigger trusted to deliver them sans a silky lock mussed-up, escort them yourself ... But beware old Toussaint that when you brush shoulders once more with fine-mannered Blanc Pissoirs, that you are not tempted to sneak back into slavery rather than continue to rub elbows with we savages.

TOUSSAINT

I spent a lifetime among fine-mannered Blancs, Biassou. It taught me that Liberty is more crucial than manners. There'll be time for manners after freedom.

BIASSOU

HA, ha—not mine, Toussaint. Too late! Biassou's manners are hopeless for improvement.

(Without break, scene shifts to ASSEMBLY. TOUSSAINT stands below the ASSEMBLYMEN and COMMISSIONERS who are arrayed atop the WHEEL. A white PRISONER is standing below also being addressed by the ASSEMBLY CHAIRMAN.)

CHAIRMAN

Have you been treated well?

PRISONER

Yes, Msieur. The rebels shared their food. We were rested, given water, and Blacks along the route were prevented from attacking us. We were treated well.

ROUME

Msieur Chairman, I propose we record this testimony attesting to the honorable conduct of the Blacks.

CHAIRMAN

This is no legal hearing, Msieur Commissioner. We keep no ledgers.

ROUME

Msieur Chairman, this envoy came to discuss matters of critical importance to San Domingo. The proceedings should be recorded!

CHAIRMAN

This outlaw is here at our discretion, Msieur. We do not confer legality upon bandits!

ROUME

Msieur Chairman—

CHAIRMAN

Commissioner!—Inform this slave brigand that the Chairman of the Assembly, representative of the King and the Government of France, does not intend to converse with anyone in rebellion against France. If he wishes to supplicate, I will reply to him through written notes—only!

MIRBECK

We approached Generals Jean-François and Biassou in good faith! Their emissary should be treated with dignity!

CHAIRMAN

We govern this Colony, Msieur Mirbeck. You have dealt with these rebels at your own instigation. Our authority prevails now, Msieurs!

(HE gestures to TOUSSAINT to speak.)

TOUSSAINT

Messieurs—I approach you respectfully . . . Regarding the unfortunate events of the past four months—I beg you to understand that we Slaves did not wish to abandon our Masters. We were driven to insurrection—provoked because of the ill treatment we suffered. I, myself, Toussaint de Breda, am fortunate to have belonged to a good Master who treated me fairly—and whose kindness I repaid by delivering his family safely here to Le Cap, protecting them against ALL harm.

However, Messieurs, throughout the sad history of San Domingo, for every good Master who showed kindness toward his slaves, another Master counteracted with brutality. Those, who, next to God, should have been our fathers, proved to be tyrants and monsters unworthy of the invaluable fruits of our labor. It was because of crimes, Messieurs—unbearable atrocities—that we were forced to resort to arms to escape the oppressive burdens of cruelty ....

Now, after calling attention to our plight, all we ask is that you acknowledge our complaints. We regret deeply the pain and discomfort we have caused you and only pray that we be allowed the opportunity like loyal children to help make restitution for our misdeeds ... Grant pardons and liberty to those leaders we cite and we assure you faithfully that our mutiny will cease and this Island will return to the tranquility necessary for its productivity. We have released two hundred prisoners to you as evidence of our sincerity.

> (*A long silence obtains as the ASSEMBLYMEN consult among themselves. Finally, the CHAIRMAN hands a written note to a CLERK and gestures that it be given to TOUSSAINT. Abruptly, the scene returns to headquarters of the Blacks where the content of the note is being read by a MULATTO AIDE.*)

AIDE

"Continue to give proof of your repentance and we will further deliberate upon your fate."

> (*Silence reigns as the BLACK LEADERS reflect gloomily; finally, BIASSOU speaks quietly.*)

BIASSOU

They rescue us ....

JEAN-FRANÇOIS

Rescue us ...?!

BIASSOU

Protect us—deliver us from ourself!... To save our own necks, we itched to betray all other niggers—the whole caboodle! Stupid Blancs won't allow us our cowardice....

JEAN-FRANÇOIS

These Commissioners cannot overrule the Assemblymen, Toussaint?

TOUSSAINT

Even when I reduced our amnesty list down from four hundred names to sixty names, the Commissioner could not get the Assembly to even discuss the offer... They are helpless—these Commissioners—three men without actual power. Their own lives are in jeopardy.

Non, mes Genereaux, the Blanc Colonists insist upon nothing but our total capitulation—"a war to the death"—and they expect shortly to overcome our superiority of numbers with troops from France.

It was foolish to have ever attempted bargaining, while other Blacks remained enslaved. Uttering the offer, the bile rose in my throat, my buttocks tightened uttering the offer... Non—Whites give us no alternative. Complete freedom is our only course.

I propose that we cease all discussions and prepare an army capable of driving the Whites into the sea. A disciplined force able to besiege their fortresses, occupy their towns and bring them to their knees. Protracted war may be ugly, but it is also necessary.

BIASSOU

Bravo! Bravo! Bravo Old Toussaint! The lamb has turned into a rhinoceros!... You are no longer fit to be doctor; I appoint you

Brigadier Toussaint de Breda of the Army of Generalissimo Biassou! From all our personal Private Armies, pick your men and start training a battalion to compare with your beloved Caesar. While you at it, the rest of us will keep the Blancs occupied—pissing blood!

> *(In semi-stylized fashion, the beginning of the BLACK ARMY is dramatized; maneuvers start raggedly and gain in expertise; guerrilla tactics are illustrated with WOMEN dancing as decoys while MEN take up positions in dead silence—then strike! Resistance prompts them to withdraw without tiring themselves out: if the enemy hesitates, HE is swarmed over by fright-yelling TROOPS.)*

VOICEOVER: ABBÉ RAYNAL

He will arise collecting around him companions in misfortune and will raise high the Pennant of Liberty. When on the move, these avengers will rage more impetuous than the torrents and everywhere leave indelible traces of their furious resentments ...

> *(The scene accelerates to climax with a representation of contending forces in diverse conflict. BOUKMAN sits Onstage observing, cross-legged, while the WOMEN's CHORUS provides commentary.)*

WOMEN'S CHORUS

Blood flowed misery mounted
Niggers mauled Whites in the North
And hacked away to the East
Slicing at the Môle sticking out of the Sea
Whites stood paralyzed in their tracks

As Blacks squeezed closer to the Forts of Le Cap
Petit Blancs couldn't fart in the West
Unless smelt by Mulattoes breathing
down their necks
Nègres supported by Mulattoes in the North

Blacks abetted Whites against Yellows
in the South
And they all kept looking across the water
Praying to France MON DIEU!—to restore Order.

(Everything freezes and a WHITE PLANTER is spotlighted)

PLANTER

The most sincere attachment binds the Master to the slave. We slept in safety amidst men who had become our children. We kept neither locks or bolts on our doors... Yet, gentlemen, a dastardly Society rose in the bosom of France preparing the destruction to which we are now subjected. Far from our being able to continue our work, this Society forces it to be suspended by sowing a spirit of insubordination among our slaves and provoking anxiety among ourselves!

It is reported that this Society will soon demand that the slave trade be suppressed altogether—that is as good to say that the profits which the slave trade earns for France will be disdained. But I say nay!... I cannot believe that this Society's romantic philosophy will ever persuade the powers of Europe that it is their duty to sacrifice the cultivation of the Colonies and betray the inhabitants of Africa to the barbarity of their savage tyrants there.

In our Colonies, under kind Masters, these redempted souls cultivate territories which, without their presence, would otherwise be left uncultivated—territories whose rich

resources are for the nations which develop them—a great source of industry and prosperity.

(Stark silence reigns as the stage is bare. Lights fade)

END OF ACT ONE

ACT TWO

(Act II opens to the stirring strains of THE MARSEILLAISE. The Tricolors of the Revolution are draped and hung from the Wheel and Other areas of the stage.

The action begins with three COMMISSIONERS from France, SONTHONAX, POLVEREL and AILHAUD, already being welcomed by COLONIAL OFFICIALS, led by DAUGNY, President of the Assembly, COMMANDER DESPARDES and BLANCHELANDE, the Governor.)

DAUGNY

In all our provinces, North, South and West, Commissioners— you will witness our citizens' submission to law.

SONTHONAX

This reversal astounds me, Msieur Daugny.

DAUGNY

Our people are like all others, Msieur Sonthonax. When they were unsure about the Mother Country's intentions, they acted with uncertainty. Now that France expresses herself clearly, they obey. Upon receiving news of the April 4th decree, we held a banquet for Men-of-Color—a few days later they reciprocated on our behalf.

OFFICIAL

Only the filthy rabble still harbors resentments, Commissioner.

SONTHONAX

Don't sneer at the 'rabble,' Msieur. In France that 'rabble' conducts a revolution. I, myself, am a servant of that revolution.

OFFICIAL

No offense intended, Msieur Sonthonax.

SONTHONAX

... Thank you, Msieurs, for your welcome. Commissioners Polverel, Ailhaud, Commander Despardes, and I are appreciative. Now—with apologies—I repeat once again that France only recognizes two classes of men no matter their color—those who are free, and those who are in slavery ... We are here to protect the rights of the former and to suppress the rebellion of the latter.

Towards this end—as of now, Governor Blanchelande is relieved of his duties and the Colonial Assembly hereby dissolved.

Commander Despardes will serve as Acting Governor. Until a new Assembly is installed, I will direct the Colony in partnership with an Interim Council appointed by me. Among whose members will be Mulattoes and even free Blacks....

DAUGNY

This is unbelievable, Msieur Sonthonax! As President of the Assembly I protest—You have no right to dismiss the elected government of San Domingo!

(Loud assents flow from the OFFICIALS)

SONTHONAX

(Topping them)

ELECTED BY WHOM, MSIEUR DAUGNY?!—A coterie of aristocrats?! . . . A cabal of incompetents who have brought France's richest possession to the brink of chaos! Whose ineptitude results in your being stalemated by a ragtag band of slaves most of whom as of yesterday couldn't distinguish a saber from a musket!

OFFICIAL

Maybe they were 'enlightened' by France's talk about 'the Rights of Man'!

SONTHONAX

True or not, Msieur—I am here to restore order and in so doing—save your ineffectual necks!

DAUGNY

All your predecessors failed, Msieur Sonthonax, because they refused to understand that our forebears did not import a half-million Blacks to this Island in order to make them French citizens!

SONTHONAX

But undeniably you have succeeded in making them your executioners! We have come to stay the verdict!

If, however, you imagine your own class slighted, comfort yourselves with the knowledge that Commander Despardes, your Acting Governor here, is a dedicated Monarchist whose devotion to the King and aristocracy is unsurpassed....

Rest assured, Msieurs, the National Assembly has no intentions of freeing the slaves—I intend to crush their revolt. Let us pray that this objective can be accomplished quickly, and peace restored to a Colony whose productivity is the very foundation of your own status....

Adieu, Msieurs—the Blacks await my attention. Long live the revolution.

> *(THE MARSEILLAISE swells as the Wheel revolves to the camp of the BLACKS... Drums are heard as the anthem begins to fade. BIASSOU sits alone Onstage, drinking. Finally, JEAN-FRANÇOIS enters.)*

BIASSOU

Eh, Jean-François—their Blanc Saints finally outdo our loas... I wonder if the good Priests of Charity have enough forgiveness in they hearts to take back a repentant sinner...? Probably twirl their holy rosary beads over my drunken carcass and pray that I end up in hell... What happens now...? You frown?

JEAN-FRANÇOIS

The Yellow bastard, Candi—has gone over to the Blancs!

BIASSOU

??? Who can blame him? . . . Why should he scramble over these devil mountains when his cousin is treated as royalty in Le Cap. Sonthonax romance half-breeds like virgins. He's even caught the White man's maladie—aching nuts for plunging between café-au-lait thighs . . . He'd better keep his pants buckled though. The closer he hug half-breeds the more he risk getting his behind sliced off by Petit-Blanc cochons . . . What news from Old Toussaint?

JEAN-FRANÇOIS

Laveaux just drove him from the Plaine-du-Nord.

BIASSOU

Laveaux!—Sacre Bleu! Old Toussaint should have read his book instead of that dead Caesar! . . . Merde, we were so close. The whole Island would now be ours—but for Laveaux! Our soldiers can't run fast enough to escape him. Toussaint is a bad prophet! . . . Ahh, Jean-François—

(Taking a big swig from his bottle)

BIASSOU (CONT'D)

—was it ever to be?

JEAN-FRANÇOIS

What?

BIASSOU

Whipping the Blancs?

JEAN-FRANÇOIS

. . . Maybe non.

BIASSOU

Ah, but what the hell! We got a fair share of they scalps. If I croak today, my ugly mug will still grin down—reminding Blancs that in mort more than enough of them keep me company... And if there's rum in the afterworld, I'll go gladly. If there's cunt, you'll be content. Maybe old Toussaint will find some books.

JEAN-FRANÇOIS

There's still time for you to pray a miracle, Biassou.

BIASSOU

I would exchange all the 'Hail Mary's on the Rosary for one volley of musket shot to get rid of Laveaux!

>*(Coinciding with BIASSOU's remark, lights blackout and immediately spotlight the Wheel—where the ringcenter opening is completely fitted out with a huge guillotine...*
>
>*The glinting razor-sharp edge of the guillotine plunges downward with a fearful clang upon landing; it draws upward and plunges down again and again.*
>
>*VOICES Offstage bellow out the MARSEILLAISE as doomed FIGURES file in and stand behind the Wheel, blotted out from view only after the blade drops. Eventually, KING and QUEEN figures take their places behind the guillotine. The blade slices down in a final fall.*
>
>*Lights blackout and the MARSEILLAISE is succeeded by drums beating steadily, conveying a sense of triumphant salvation. This feeling carries through three scenes which follow.*

The immediate scene opens at TOUSSAINT's camp where DESSALINES, a guide, formerly seen at the opening of the play as the BLACK who spat upon the dying MULATTOES; and CHRISTOPHE, TOUSSAINT's Le Cap informant, seen earlier in the Drinking-Inn as the WAITER are talking.)

TOUSSAINT

Is it definite, Christophe?

CHRISTOPHE

Oui, Commander. When news reached Le Cap that King Louis and his Queen, Marie Antoinette, had their heads chopped off, Sonthonax' French officers started deserting him. At the inn they grumble in my presence, not caring who hear them.

TOUSSAINT

So... Laveaux should have been our Frère-in-Arms. Why did not France see this...?!

DESSALINES

She is White, we are Black, mon Générale. That blinds her to all else.

TOUSSAINT

... And Laveaux now?

CHRISTOPHE

He is on his way to Môle St. Nicolas, repositioning his troops to guard against a British invasion from Jamaica.

DESSALINES

Le Cap is weak for the taking!

CHRISTOPHE

Oui, Sonthonax has no one he can trust but the Mulattoes.

DESSALINES

Shit on Yellow breeds! . . . General Toussaint . . . ?

TOUSSAINT

Consider . . ., even with Sonthonax weakened, we would not stand a chance. Laveaux has inflicted too much damage. No, our soldiers are too valuable. Warring with both Britain and Spain, France will surely send more troops to defend San Domingo . . . No—we will wait . . . .

> *(Quickly, scene shifts briefly to SONTHONAX' headquarters where an AIDE has just brought him a message; the drumming continues.)*

SONTHONAX

Galbaud! . . . Merdes! Canailles! . . . We chase Blacks, we snuff out Planter-rebellions, and now we face Britain and Spain—who does France send to Govern—Galbaud! . . . Why not send the reactionary president of the Massiac Club! Why not sew King Louis and Marie Antoinette's heads back on their skeletons and ship them here . . .?!

> *(Scene shifts back to BLACKS where an AIDE is reading a communiqué from the SPANISH.)*

AIDE

"Liberty now and forever. The rights and prerogatives of Spanish citizenship. Valuable land for all rebel chiefs in French or Spanish parts of the Island. Plus ample monies and supplies for you and your armies."

... Signed by the Spanish Counsel, representative of the King of Spain.

BIASSOU

(*Ecstatic*)

Ha, ha, ha! Did you hear that, Jean-François?! My Blanc prayers have been answered! Hail Mary, Jesus favor us! We scamper up and down these damn mountains, spill blood to fill ditches—and just when the rodent is about to choke us down his gullet—we get liberty, not from France but Spain! Ha, ha, ha!

TOUSSAINT

Be suspicious of gifts, Biassou.

BIASSOU

Shit on your suspicions, Toussaint! We shouldn't have bothered with the French. Just scoot past the border and pick up freedom from the Spanish for the asking!

TOUSSAINT

They need us.

BIASSOU

And we them! ... We were finis, Toussaint—you hear me?! Finis! ... Look at us now—ragged, hungry, scurrying like rabbits one stop ahead of Laveaux' hounds. Spain saves us, you hear! Saves us!

TOUSSAINT

And when our usefulness ends?

BIASSOU

Merde on the future! Until today a nigger couldn't beg a chew off a cane-joint. Now we are handed guns, ammunitions—commissions in the Spanish Army and PERMISSION to kill Blancs! That's all the future I need know!

TOUSSAINT

The Spanish mention only we chiefs—nothing about other slaves.

BIASSOU

We kissed French asses for less! Begged to lick their boots and rewarded with insults! Remember, Toussaint—you played the beggar! . . . God bless Spain—Damballah, too! . . . Oui, the Spanish are très genereaux—but it figures, they never treat us bad as the French—too busy screwing our wenches to work us to death. They don't care about prosperity; all they want is to fuck! Why they district populate with more mixed-breeds than slaves!

TOUSSAINT

And need us to fight!

BIASSOU

And you don't trust them, eh, Toussaint? . . . But you have enough faith to hide your family behind their border! . . . You tired of fighting the French, Toussaint—? You afraid you might bayonet your so loved Mistress de Libertat in the twat? Did you stow her away safe in Le Cap because you dream of stabbing her with a meatier saber?

TOUSSAINT

Don't insult me, Biassou . . . !

JEAN-FRANÇOIS

ARRÊTE, ARRÊTE! ENOUGH!... Our decision is clear... Biassou is right... France does not stand a chance fighting against both Britain and Spain. If we keep our own armies, we control this Island. It doesn't matter what purpose the Spanish think they use us for... France lost its chance. It could have had us with a grin and a pat... Now she will pay for her error in blood.

TOUSSAINT

I will only bargain with the Spanish on my own terms.

JEAN-FRANÇOIS

By all means—long as your Army remain under our joint command.

BIASSOU

We give you permission to negotiate, Old Toussaint. But take care that your fear of shiny gift wrappings don't blind you to the sweet bonbons inside!

> *(Drumming ends as scene shifts without break to GALBAUD's headquarters. GALBAUD is pacing around, angrily addressing an AIDE.)*

GALBAUD

This is an insult! Sonthonax and Polverel deliberately ignore me! I ordered them to return to Le Cap a month ago.

> *(SONTHONAX AND POLVEREL enter.)*

SONTHONAX

Msieur Galbaud, bonjour.

POLVEREL

Bonjour, Msieur Galbaud.

GALBAUD

Well, Msieurs, I have waited impatiently for your return. What delayed you?

SONTHONAX

We were occupied, Msieur Galbaud... Insurrections are no small occasions.

GALBAUD

France is at war, now! Total War is more critical than local insurrections!

POLVEREL

Insurrections against the revolution wherever translate into war, Msieur Galbaud.

GALBAUD

I am responsible for defending all of San Domingo. You were sent to put down riots, I have been assigned to resolve a conflict between nations!

SONTHONAX

Msieur Galbaud, we were sent to San Domingo to enforce the April fourth decree of the National Assembly, then to suppress a revolt by Black slaves. For this we were invested with supreme authority. The weight of that authority has already resulted in Governor Blanchelande being shipped back to France and arrested. Subsequently, Acting Governor Despardes was removed for traitorous actions against the Republic and paid dearly under the guillotine... Msieur Galbaud, until we receive direct instructions from France's National Assembly, our authority subordinates itself to no one.

GALBAUD

I bring you direct orders from the Executive Council of the National Assembly, don't you understand that? . . . I am Governor of this colony!

SONTHONAX

Sworn to uphold all laws—including the April 4th Decree?

GALBAUD

Minus excesses! . . . Your favoritism towards Mulattoes disadvantages the cream of San Domingo society!

SONTHONAX

As the late beheaded King Louis was the "creme" of French society, Msieur Galbaud?

GALBAUD

The King has nothing—

SONTHONAX

YES-MSIEUR GALBAUD, LIKE THE KING! . . . The "cream" of San Domingo society who constantly defy the revolution! Incessantly scheming and plotting—opposing the Republic by every means of subversion, including resort to arms!

GALBAUD

You insist upon defying me, Commissioner Sonthonax?

SONTHONAX

You have no legitimate authority to contest, Msieur Galbaud.

GALBAUD

Authority conferred by France's highest tribunal!

SONTHONAX

(Remaining calm)

Your appointment is illegal, Msieur Galbaud. The National Assembly . . . or more accurately, a committee of the National Assembly—caught up in the confusion of crisis, overlooked the law—an oversight hastily exploited by your Colonial amis to obtain your appointment.

GALBAUD

What do you mean?

SONTHONAX

Before accepting your assignment, Msieur Galbaud—did you sell your property—your coffee plantation and other holdings here in San Domingo?

GALBAUD

My holdings have no bearing on my appointment!

SONTHONAX

Upon taking power the National Assembly enacted a law, Msieur Galbaud—a regulation forbidding any property-owner in the West Indies to serve as Governor of any Colony where his property is located.

GALBAUD

You are not authorized to question my appointment!

SONTHONAX

That law gives me the right! It has not been rescinded ... Upon your return to Paris, you will enlighten the Executive Council of their oversight.

GALBAUD

I have no intentions of returning to France!

SONTHONAX

Then despite your intentions.

GALBAUD

You dare order me back to France?!

SONTHONAX

Msieur Galbaud—a ship is presently anchored at harbor. As soon as you and your staff have collected your belongings, it will sail. If you resist departing voluntarily, be assured that I am prepared to see that you are escorted on your voyage back to France.

> *(SONTHONAX signals and a SQUAD OF MULATTO SOLDIERS enters and takes up positions ... GALBAUD stares at them silently. After a long pause, HE realizes the hopelessness of circumstances.)*

GALBAUD

... I see, you give me no choice, Sonthonax. I bow ... not because I am intimidated by your Mulatto henchmen ... but because of my love for San Domingo. I quiver at the civil strife she will face ... No, I will leave you to be dealt with by the National Assembly—confident that your insane defiance will brand you an outlaw to be tracked down like the Black rebels whom your policies facilitate against France's best interests.

SONTHONAX

Spare me lectures, Msieur Galbaud!... When, from the very moment you set foot in San Domingo to the cheers of Royalists, you have been conniving with traitors of the Republic!

You are not a believer in the revolution, Msieur Galbaud—but a deceitful worm of the Massiac Club, pretending support for revolution while secretly plotting to regain the lost privileges of your aristocratic class, parasites intent upon gorging yourselves, leaving nothing but cast-off dregs for minions below you!... Spare me your sentiments, Msieur Galbaud—they are dubious upon the enunciation. Adieu, Msieur.

> *(The ensuing scenes occur simultaneously at various locations. Centerstage is dominated by a celebration taking place in the dance hall where SONTHONAX, POLVEREL and MULATTOES toast their ousting of GALBAUD.*
>
> *LUSCIOUS FEMALES of ebony and color caress and entertain the CELEBRANTS. A majority of the WOMEN are engaged in a dance. THEY are clothed in diaphanous gowns hugging their shapes; then, gradually, THEY add elegant 'ladies' apparel piece by piece—a reverse striptease contrasted to their performance at the beginning of the play...*
>
> *While this transpires, Upstage, atop the Wheel, which now represents a ship deck, GALBAUD is seen conversing with SAILORS.*

Stage Left has an area which will be pinpointed with light as TOUSSAINT is observed meeting with the SPANISH MARQUIS DE HERMONA...

A similar area, Stage Right, will be pinpointed as a MULATTO AIDE OF TOUSSAINT meets with LAVEAUX.

When the other brief scenes intrude, noise from the dance hall celebration subsides into silence, then resumes.

Lights pinpoint HERMONA and TOUSSAINT.)

HERMONA

Colonel Toussaint, I deplore Governor Don Garcia's rejection of your proposal. I think it splendid. Emancipating slaves in Spanish San Domingo would certainly attract Black support to our war effort against France on both sides of the border. However, I am afraid I must defer to Governor Garcia's superior authority.

(Lights fade and then pinpoint LAVEAUX replying to TOUSSAINT's MESSENGER.)

LAVEAUX

Tell your 'Colonel' Toussaint that I am not authorized to accept his offer. France is not in the habit of bestowing amnesty and freedom upon those rebelling against her—even if it would strengthen her against our Spanish enemy—

(Lights fade and noise from the dance hall rises. Now, the WOMEN are dressed in full elegance and the CELEBRANTS are drunker and more raucous.

When toastings are climaxed, the WOMEN turn abruptly and once again address the audience.)

WOMEN'S CHORUS

**Once again Msieur Sonthonax proved a winner
But his loa was soon to express its displeasure
Just when fortune seemed to bestow reward
Fickle Gods intervened to cause his spirit discord
Galbaud his foe, he thought, was making ready to sail Instead the trickster was cooing in shipmen's ears since there was little love lost between seamen in the harbor
And cheeky Mulattoes astrut the town's quarter
Galbaud had no difficulty
Stirring up disorder**

(Atop the Wheel, GALBAUD draws attention to a fistfight between a SAILOR and a MULATTO. OTHER SAILORS stream down the Wheel, weapons raised, joining the melee.

Offstage, the sound of gunfire erupts all over the city.

Downstage, a SOLDIER rushes into the dance hall shouting.)

SOLDIER

SAILORS ATTACKING THE CITY! SAILORS ATTACKING THE CITY!

SONTHONAX

Get to your positions! Hurry! We must stop Galbaud!

(As THEY ALL race Offstage, the WOMEN'S CHORUS remains to narrate the details of the conflict which is shadow-depicted upon the Upstage scrim from the rear.)

WOMEN'S CHORUS

Barricades made of barrels, boxes and
bales of cotton
From windows, buildings and the roofs of houses
The battle raged as Galbaud's
regiments pressed on
Mulattoes at the Arsenal all massacred
After their Royalist officers' turncoat against them
National Guard and Soldiers of the Line
Divide and fire at each other without decline
Galbaud swept on
Past the Rue Penthièvre
Down the Rue Dauphine

Stalled by Loyalists holed up in the Cathedral
Then plunged on across the Rue Vaudreuill
Fighting promised to end by night
With Galbaud ogling victory in sight

But Sailors pausing with kegs of rum made delay
Causing strife to spill into another day
At last Galbaud shelled the Government House
Setting Sonthonax and his men to rout
By nightfall Galbaud's Sailors ruled over Le Cap

With Sonthonax nursing his wounds beneath
a mountaintop A great hurrah swept
through the town
Royalists frolicked 'til daylight
Celebrating Galbaud's renown
And the salvation of the Crown.

(Led by victorious SAILORS, the stage is peopled with CELEBRANTS engaged in bacchanalian orgies, drinking into stupors. The revels are accompanied by the sound of Black drums, imperceptible at first, then steadily growing louder and louder.

Soon, along the edges of the stage, the presence of ragged, fierce-looking BLACKS reveals itself. Stealthily, THEY take up positions, surrounding the REVELERS. THEY are poised and silent, machetes and muskets drawn.

The drums reach a climactic crescendo and the BLACKS explode down upon the CELEBRANTS, hacking away, running amok across the stage, directed by two leaders, MACAYA and PIERROT.

The massacre sweeps Offstage and its continued fury is indicated by Offstage sound effects and shadow play enlargements behind the scrim.

GALBAUD's FORCES are overwhelmed by the furious onslaught of the BLACKS, aided by revengeful MULATTOES and loyal WHITE REPUBLICANS.

The action spills back Onstage with GALBAUD and some of his FOLLOWERS illustrated making their final escapes, swimming toward the Wheel-ship.

At the moment when BLACKS are poised to commit their final atrocities against WHITES, the scene is frozen into suspended-tableaux.

Play I: The Rise of Toussaint L'Ouverture

BOUKMAN *appears Downstage and confronts the audience.)*

BOUKMAN

Like le chat, Msieur Sonthonax had many lives. Once again he had snatched his tail out the bramble bush... As old Toussaint's book might say: "Policy change through necessity"... As I would put it, 'You'll gladly eat shit when it look like you won't be around for breakfast.'

Remember what Sonthonax said when he first landed in San Domingo? That he'd rather see niggers dead than free? Well, after Galbaud beat him avec sword and saber, Msieur Sonthonax proved a very practical man. What good is a mission if the missionary not around to see it through?

Still licking his wounds, Sonthonax could hear Galbaud celebrate inside Le Cap. But not too far away, he also saw the flames of some campfires. Black outlaw rebels there!—-Poof!—Sonthonax, the missionary, smooched his old mission goodbye!—and hurried off a messenger to the nigger camp, inviting them for a chat....

SONTHONAX

If you join me and the Republic, Chiefs Macaya and Pierrot, all your men will be pardoned and everybody under your command freed. You'll be equal with all men and granted all the rights and privileges of French citizens.

MACAYA

In exchange for what?

SONTHONAX

Recapturing Le Cap. The Royalist Galbaud occupies the city and if he retains it, Blacks will remain enslaved forever and the entire Island will be lost. But together our joint armies can reconquer the city for the Republic.

PIERROT

Spare your talk of freedom. What's in it for us maintenant?!

SONTHONAX

—All the loot you can carry.

> *(The freeze ends abruptly and the BLACKS complete their final savagery; the action swirling through the center of the Wheel, moving Offstage.*
>
> *The stage is vacant as the sound of crackling flames and the sight of glowing embers loom, cast by the torching of Le Cap.*
>
> *A huddled stream of MARCHERS file Onstage, slowly and dejectedly mounting the Wheel. Bundles in hands, silhouetted by firelight, THEY gather atop the Wheel to gaze mournfully into the audience. Against the illumination of the monumental fire-holocaust, THEY appear very tiny and pitiful.)*

BOUKMAN

Ten thousand Whites—more than half the population in Le Cap—crowd the decks of one hundred ships—and on the night June twenty-fourth, seventeen ninety-three— they snuck outta the harbor—heading in the moonlight toward any port might shelter them from San Domingo nègres. Their favorite destination: the nouveaux United States of America...

Except for clothes on their backs and whatever else they clutch in two hands; haste didn't allow them to salvage much more..

They were fortunate ones—Unluckier Blanc brethren stayed behind, stinking corpses stacking up the streets of Le Cap, rotting and decaying away to maggots' flesh... As the sailway survivors cruise off, they look back a last time, but the Le Cap they had once pirouetted and minuetted through golden days of splendor... the Paris of the Antilles... jewel of the richest Colony in the world—was flaming to ashes, two-thirds of buildings already scorched to embers and hundreds of millions of Francs disintegrating every wisp of smoke... In just four days, White San Domingo lost what it took Black slaves more than two hundred years to construct.

The slaves had given, now the slaves was taking away—blessed be the vengeance of Damballah... Sonthonax triumphed anew, but this time victory was like diarrhea. All he had left was a gut-out city and thousands of rampaging niggers. Even blue-blood officers defected to Black Spanish armies. His torrid affair avec the Mulattoes even fizzled. Like Blancs they had no interest in watching crazy darkies stagger around shouting liberty and fraternity... But the unkindest cut of all was Macaya and Pierrot, Sonthonax' Black rescuers—after sacking up everything they could plunder—instead of sticking around—picked up and led twenty thousand niggers back to the mountains—where they too hired theyselves out to the Spanish....

Having won a skirmish but about to lose the war, Sonthonax decided to lay cards face-up and play his strongest suit... five hundred thousand niggers was in the pot....

On August twenty-ninth, seventeen ninety-three, he issued his personal emancipation proclamation:

SONTHONAX' VOICEOVER
"ALL SLAVES ARE HENCEFORTH FOREVER FREE."

BOUKMAN

His petro was unkind—he was already being trumped.

(Lights pinpoint TOUSSAINT atop the Wheel)

TOUSSAINT

Brothers and friends, my name is known to you. I am Toussaint L'Ouverture. I was the first to champion your cause and I intend to press on. I will allow no one to rob me of the initiative nor rest until complete liberty and equality is achieved in San Domingo. Come fight alongside me and you will gain the rights of freemen quicker than any other way. I am a Black like you. Neither Whites nor Mulattoes have influenced me in my determination. It is God alone to whom I owe my inspiration. I was the first, I have kept on and I know how to proceed until victory is won . . . .

(Lights fade)

BOUKMAN

Signed "Toussaint L'Ouverture" . . . L'Ouverture? . . . 'Papa Legba, ouvre les barrières pour moi'—Papa Legba open the gate for me . . .??? Could old voodoo-hating Toussaint de Breda have been cogitating about Papa Legba, our beloved voodoo God . . . keeper . . . opener of the Gate of Destiny . . .???

Whether yes or nay—the Gods had counsel him wisely. "L'Ouverture, the opening"—Toussaint Breda no more—but "L'Ouverture"! . . . 'Only a courageous chief was wanted and he appointed himself.'

(WOMEN'S CHORUS narrates TOUSSAINT's ARMY's dramatic course; dividing lines individually.)

Play I: The Rise of Toussaint L'Ouverture

WOMEN'S CHORUS

Six hundred crack-jack soldiers
A staff of Whites, Mulattoes, but mostly Blacks
His nephew Moïse
His brother Jean-Paul
Officers Parapet, Noël and a mean nigger rising
in the ranks
Called Dessalines
Toussaint swept down on French Domingo
Carrying everything in his path before him

"He disappears! Has flown as if by magic!
Now he reappears again where least expected
He is ubiquitous!
One never knows where his army is,
What it lives on, how he recruits it, what mountain
fastness He stashes his supplies and his treasury!
Yet he always knows what goes on in our camp!"

Thousands of niggers in the ranks of the French
Come over to him without a shot
Fifteen hundred men captured without a fight
When second-in-command White Pacot
Betrays his Colonel Brandicoot
Twelve hundred more when Mulatto Vernet
defects at Enery

(The scrim is illuminated with a huge battle map pinpointing TOUSSAINT's campaign victories.)

WOMEN'S CHORUS (CONT'D)

Chanalatte delivers all his troops in Plaisance
Garrisons defect at St. Marc, Archayle
and Verrettes,
Gros-Morne, Marmelade, Plaisance, Acul, Limbe,

Port-Magot, Le Petit-Louis and Terre Neuve—
All fell

The cordon of the West from the Spanish border
To the sea was held
Every fortified position in the North
except for Le Cap
Spain controlled as well

Britain invaded the South and West
Creating more woe
Sonthonax made ready to put torch to France's
last hopes in San Domingo
But before he could light the match to ignite
a fiery wreck
Paris ordered him back to face the guillotine being
sharpened For his neck
Barricaded at Port au Paix
Only Laveaux remained in command
Waiting the end which seemed close at hand

(Lights pinpoint LAVEAUX. Sad strains of the MARSELLAISE are heard.)

LAVEAUX

For six months, my officers and men are reduced to six ounces of bread a day. Since the thirteenth of this month, we have no bread whatsoever. Our misery is truly great. We have no shoes, clothes, soap, tobacco. Like the Africans, most of my soldiers stand guard barefoot. We have not even a flint to give our men . . . .

(The MARSEILLAISE fades, supplanted by African drums and the jubilant noise of CELEBRANTS Offstage. Scene shifts to the

headquarters of TOUSSAINT, who is alone in his chambers. CHRISTOPHE enters and pauses as HE notices the somber mood of his chief.)

CHRISTOPHE

Why so sad, mon Colonel?

TOUSSAINT

... Christophe—when Spain's new ally the British recently invaded Jérémie in the South, at whose invitation did they answer to?

CHRISTOPHE

Invitation, Colonel...?

TOUSSAINT

(Supplying his own answer)

Loyal French planters of the South... These Slave-masters stood cheering on the wharf—rich Mulattoes too...Why do these French citizens welcome the hated British so warmly?

CHRISTOPHE

They dislike the new French Republic mon Colonel.

TOUSSAINT

Perhaps they like slavery more... Could the British have promised them what they cherish most...?

(HE sits)

TOUSSAINT (CONT'D)

I am fatigué, Christophe—weary, confused... sit.

(CHRISTOPHE *obeys.*)

TOUSSAINT (CONT'D)

This alliance we share with Spain . . . what strange bedfellows . . . they hug us—but will they smother us? . . . They press monies, gifts upon us—To what purpose . . . ? . . . We Blacks seem always to be stranded in the midst of White men's' ambitions. Hundreds of years, machetes in hand, we were the muscles of their prosperity. Do they use us now to harvest a different yield . . . ? If so, we stand as much slaves upon the battlefields as in the canebrakes—as ill-used in our glittering uniforms as once in our tattered breeches.

CHRISTOPHE

It is you who control San Domingo, Colonel.

TOUSSAINT

I control the battlefield, but I do not master circumstances . . . we are too much in the dark—still shackled to ignorance, unable to penetrate to the heart of the White man's intentions . . . When I joined the Spanish, I hoped everything would be resolved—we would hack our way to a sensible future promising liberty . . . Those sounds of gaiety outside?—are they premature . . . ?

. . . I pray that Mon Dieu would deliver me from uncertainty . . .

> (*The drum sounds are once again supplanted by the MARSEILLAISE as the scene shifts back to the National Assembly where a tumultuous session is underway.*)

CHAIRMAN

Since seventeen eighty-nine the aristocracy of birth and the aristocracy of religion have been destroyed—but the aristocracy of the skin remained . . . Today at last that too is in its final throes and equality is on the verge of consecration. Citizens, your Committee has verified the credentials of the Deputies from San Domingo. I move that they be admitted to their places in the Convention . . . Bellay, a Black man, an ex-slave, purchaser of his own freedom, and Mills, a Yellow man, are about to join this Convention in the name of the free citizens of San Domingo!

> (BELLAY, the Black; MILLS, the Mulatto; along with DUFAY, a White, enter to the sound of great applause. LACROIX of Eure-et-Loire rises.)

LACROIX

For some time, this Assembly has been anxious to include in its ranks some men of color, perpetual—sufferers of oppression! Today it is privileged to have two of them! I La Croix, of Eure-et-Loire, propose that their introductions be honored with the President's fraternal embrace!

> (The proposal is greeted with thunderous assents. The PRESIDENT rises to comply.
>
> HE busses the two MEN, saving his last kiss for BELLAY—causing an even greater eruption of acclaim.
>
> Scene shifts back to TOUSSAINT's headquarters where MOÏSE, DESSALINES, CHRISTOPHE and OTHERS are present. A WHITE AIDE is reading.)

AIDE

"The National Convention declares slavery abolished in all the Colonies. Furthermore, it declares that all men living in the

Colonies without distinction of color are French citizens and are entitled to enjoy all rights assured under the Constitution."

TOUSSAINT

When did this happen, Christophe?

CHRISTOPHE

In February, Colonel Toussaint, almost four months ago. French troops only now arrive with the news. They claim that a man called Robespierre is sending hundreds of slavers to the guillotine.

DESSALINES

Merde! They lie!—But even so, it's too late! France hand out freedom after we took it!

TOUSSAINT

It is never too late, Dessalines. Without legality, freedom is fragile. Look at us here—as fast as we enforce liberty at saber point, other Blacks barter it away for pouches of silver . . . Governor Laveaux?—how does he react, Christophe?

CHRISTOPHE

He enforces the decree before its official confirmation, Colonel.

TOUSSAINT

Then we must follow his example ici in Spanish territories we control.

> (*Without break, the scene shifts to JEAN-FRANÇOIS and BIASSOU being briefed by a MULATTO AIDE.*)

AIDE

Despite Spanish policy, he violates sacred orders of the King, arming slaves, telling them they are free—including those who are perfectly content to continue toiling without freedom! Toussaint calls himself Chief of the Blacks and preaches disobedience.

BIASSOU

And gets promoted for it! . . . How do you like that, Jean-François?—Old Toussaint do as he please even if it is not what is wished and the Spanish promote him for it. Soon he'll be our chief—instead of just costing us money—you more than me, of course!

JEAN-FRANÇOIS

You supply as many slaves to traders as I do, Biassou.

BIASSOU

Just enough to keep my rum supply flowing. Your uniform and pussy debt is costlier . . . But why should Old Toussaint fret? While I guzzle and you fornicate, he's built the best army in San Domingo. He can afford to tell us to stick our nose up his ass-crack.

JEAN-FRANÇOIS

Soon I will clip the gray burrs on Toussaint's tête to a bald shine . . .

> *(Lights fade as there is a SHADOW SCRIM depiction of TOUSSAINT being suddenly ambushed while riding horseback; an ambush which fatally wounds his brother Jean-Pierre . . .*

Scene shifts to TOUSSAINT's chambers where he is in the midst of praying. DESSALINES enters, delays until TOUSSAINT rises from his knees.)

DESSALINES

The Marquis de HERMONA est ici, General, aussi General Biassou and Commander François! Sacre bleu! Les chats pretend the mice never got pawed! Let me cut cochons' throats, mon Général?!

TOUSSAINT

No, Dessalines.

DESSALINES

If not for you, General—for your brother, Jean-Pierre, who they assassinated!

TOUSSAINT

We cannot afford revenge maintenant. Show them in.

(DESSALINES exits and TOUSSAINT occupies himself putting away his rosary and praying articles. As HE does so, the MARQUIS, BIASSOU and JEAN-FRANÇOIS are ushered in by DESSALINES.)

BIASSOU

(Observing TOUSSAINT's obviously-concluded religious rite.)

You embarrass me Toussaint! I who spent so much time next to God's helpers, you put me to shame with your reverence!

MARQUIS

If God descended upon earth, he could take refuge in no purer heart than the heart of Toussaint L'Ouverture!

BIASSOU

But since God needs be occupied elsewhere, today, Toussaint will have to be satisfied with consecrations from God's earth representative—our Catholic majesty hisself who is waiting to preside where citizens shout hoarse to the sound of Ole's!

JEAN-FRANÇOIS

I hope this honor will ease your grief, Toussaint. My condolences for your brother, Jean Pierre—but for the brave to fall in battle is the supreme honor.

DESSALINES

(*Unable to control his outburst*)

No honor to be slayed in a coward's ambush!

JEAN-FRANÇOIS

In war???

(*Training a severe gaze upon DESSALINES*)

DESSALINES

Captain Dessalines.

JEAN-FRANÇOIS

In LaGuerre—Captain Dessalines, all manner of soldier's deaths occur in 'battle' . . . I gather, Toussaint, that when you were intercepted, you and Jean-Pierre were hurrying to intercede for officers detained in my custody. How unfortunate. Just think—

if your officers had not interfered in my affairs, Jean-Pierre might still be alive.

TOUSSAINT

They were acting on my instructions, Jean-François.

JEAN-FRANÇOIS

Who gave you the right?! What right do you have meddling in my districts?!

TOUSSAINT

I sent my officers to intercede with the royal Governor on behalf of slaves being sold to traders.

JEAN-FRANÇOIS

Why should that concern you?!

TOUSSAINT

Whatever affects the morale of my troops concerns me, Jean-François. How can I ask soldiers to risk their lives while their kinsmen are re-enslaved and shipped out of San Domingo?!

MARQUIS

Generals—let's not quarrel! But rejoice! Port au Prince has just fallen to the British. The French will soon be driven out of San Domingo. Once France and its Republic of King-Murderers is no more, in time all disagreements will be resolved... Now, come let us make way to celebrate—and allow Spain to pay homage to General Toussaint whose brilliant campaign has led us to the eve of decisive victory! Let us salute him!

BIASSOU

To the Arena! Where l'homme who pit hisself against a dumb but wily brute wait to entertain. The French will soon be driven out of San Domingo. We couldn't find a lion, Toussaint, you will hafta be content with the dead ears of a bull....

(Suddenly, the sound of intense battle erupts as lights change quickly. SOLDIERS are heard screaming in agony. Clashing saber-din and musket-fire are continuous. Time flashes forward ... Finally, TOUSSAINT emerges out of darkness, approached by DESSALINES from the opposite direction.)

TOUSSAINT

Did you capture him?

DESSALINES

Non, non, mon , the merde escaped!

TOUSSAINT

(Collecting stray objects)

... Too in a hurry to take his gold watch and diamond snuff-box?

DESSALINES

Not even his precious horse and carriage.

TOUSSAINT

He truly was hurrying!

DESSALINES

He can't get far on foot! We can overtake him—

TOUSSAINT

No—let him escape.

DESSALINES

Let him go free?!

TOUSSAINT

Let him be—oui... Gather all his belongings—even his horse and carriage—and have them delivered to the Spanish high command with my compliments—especially his rum. He will be delirious without it...

DESSALINES

The drunken sot should be shot for assassinating Jean-Pierre!

TOUSSAINT

Non... I owe Biassou favor. Besides—the ambush had all the trademarks of Jean-François, not Biassou... I might kill Biassou yet now that we are French Republicans—but I can't stop being fond of him.

Picturing the shock on his face being so rudely interrupted upon is revenge enough... Let's move on. A more personal score to tend to...

> *(There is a flourish of drum-thunder, then lights contract to pinpoint TOUSSAINT dictating a letter to an AIDE.)*

TOUSSAINT (CONT'D)

Mon Père, Laveaux, I almost captured General Jean-François himself. He barely escaped with his life by diving into thick weeds. Altogether during my campaigns, I have taken many prisoners... We have moved so rapidly, my army has run out of supplies—my men have no coats, shirts or trousers, only a few rags scarcely covering their bodies—But without these encumbrances we are able to move faster.

We have little to eat—but, we have always been close companions to starvation. The ecstasy of fighting for freedom—a freedom finally bestowed upon us by the Mother Country without qualifications—compensates for our hardships. Brave French Republicans like Moïse, J. B. Parapet, Dessalines and Noël speak for all our Chiefs—swearing that they will brave any difficulty to the end.

... Nothing can resist the bravery of French Sans-Culottes like our soldiers ... In one battle, after all ammunition had been spent, they continued to fight with stones. If I had some artillery, I would sweep the British into the sea. Lacking such weapons, I find more ingenious ways to outmaneuver them.

(MOÏSE enters on cue)

MOÏSE

Oui, Uncle. According to information from Generals Rigaud and Beauvais, Diodonne, the Maroon Chieftain in the West is thinking of joining up with the British... He has more than five thousand men under his command.

TOUSSAINT

We can't allow a defection of that size, Moïse. Send this message to La Plume, Diodonne's Chief Lieutenant—my Secret Ally. He will know what to do.

(As TOUSSAINT delivers the message, lights simultaneously focus upon LA PLUME miming the oration before DIODONNE'S MEN.)

TOUSSAINT (CONT'D)

Mon frère Diodonne, I cannot believe the painful rumors about you joining the British. Can it be possible, dear ami, that at the very moment when France achieves victory over all Royalists and adopts Blacks as her children—that you could be deceived by England, sworn enemy of our freedom, ancient tyrants who plot to misuse half of us to keep the other half in chains??? Yes—their ally, the Spanish, had me blinded for a time, but it didn't take long for me to see through their trickery. Upon recognizing their rascality, I abandoned them and proceeded to beat them well.

I implore you, dear brother, to take heed of my example. If you have reasons to mistrust Generals Rigaud and Beauvais, or even Governor Laveaux in whom our Mother Country invests its confidence—then I trust you will not reject me who am Black like yourself and who wish nothing more than to see you and all our brethren happy.

It is underneath the flag of the French Republic that we are truly free ... If, possibly, the English have succeeded in deceiving you, come to your sense and disown them as I disowned the Spanish. Unite with honest Republicans and let us all chase these Royalist oppressors from our country—these wretches who strain to reshackle us with chains we have suffered so much agony breaking ....

> *(TOUSSAINT's message ignites the MEN. THEY mime hurling invectives upon DIODONNE whom LA PLUME orders arrested, to the enthusiastic approval of the MEN.*
>
> *Lights blackout on the DIODONNE area; TOUSSAINT resumes as lights also pinpoint JEAN-FRANÇOIS and BIASSOU.)*

TOUSSAINT (CONT'D)

Jean-François, your King of Spain supplies you with abundant arms and ammunitions. Use them to tighten your fetters. As for us, we need nothing more than sticks and stones to make you dance the Carmagnole ... Enjoy your commissions, your liveries and your parchments. One day they will serve you as the fastidious titles of former aristocrats serviced them—uselessly!

... How dare you offer us the protection of your despicable royal master ... Listen well and tell Caso Calva, your Spanish Grandee, that Republicans cannot treat with a King. But we urge him to come anyway and you along with him—we are ready to welcome you as Republicans should!

(Lights fade on the DOINDONNE SPOKESMAN and remain on JEAN-FRANÇOIS and BIASSOU)

BIASSOU

... Old Toussaint, our courageous leader ... He offer a invitation more compelling than yours, Jean-François. I'm tempted to accept ... if I could trust he won't wring my neck. He allow me one escape already, I wouldn't want to tempt him again.

Ha, ha, ha, ha—what a joke on us, ay, Jean-François? Just when France is ready to call the pallbearer and bid adieu to San Domingo, Old Toussaint change side and reverse the war—bang the door on Spain and Britain and carve out a new opening for the Ghost of France ... He musta been in touch with old Frenchy Laveaux all the while. Even before our great Spanish Majesty of God on Earth himself could finish pinning medals on Toussaint, he pounce on us—barely give me chance to swallow my rum and caught you mid-dick-stroke without time to sheath your leaky rod or hitch up your britches! Ha, ha, ha! ... All the territory he once conquered for Spain, he's already given back to France ...

JEAN-FRANÇOIS

Toussaint is a jackass—loyal canaille to French merdes who kept him in slavery the best years of his life?

BIASSOU

He seeks liberty for all.

JEAN-FRANÇOIS

He'll never get it!

BIASSOU

But he'll kill us trying! . . . Face it, Jean-François. He's a better garçon than us. My ambition last no longer than it take my rum stupor to lift—and your aspiration stretch no farther than the shadow cast by your dick. But old Toussaint always had greater vision . . . You and me primp and prance—dizzy by sweet muttering from the Blancs—San Domingo exile scum who wouldn't stoop to spit on us a few years ago! . . . Now they flatter us! "Great generals of antiquity, you warrant our deepest admiration . . ."

Merde! The asslickers depend on us to recapture they property! . . . Toussaint—even when he was on their side, they never fawn over him. Cursed him behind his back because his obsession about liberty was contrary to theirs! . . . Isn't it strange, Jean-François, that you and me who once struck terror in the hearts of the Blancs should end up their chéris, while they protector Toussaint is now the gargoyle of their sleep . . . ?

JEAN-FRANÇOIS

Toussaint's "liberty for all" is delusion—a chimera! These Blancs—French, Spanish, British, whoever—will never surrender it! Liberty for some niggers, yes—but for all—NEVER! Jamais! . . . No, Jean-François fights for Jean-François! I have no illusions about the Blancs. Even now, Laveaux begs me to quit the Spanish. Shit! He has too little to offer!... France's prattle about liberty is fantasy! Until I see Laveaux and his French gentlemen of quality offering their daughters in marriage to Nègres—only then will I believe in their precious "equality"!

BIASSOU

PRECISELY, Jean-François—as I said, your aspiration stretch no farther than the length of your dick....

(Lights fade simultaneous with BOUKMAN picking up on BIASSOU's assertion.)

BOUKMAN

Which didn't stretch far enough. About one year after old Toussaint's switch, the Spanish yanked the rug from underneath Jean-François and Biassou and made peace with France—surrendering Spanish Domingo, stipulating that White Spanish troops should stay until equally-White French soldiers could replace them. No niggers need apply. All the Black armies—disbanded.

But, lo and behold, Jean-François landed on his feet upright—all the way across the ocean at a place called Cadiz in Spain. In splendid retirement, general's rank intact and a chest full of gold to boot—he had all the time and money in the world to parade around in fine jewelry and dazzling uniforms—a lion of society, exercising the stiff "reach" of his aspiration upon the many White women who panted after its length, width, and slaying power...

Old stink-mouth, hard-drinking Biassou ended up in the United States of America where news has it that he got himself killed in a barroom brawl. Neither he nor Jean-François ever set foot in San Domingo again ...

As for Toussaint—by seventeen seventy-six, the French Government was promoting him to—

> *(Scene shifts to RIGAUD's camp where BEAUVAIS and PINCHINAT are also present ... RIGAUD rages.)*

RIGAUD

Brigadier General! Less than five years out of slavery and the old Black is made Brigadier General!

BEAUVAIS

Laveaux is helpless without him.

RIGAUD

And us?! Where would Laveaux be if we did not keep the British at bay?! Does he promote us?—we who remained faithful to France while Toussaint was killing her sons!

PINCHINAT

Unlike us, Toussaint appeals to Laveaux' vanity,—addresses him as 'father.' The old Postillion caters to all Whites. Pardons former emigres and enrolls them in his army. While we, Msieurs, exclude all Blancs from office in our districts and keep them under strict surveillance.

RIGAUD

And will continue to do so! We've had our fill of White treachery!

PINCHINAT

Toussaint's magnanimity ingratiates, while our behavior condemns us to Laveaux's neglect.

RIGAUD

We are the rightful heirs to San Domingo! We did not shed our blood to be usurped by ignorant Blacks—Blacks scarcely out of bondage—our masters?!

BEAUVAIS

Be sensible, Rigaud. If Toussaint had not defected from Spain, we might not be here to fulminate.

RIGAUD

You wish to baiser Toussaint's ass?!

BEAUVAIS

I defer to no one in promoting the interest of our class, but we must be realistic. As ignorant and uncultured as the slaves may be, they greatly outnumber us, and despite their purported ignorance we rely upon them to fight our own battles.

RIGAUD

You expect Blacks in our province to remain deferential knowing that a Black as pure in color as themself
—struts around with the rank of Brigadier General?!

BEAUVAIS

They will remain docile as long as our policies benefit them.

RIGAUD

They will obey as long as we enforce our supremacy! Weakness will earn us the same fate as the Blancs!

PINCHINAT

Mes amis... The issue reduces to the simple proposition—do we remain impotent faced with Toussaint's elevation... Don't quarrel with Laveaux—He is merely practical... However, it is not too late for our fortunes to be revitalized.

San Domingo's key city, Le Cap, is ruled by Villate—our ambitious Mulatto kinsman, known to have little affection for Laveaux or Toussaint. A confrontation between Villate and Laveaux has long been in the offing. If we can manage to bring Le Cap under our influence, we can gain control of the Northern Province and eventually rule the entire Island.

BEAUVAIS

And what fantastic alchemy shall produce such a fortuitous happenstance?

PINCHINAT

... First, Laveaux must be discredited among the Blacks.

BEAUVAIS

They idolize Laveaux almost as much as Toussaint!

PINCHINAT

Not after successful rumors have been spread that he has sold out to Britain and intends to restore slavery. Once such rumors have congealed into belief, Laveaux can be dispensed with—preferably deported back to France... This accomplished—we fuel Villate's vanity by installing him as Provisional Governor. Then, with the support of Mulatto sympathizers occupying key positions in the Colony, along with Free Blacks whose cultural habits make them our natural allies -we, mes amis, effect our takeover of the entire Island.

BEAUVAIS

What will General Toussaint be doing? Knotting his madras headpiece?!

PINCHINAT

Once Blacks have soured on Laveaux, Toussaint's influence will be neutralized. Because of the old gladiators' often-expressed—but nevertheless sincere—aversion to civil war, I expect him to stall until it is too late.

RIGAUD

Your scheme's success hinges upon Laveaux being superseded by Villate. Yet, they rule from distant outposts.

PINCHINAT

Laveaux, determined to overthrow Villate's despotic rule, has already transferred his headquarters from Port au Paix to Le Cap upon instructions from the Paris Convention. Villate fumes at being made subordinate to Laveaux. The situation is incendiary. A spark can ignite it—and we can provide that spark.

RIGAUD

So far away?

PINCHINAT

In a few days, I intend to board a ship to Paris. I, however, will never debark at that glorious capitol. But secretly land in Le Cap, where I will light the fuse of mischief, after which I will make a flamboyant, public return here to Port au Prince and regale you with the vicissitudes of my invisible Parisian stay.

BEAUVAIS

You are unmatched in cunning, Pinchinat. However, I suspect that events seldom conform to the symmetry of the best conspiratorial calculation. You underestimate Toussaint.

PINCHINAT

My admiration for the military astuteness of our grizzled Black adversary is unsurpassed, Beauvais. Yet, no matter his genius on the battlefield, only five years out of slavery is insufficient time to decipher the insidious complexities of sophisticated intrigue. On this front, Toussaint is a rank novice.

BEAUVAIS

Don't wager on it.

> *(Scene shifts without break to the Wheel and, separately, to TOUSSAINT's headquarters. A two-part representation occurs: LAVEAUX being abducted upon the Wheel, and the incident being described to TOUSSAINT. Scene upon the Wheel activates.)*

LAVEAUX

What do you want, citizens?

> *(A punch is thrown which LAVEAUX dodges, grappling his ASSAILANT to the floor.)*

LAVEAUX (CONT'D)

I am not armed!

> *(OTHER ATTACKERS overwhelm him)*

ATTACKERS

Take him to jail!

LAVEAUX

I demand to see the Municipal Councilors!

ATTACKERS

Move rascal!

LAVEAUX

You are assassins! You do not represent the People! Not a single Black, or a single White among you!

(Blows rain down upon HIM as HE yells)

LAVEAUX (CONT'D)

ROBERT! ROBERT!

(ROBERT, his aide-de-camp rushes in and is felled. LAVEAUX continues to struggle until silenced and subdued by fists and sticks. HE is dragged out by the hair.)

TOUSSAINT

What?! In prison?! . . . They will free Laveaux or I will take a thousand lives for one!

AIDE

Major Christophe already carries a threat from Colonel Michel to level the town if Governor Laveaux is not released.

TOUSSAINT

What about Le Cap's Municipal Council?

AIDE

The very ones behind Governor Laveaux's arrest. They have replaced him with Villate.

TOUSSAINT

Ah, these Mulatto dogs! Scoundrels, rogues!—Ungrateful wretches never tire of seeking to deliver me to my enemies . . .

Order Moïse, my nephew Belair and Dessalines—by all means Dessalines their sworn nemesis—to link up with Michel at Haut-du-Cap. Round up all the Mulatto officials in the district and detain them.

(HE declaims as if addressing LE CAP directly.)

TOUSSAINT (CONT'D)

Citizens of Le Cap—in disrespecting Governor Laveaux, you disrespect France! What will France, the Mother Country, say when she learns of your insulting treatment of her representative . . . ? Cast your eyes upon the Artibonite district and cringe at the depravities heaped upon your kinsmen by the English. Hundreds drowned at sea—others branded and chained as galley slaves—Mulatto women forced to flee, taking cover in woods to escape English defilement and barbarity.

But you under our protection live in serenity and peace—yet insist upon sowing confusion and treachery! . . . Continue this course and you will pay dearly. Nothing is more awesome than the wrath of Toussaint L'Ouverture bringing his arm down to rescue justice from being debased by the unjust . . .

AIDE

Should I gather your troops, General?

TOUSSAINT

That won't be necessary. Michel, Moïse and the others, are enough military might. Back them up—instruct thousands of laborers of the Plains-du-Nord to pour into Le Cap. I will remain here in Gonaïves and wait.

> *(Scene shifts to LE CAP, the Stage gradually filling with BLACKS taking up positions. Tattered BLACK LABORERS race back and forth over the stage shouting: "POWER TO LAW, POWER TO LAW!" Drums pound menacingly.*
>
> *Soon, a DELEGATION of the Municipal Council marches Upstage to the Wheel. LAVEAUX, just-released, descends and moves Downstage where the DELEGATION awaits him, their fright showing.)*

COUNCILMAN

Governor Laveaux, there's been a terrible misunderstanding. We prostrate ourselves before you tending our most humble apologies for the behavior of a few misguided fools. We are outraged at the insult you have suffered. By unanimous consent the Municipal Council votes to condemn the travesty and reaffirm our loyalty to you. We regret any discomforts you have endured as a result of this appalling error.

> *(LAVEAUX moves away and walks through the CROWD greeting him with tumultuous applause. Scene shifts to TOUSSAINT.)*

AIDE

He is free, General—without a shot fired.

TOUSSAINT

The threat of force often makes its use unnecessary. What news of Villate, Lieutenant?

AIDE

He has fled, General.

TOUSSAINT

Find his hiding place and get him to return. Tell him the entire incident has been a misunderstanding.

AIDE

??? Sir...???

TOUSSAINT

I prefer Villate where I can watch him. Villate is a scoundrel, but I discern more expert calculation behind his maneuvers ... I wish no further confrontations with the Mulattoes... Long as the British occupy our harbors, civil conflict must be avoided. If Villate is too cowardly to cooperate, only then will I have Laveaux dismiss him. Meanwhile, have Laveaux escorted to Haut-du-Cap. Our troops will greet him with full military salutations and courtesy.

> *(The entire stage becomes the site for a tumultuous welcome for LAVEAUX; HE and TOUSSAINT fall into EACH OTHERS' arms; then THEY BOTH mount the Wheel, entering Le Cap to the momentous reception of the ENTIRE POPULATION- BLACK, WHITE, MULATTO, WOMEN, MEN, CHILDREN, RICH AND POOR; the MARSEILLAISE and African drums play simultaneously as wave after wave of smart-*

disciplined but not-so smartly-dressed BLACK TROOPS parade On and Off the stage, creating the illusion of thousands.)

LAVEAUX

(Pointing to TOUSSAINT)

I hereby appoint Toussaint L'Ouverture to be my trusted assistant, without whose advice I vow to take no actions in this Colony! Whose confidence and guidance I will always seek! Toussaint L'Ouverture is hereby appointed Lieutenant Governor of the Colony of San Domingo!

(When the cheering crests, TOUSSAINT moves forward and shouts)

TOUSSAINT

APRES MON DIEU, LAVEAUX!!! APRES MON DIEU, LAVEAUX!!! AFTER GOD, LAVEAUX!!!

END OF ACT TWO

ACT THREE

(Act III opens in the inner offices of TOUSSAINT as the dying strains of the MARSEILLAISE are heard. SONTHONAX, who has recently returned from France, is present along with GOVERNOR LAVEAUX. After the music fades, a long beat of silence prevails. Finally, TOUSSAINT speaks.)

TOUSSAINT

... Fortune is a very mysterious oracle, isn't she Commissioner Sonthonax? We stalked each other like panthers a few years ago. Who could predict that we would meet again as comrades?

SONTHONAX

Credit the Revolution, Commander. Upon being removed from San Domingo, I feared that I was being escorted to the guillotine. But even before the vessel docked, my detractors had been silenced and themselves suffered the fate I had ordained for myself... Revolutionary justice spared me to return to San Domingo even more determined to implement the ideals of our Republic... If you favor me with the same cooperation that you have given Governor Laveaux, I am confident Commander that San Domingo can be restored to her rightful place as the Greatest Colony in the world.

TOUSSAINT

I will continue to give evidence of my loyalty, Commissioner ... However, there will be many others not so pleased by your return.

SONTHONAX

I am fully aware of that, Commander. I intend to make a thorough investigation of Msieur Villate's abortive coup.

TOUSSAINT

I suggest you proceed carefully, Msieur Sonthonax. Despite their mischief, Mulattoes, especially of the South, have contributed greatly to our retaining San Domingo. Such contributions must be balanced against their alleged involvement in the Villate affair.

SONTHONAX

I am surprised at your restraint, Commander, since it is well-known that it is your own success which most enrages the Mulattoes?

TOUSSAINT

I must overlook the jealousy of ambitious men, Commissioner, and seek not vengeance but collaboration. France needs it, also San Domingo. Mulattoes must not be provoked into greater disenchantment but reasoned into steadier loyalty.

SONTHONAX

I will be circumspect, Commander. If I uncover evidence implicating Mulatto leaders—especially Msieur Pinchinat—I will personally apprehend them.

TOUSSAINT

I advise against it, Msieur Sonthonax—particularly in regards to Pinchinat. He is the idol of the South. The Mulattoes will object to him being so treated. It will incite others—especially General Rigaud, the most volatile of their leaders.

SONTHONAX

We have already taken steps to guard against repercussions, Commander. General Desfourneaux, my staff chief, is placing all Mulatto regiments under his command and Rigaud will be dealt with by Commissioner Rey.

TOUSSAINT

??? Rey . . .?! Above all, Commissioner Sonthonax—not Rey! He is a sworn enemy of Rigaud. Rumors say he once attempted to have Rigaud assassinated in Les Cayes! I beg you not to include Rey in your delegation!

SONTHONAX

Commander, we will do our utmost to avoid alienating peoples of the South. But I have sworn an oath to the National Convention to not waste time acting against suspected enemies of the Republic . . . However, please let us not be distracted by trivial matters.

I have returned, Commander, for a far more joyous purpose; to establish the unchallenged leadership of you and your Black brethren!

Not only will France increase the strength of your armies, but weapons will be distributed to Black laborers. Loaded muskets are the only guarantee of their liberty and we will instruct them that whoever attempts to strip away their weapons intends to re-enslave them.

Never again will their color be a leprous badge disbarring them from enjoying the same rights as the highest-born aristocrat. I dedicate myself so thoroughly to this mission, Commander, until I envy you, wishing that I were as Black as yourself.

TOUSSAINT

God did not deem the dusky acquisition necessary, Commissioner, but I am certain he would applaud your sentiment.

SONTHONAX

Merci . . . Now, Commander—to celebrate your promotion as Commander-in-Chief of France's army in San Domingo, I have been delegated to present you with these tokens of our mother country's esteem.

> (HE presents TOUSSAINT with a magnificent sword and a brace of pistols.)

TOUSSAINT

Merci, beaucoup, Msieur Sonthonax. These are truly magnificent. Oui, Governor Laveaux?

LAVEAUX

They are worthy of their recipient.

TOUSSAINT

I am indeed honored. Msieur. Apart from my practical interest, I am an even more dedicated hobbyist. These firearms will be the prize of my collection.

SONTHONAX

As additional evidence of her indebtedness, Commander, France wishes to provide your two sons with the finest education she is capable of. I have been instructed to obtain your approval for their taking up residence in Paris.

TOUSSAINT

... This overwhelms me, Msieur Sonthonax ... the request is more than flattering ... Despite my joy at my sons' extreme good fortune—to imagine them so far removed—across an entire ocean—is unsettling ... But give me some time, Msieur Sonthonax. I will consult their mother and in due course inform you of our decision.

SONTHONAX

A favorable answer would please France ... and I ... Now if you will pardon me, Commander, Governor Laveaux, I must return to Le Cap. I remain your servant, Commander. Adieu, Msieurs.

(SONTHONAX exits. A long silence ensues.)

LAVEAUX

... Well, mon ami, how does he impress you?

TOUSSAINT

... How Msieur Sonthonax has survived—only God can give account ...

LAVEAUX

He hates aristocrats so passionately; he would gladly banish them from all earthly precincts.

TOUSSAINT

... a man hard put to be placated with half-measures ...

LAVEAUX

He will be difficult to restrain.

TOUSSAINT

Pour vrai ... but—Although Msieur Sonthonax flattens obstacles in his path like a cannonball, he can be of service. He is highly regarded among our people who have not forgotten that he was the first Blanc to announce freedom. As long as he promotes their progress, I can contend with his failings ... It would have been asking too much for him to be as perfect as you, mon ami.

LAVEAUX

You are too kind, mon frère. If I was younger, I would remain here beside you.

TOUSSAINT

(Embracing him)

Mon cher ami, you have already sacrificed too much for us—your health, your family, your personal life. In all the years served in our behalf, you have not made one trip back to France. Now it is time for you to rest.

LAVEAUX

You are no longer young, mon ami, yet your energy does not flag.

TOUSSAINT

Because I am still an infant—born the minute my enslavement ended. So truly I'm no more than a babe. But you my confrère—France beckons you home. With you there, I can relax ici—knowing that San Domingo's interests are well-protected.

LAVEAUX

Dear comrade, I will do everything to justify your confidence -- on whatever front. But I cannot help but be vexed. Commissioner Sonthonax is not an elixir for tranquility . . .

(THEY gaze at each other in silence as scene shifts to RIGAUD's headquarters where PINCHINAT and BEAUVAIS are present also.)

RIGAUD

Canailles! Merdes! We treat the cochons avec respect and what do they do? Incite Blacks against us! . . . What must we do to bring French chiens to their senses?!

BEAUVAIS

They are delirious. Our district intoxicates them; busy carousing, gambling, piling up debts and chasing every whore in Port-au-Prince.

PINCHINAT

Ahh, scratch the last; do not begrudge them love of fornication, Beauvais!

BEAUVAIS

Especially since it could never rival with your own.

PINCHINAT

I stand convicted! A lubricious avocation you could easily excel me—being young and devilishly attractive to women who weep in despair at your preference for the life of a monk . . . It is not the sportive pastimes of Sonthonax's minions that worry me—but their meddling in affairs-of-State. No matter how decently we treat them, they are determined to obstruct us. Obviously, Sonthonax does not intend to rest until he has us in the stocks.

RIGAUD

I force myself to abide these scum, but my patience runs thin!

(RIGAUD's AIDE enters)

AIDE

General Rigaud, Commissioner Rey wishes to know when you will fetch him?!

RIGAUD

Fetch the fuck?! I should fetch his tête off with my saber!

PINCHINAT

If you can bear a second without managing that decapitation, Rigaud, rest assured that your patience is infinite!

(Exiting)

RIGAUD

Tell my fiancée, Marie, that I will send a carriage for her as soon as I am finished with Msieur Assassin Rey.

(Scene shifts to the Wheel which is now transformed into REY's living quarters. RIGAUD ascends the Wheel where REY greets him enthusiastically.)

REY

Rigaud! Rigaud! Discussions of State can wait! I shall introduce you to the most beautiful wench you have ever sighted—but you must swear to tell no one about her! Her identity must remain secret between you and I!

> (HE guides RIGAUD towards a curtained room. REY parts the curtain and a beautiful YOUNG WOMAN is exposed, propped languorously upon pillows in a resplendent bed. SHE is ravishingly nude.
>
> Simultaneously, SHE and RIGAUD gasp. SHE then attempts hurriedly to scramble under the covers. Momentarily, RIGAUD is frozen in astonishment as REY laughs uproariously. RIGAUD erupts shouting)

RIGAUD

MARIE! MARIE!

> (Violently raging, RIGAUD knocks REY down, then lifts him up and is about to hurl him from the Wheel when SERVANTS rush in and restrain him. In a simultaneous, but unconnected action, Downstage, a MULATTO rushes Onstage shouting)

MULATTO

Commissioner Desfoumeaux just arrested a Mulatto officer!

(MULATTOES stream Onstage as the ARRESTED OFFICER is marched in by EUROPEAN SOLDIERS. The OFFICER wrenches free from his CAPTORS and dashes to safety among the MULATTO CROWD.)

Both sides gird for a clash. The scene freezes. BEAUVAIS rushes to RIGAUD, still standing atop the Wheel, and shouts excitedly)

BEAUVAIS

They're fighting in the streets! Sonthonax will charge us with insurrection!

RIGAUD

(Without budging)

How terrible is the rage of the people...?

BEAUVAIS

Your brother stirs up Blacks—accusing the Commissioners of planning to restore slavery! Rey and Desfourneaux have already fled. Only you can prevent a slaughter, Rigaud!

RIGAUD

How terrible is the rage of the people...?

BEAUVAIS

Reason with them, Rigaud! Or Sonthonax's men will be massacred!

RIGAUD

Terrible is the rage of the people...

(BEAUVAIS gives up in frustration and runs off, leaving RIGAUD alone atop the Wheel observing the scene below which now unfreezes.

The postponed clash between the EUROPEAN SOLDIERS and the MULATTOES erupts, with additional brutalization of the Whites' shadow—depicted behind the scrim.

When the action is completed, RIGAUD exits, commenting)

RIGAUD

How terrible is the rage of the people...?

(Scene shifts back to TOUSSAINT, with SONTHONAX and LAVEAUX present.)

LAVEAUX

It was a mistake, Commissioner.

SONTHONAX

Treason! How dare they defy French authority!

TOUSSAINT

Desfourneaux and Rey provoked defiance. They could not have done more harm if they had willed it! Rigaud sends a delegation to us—he still seeks a peaceful accommodation.

SONTHONAX

I will not meet them! France is not in the habit of negotiating with rebels!

TOUSSAINT

(Chuckling wryly)

I recall that statement before, Governor Laveaux...

LAVEAUX

Fortunately—I was privileged to reconsider.

TOUSSAINT

Commissioner Sonthonax, if you do not meet with Rigaud's envoys, he will have no other choice but to give ear to the British! We can ill-afford his defection.

SONTHONAX

I respect your judgment. Commander—but the Mulattoes must be made to understand that if they do not bow to French supremacy, they will face the Republic's retribution. I will warn them for the last time!

(Scene shifts to RIGAUD's headquarters where PINCHINAT and BEAUVAIS are also present.)

RIGAUD

How fares Msieur Sonthonax's proclamation parchment?

PINCHINAT

Dragged through the streets of Les Cayes tied to the tail of an ass.

RIGAUD

How fitting—the rantings of a two-legged fart flapping at the braying hole of his four-legged brother!

(THEY laugh)

BEAUVAIS

When your hilarity ebbs, mon amis, consider that this affront seals our break with France.

PINCHINAT

Not with France!—This fanatic does not represent France!

BEAUVAIS

While this "fanatic" governs—he is France! Paris already disregards our own delegated spokesmen.

RIGAUD

White scum who betray us instead of pleading our cause! . . . We must appeal to Toussaint to intervene on our behalf.

BEAUVAIS

The "nigger" whose very name drives you to fury, Rigaud?

RIGAUD

Whether I like him or non—he is the only one capable of suppressing that revolutionary fanatic!

PINCHINAT

Yes, we must enlist Toussaint's intercession.

. . . How strange . . . A few years ago, we Half-Breeds would never have suffered the sight of that old, low ugly slave, Toussaint de Breda . . . Now we prepare to grovel before him . . . .

BEAUVAIS

Not very strange, Pinchinat—when we remind ourselves that our mothers were as Black and lowly as he—if not so ugly.

PINCHINAT

But—wouldn't it be simpler to be wooed by the ardent entreaties of the British than to forever insist on risking our pale necks on behalf of ungrateful Frenchmen who fail to appreciate our desirability?

BEAUVAIS

Maybe it is the blood of our fathers which attaches us to France. We disown our mother's legacy so thoroughly until there is little left to prevent us from drifting in a limbo of torturous uncertainty . . . .

> *(THEY remain staring as scene shifts to TOUSSAINT instructing an AIDE; then to a two-part alternation between the PARIS CONVENTION and TOUSSAINT's headquarters.)*

TOUSSAINT

Assure General Rigaud that I will handle Commissioner Sonthonax—but the Mulattoes must do no more to provoke him . . . San Domingo cannot afford discord within. Once again, we are threatened from agents without.

> *(Atop the Wheel, the PARIS CONVENTION is indicated being in session with a reactionary delegate, BOURDON speaking.)*

BOURDON

Reports of new massacres are received every day! In less than six years the White population of San Domingo has been cut in half—from forty thousand, five hundred to twenty thousand citizens! . . . Why?! Are Blacks being armed to destroy our White brothers and sisters? We in France grant compassionate pardons to former followers of the King, while in San Domingo these same citizens are brutally persecuted.

> *(The CONVENTION scene freezes as lights pinpoint TOUSSAINT, dramatically addressing the CONVENTION, although his real means of communication is epistolary.)*

TOUSSAINT

In San Domingo, we remain triumphant because hatred for the English unites French citizens of all colors.

> *(Applause registers as the freeze of the CONVENTION breaks. VAUBLANC, another reactionary, jumps up.)*

VAUBLANC

You demand that this pack of lies be printed in this Convention's records...?! Yes—I declare Commander Toussaint's mouthings "a pack of lies"—contrived to elicit your applause in order to cloak Sonthonax's criminal rule—this maniacal assassin who drips with the blood of Whites abandoned to revengeful Blacks! This monster who has enacted atrocious laws which the tigers of Libya would not endorse if tigers had the misfortune to pass laws!

It is Sonthonax and his predecessor Laveaux who are responsible for inciting Blacks to insubordination and misrule. Blacks are merely the servile instruments of their machinations!

> *(Lights rise on TOUSSAINT)*

TOUSSAINT

Gentlemen... the foolish and inflammatory diatribes of Msieur Vaublanc do nothing more but alert us to the conspiracy that the Colonists of San Domingo fashion against us—backed by their allies in France, San Domingo exiles in the United States and base colon traitors serving under the British flag. Without a doubt these conspirators intend to restore slavery in San Domingo—and their determination requires that they cloak themselves in the mantle of liberty in order to strike liberty a deadlier blow.

Presently their emissaries have sneaked into San Domingo to foment a destructive leaven shaped by poisonous hands.

To achieve their purpose, they rely upon my complacency—expecting me to be incapacitated out of fear for my two children in France... It is hardly astonishing that men who would sacrifice their country to promote their own interests—that such caliber of men would be incapable of understanding how much a better father I am than they are—a father who possesses a genuine love of country, since I base the happiness of my children upon the progress of my country—

Citizen directors—it is your solemn duty to sweep back this storm which eternal enemies of freedom whip up in secret shades of silence—your task is to restrain these predators from overrunning our embattled shores attempting to sully our banks with new crimes.

I trust that your wisdom will enable you to avoid the snares they dangle to entrap you.

As for me—my knowledge of my people and my loyalty to France make it urgent that I inform you of the oath we in San Domingo all swear—that revitalized by liberty we will bury ourselves under the rubble of a blood-stained isle rather than return to slavery!

Do these despots think that men like ourselves who for the first time have enjoyed the blessings of freedom will stand by calmly and see it wrestled away?

We once endured our chains so long as we were not acquainted with any other condition of life better than slavery—but once freed—if we had a thousand lives to live, we would sacrifice every one of those lives rather than be forced back into bondage!

Msieurs, I am confident that any trepidations I might have about my two sons' safety are baseless—since it was to the solicitude of the French Government that I entrusted them. I would tremble in horror if it transpired that they have been delivered into the hands of hostage-takers . . . But even so, let these would-be assassins reflect—that in punishing my two children for the naive trust of their father, these fiends would only be increasing their barbarity without any hope of deterring me from my duty.

Blind as these wretches may be, they cannot fail to recognize how their conduct would only signal new disasters in San Domingo—and far from enabling them to regain the lost privileges which liberty for all terminated, they expose themselves and the colony to total devastation.

Distinguished Deputies—I know I worry unnecessarily. Surely, it could not come to pass that the same hand of France that freed us of our chains will now sacrifice us to our enemies—will permit her sublime morality to be subverted—her principles degraded—her edicts which so ennoble humanity to be revoked . . .

However—if to reestablish slavery in San Domingo all this was done—then I vow that you would be attempting the impossible . . . We have known how to face danger to win freedom—we will know how to brave death to maintain it . . .

This, Citizens Directors, is the morale of the people of San Domingo. These are the sentiments which they transmit through me to you . . .

> *(Lights rise on CONVENTION as scene unfreezes with VAUBLANC haranguing.)*

VAUBLANC

General Martial Besse—fresh from San Domingo—presents conclusive evidence of the wildest disorders tearing the Colony apart! . . . I demand that Commissioners Sonthonax, Roume and the Mulatto Raimond be recalled! Force is the only solution for protecting the lives of our unfortunate White compatriots! I demand that troops be dispatched and San Domingo be put in a state of siege until order is restored! The council of Elders vote to recall the murderer Sonthonax and his henchmen. Peace can now be restored in San Domingo!!!

> *(Cheering resounds as lights flash upon SONTHONAX with TOUSSAINT.)*

SONTHONAX

Why must these reactionary canailles keep rising from the ashes of defeat to harass me?! . . . Commander . . . I wonder if San Domingo's progress does not rest with severing ties with France and having done with these abominable colonists!

> *(Immediately lights rise upon the WOMEN's CHORUS whose narration begins as the cheering dies.)*

Play I: The Rise of Toussaint L'Ouverture

WOMEN'S CHORUS

One Two Three Four Five Six Seven Eight Nine
Even le chat must expire sometime

The Bells Tolled
Heads Rolled

In France the Revolution was like a
wheel of fortune
Each turn of its bloody occasion
Thrust into prominence peoples of
different persuasions
Brissotins, Girondins and Jacobins
Each had a stab at posterity's pretensions

One faction up, another faction down
Switching betwixt liberals, rebels and secret
supporters of The Crown
Life was slippery
Fame was risky
When so many had a stake in victory

The Bells Tolled
Heads Rolled

An instant in the seat of power
Was preparation for
Destiny's hour
A scramble up the ladder of high office
Was invitation to sudden departure

Bells Tolled
Heads Rolled

Alliances shifted with dazzling speed
A friend today, tomorrow's foe indeed
Loyalist of the Crown defied being split asunder
A new Bourgeoise dreamed of fresh
worlds to plunder
The young proletariat awoke to a status bereft
Sans-Culottes banded together to dole out death
The tide would turn, the barricades would break
Confusion would usher in a different stroke of fate

Bells Tolled
Heads Rolled

No candidate could be counted off the scene
Until struck down by the guillotine
Barnave, Brissot, Bourdet, Condercet, Gaudet,
Murat, Danton, Mirabeau and Robespierre
All held a grip on the levers of power
Before being flung from history's tower
A moment to stir up tremors of fear
Before being hurled onto eternity's bier

Bells Tolled
Heads Rolled

(Having entered unnoticed, BOUKMAN assumes the narrative as the WOMEN's CHORUS slowly exits.)

BOUKMAN

One Two Three Four Five Six Seven Eight Nine Even le chat must reach the end of the line.

To Blacks, Msieur Sonthonax remained the hero supreme.
But his enemies' pursuit of relentless ambition
Strove mightily to vault his bulwark of opposition

But no matter the statutes they legislated,
Msieur Sonthonax, shielded by San Domingo's isolation,
persisted in not being exterminated.

Once again it seemed his executioners were doomed to disappointment.
If Fate had not stalked Sonthonax from a contrary dispensation.

(Lights fade, then rise upon SONTHONAX and TOUSSAINT)

Why, Commander...? Why—why?!... You know I love you and your people as if I was one of you!

TOUSSAINT

You plot against me, ami Sonthonax...

SONTHONAX

? It was I who secured your promotions, Commander!? You sponsored my election as Senator for San Domingo—why have you suddenly turned against me...?!

TOUSSAINT

You ignored my advice... Courted my officers, raising their salaries against my orders... withheld supplies from troops in the field, causing resentments and in even one—mutiny...

SONTHONAX

If I have buttressed my power, Commander, it was not to compete with you but to promote our common objectives. If you had alerted me, I would have done everything to satisfy your objections!

TOUSSAINT

You are an official of France, Commissioner Sonthonax—it was not within my power to challenge you...

SONTHONAX

Yet you order me to vacate the Colony!!!?

TOUSSAINT

It is France who recalls you, Commissioner...

SONTHONAX

I received no such directive! I am responsible only to the Supreme Council of the Revolution! Only enemies of the Republic seek my recall!... Those same conspirators who scheme to destroy everything that you and I have struggled to accomplish—the same villains who seek to re-enslave you and your people! Reactionaries who are sure to be ousted as before!

TOUSSAINT

Are you certain of that, Commissioner...?

SONTHONAX

As confident as I am of our victory here!

TOUSSAINT

I pray that your confidence is rewarded when you confront them.

SONTHONAX

I hope for no greater epitaph than the disapproval of anti-Republican traitors!

TOUSSAINT

I, myself, have run out of optimism . . .

SONTHONAX

Our enemies' gains are only temporary!

TOUSSAINT

Sonthonax . . . I do not fear the machination of a handful of slavers as much as I am alarmed by the twists of the Revolution itself . . . It is less than ten years since we Blacks fled slavery . . . But now, after sipping the nectar of freedom we have developed a thirst which can only be quenched by death . . .

This Isle groans from our martyrs . . . But it seems no matter how great the sacrifice, we novices-in-freedom fail to discourage those who envision no other destiny for us except under the whip. Their hunger for our servitude is insatiable . . .

I am not sophisticated in the ways of politics, mon ami. I am knowledgeable about only one cause—that neither I nor my people will ever be re-enslaved. This simple determination is the beginning and end of our intention . . .

Even in the desperate days of our rebellion, I remained— an orphan son of France. Even when I commanded armies against her—her ideals sustained me. Once placed under her tricolors, I never expected to witness my natural right to liberty constantly juggled over the quicksands of her indecisions.

As you are well aware, Msieur Sonthonax, old enemies like ex-Governor Barbemarbois, who we chased from the Colony at the start of our revolt, have regained power in France. These refugees conduct a chorus clamoring for our re-enslavement, and since they can no longer voice their intention baldly—they threaten us under the subterfuge of eliminating our misrule . . . I have no stomach for challenging France, but even more compellingly, I can no longer entrust our freedom to the vacillations of others.

SONTHONAX

Foes and friends alike will interpret my expulsion as evidence of your desire for absolute command, Toussaint!

TOUSSAINT

It was you, not I, Sonthonax, who proposed breaking ties with France—murdering all San Domingo Whites....

SONTHONAX

I never meant it!

TOUSSAINT

Nevertheless, I would not be straining credulity by disclosing that I have heard you voice such desires....

However—the matter is inconsequential. Upon your leaving San Domingo, I will provide comfortable accommodations for you, your beautiful Mulatto bride, your entire staff and all others wishing to accompany you back to France.

SONTHONAX

... Even to face the guillotine, Toussaint?

TOUSSAINT

My superstitious kinsmen believe that your loa protects you, Sonthonax. Even a disbeliever like myself am convinced that yours is indeed a charmed life.

SONTHONAX

Many San Domingoans will not react favorably to my expulsion!

TOUSSAINT

Why do you insist upon describing my request as an 'expulsion' Commissioner? I am merely asking that you assume the duties we elected you to perform. You are valuable to us—San Domingo's adopted son. You have risked her dangers—shared her agonies... That is why I need you to defend her upon France's distant shores.

SONTHONAX

While you remain to rule San Domingo alone?

TOUSSAINT

I have no appetite for solitary rule, Sonthonax—but as long as Britain occupies our territory, I cannot fight on all fronts.

SONTHONAX

If France does not interpret your act as a thrust for independence, she is certain to view my ouster as a step toward your making peace with England.

TOUSSAINT

My making peace with England?!!!... What travesty... Are you not aware, Msieur Sonthonax, that the same courier who brought news of your recall—that same courier also supplied me with information of France's secret peace negotiations with England?...

If a bargain is struck between France and Britain, shall it evolve that once French soldiers have been relieved of vying against Britain—will they certainly then be unleashed once again to besiege our corpse-ridden shores...?

SONTHONAX

All the more reason for you to assure the presence of friends!

TOUSSAINT

... I fear that your policy exposes us to too many risks, Commissioner.

SONTHONAX

By sacrificing me you think you purchase time—that your enemies will be placated for the moment.

TOUSSAINT

... I merely ask you to assume your elected duties, Sonthonax. I beg you to take up your position in the Paris Assembly where you can benefit us most.

SONTHONAX

You won't reconsider your decision...?

(TOUSSAINT doesn't reply)

SONTHONAX (CONT'D)

Then I will not incur your displeasure, Commander. I again invest my faith in the Revolution... I will sail immediately and gladly assume the responsibilities you and the citizens of San Domingo have elected me to perform...

But to strengthen my Paris reappearance, I ask that you supply me with a letter from you and your staff officers—thanking me for services to the Colony, urging me to occupy my seat in the Assembly. This document will allow me to dissuade those who still fear the full force of your wrath.

TOUSSAINT

By all means, Commander—compose the letter and we will sign it.

Play I: The Rise of Toussaint L'Ouverture

SONTHONAX

Three days and I will be ready to sail.

(SONTHONAX exits as lights fade to black—then arise upon TOUSSAINT, now surrounded by his OFFICERS.)

WOMEN'S CHORUS

Sonthonax left in despair
Depressed about
Quitting the land he
Come to cherish beyond compare
Where his mutual embrace
Adopted of citizens
Led to even being
New Island-Bride
Intoxicated
Ordered to relocate
To France's chillier clime
His mortal existence
Strung like
A thread on the line
He strengthened his resolve
To circumvent Toussaint's Sphinx-type logic
And plotted to defy the expulsion order.

LEVEILLE

Commander, I cannot sign this letter.

MENTOR

Nor I.

MULATTO OFFICER

I will only sign if Commissioner Sonthonax requests it of me in person.

OFFICIAL GENERAL

I have just consulted with Commissioner Sonthonax. He was so evasive until I have doubts as to its genuineness.

TOUSSAINT

Mes amis—Commissioner Sonthonax wishes to travel to France and assume his duties as Deputy from San Domingo. You may sign the letter or you may refrain. Commissioner Sonthonax requests it, I invite you to comply. The choice is all yours.

> (MOÏSE and CHRISTOPHE step forward and proceed to sign.)

MOISE

I once threatened to resign if Commissioner Sonthonax was ever recalled to Paris. Now, I bow to his wishes.

> (OTHERS start out, hesitating before exiting, then return to affix their signatures. TOUSSAINT prevents them.)

TOUSSAINT

No, Msieurs, no—you may not sign. You had enough time. I did not force you. Now, I will not permit it. I am prepared to sign this letter alone and assume full responsibility for it.

> (The OFFICERS file out as lights contract to leave TOUSSAINT in isolation as HE speaks; actually, addressing SONTHONAX.)

TOUSSAINT

It grieves me to learn that at the same time you reassure me how gratifying it will be for you to fulfill the honorable mission the people of San Domingo have entrusted upon you—that you are assembling officers of Le Cap's garrison to protest your departure... I hereby warn all leaders in Le Cap that they will be held responsible for any bloodshed which results from their military provocations...

WOMEN'S CHORUS

>Spurred by memory of
>Old foe Galbaud
>Who cooed in Sailor's ears
>To ward off deportation
>Sonthonax strove to emulate
>Same ploy
>Set up warm sentiments
>And rouse citizens to prevent
>His banishment
>Like Galbaud
>Sonthonax miscalculated
>The strength of his forces
>And now faces
>Potential disaster

(Lights crossfade and rise upon SONTHONAX, still in nightclothes, confronted by GENERAL AGE, TOUSSAINT'S White Chief-of-Staff, accompanied by ARMED GUARDS.)

AGE

If you and your entourage are not aboard the L'Indien by sunrise, Commander L'Ouverture will enter Le Cap and deport you forcefully. If you resist, he will crush you.

SONTHONAX

Haven't I already given Commander Toussaint my word?!

AGE

Commissioner—you, least of all, should play Commander L'Ouverture for the fool. Your deadline has long been overstayed. Isn't it peculiar that during this delay—suspicious troop activity and much agitation by your dedicated supporters have taken place? ... Only the deaf and sightless could misjudge the implications of such coincidences ... Certainly not Commander Toussaint, who is already marching towards Le Cap with his troops.

SONTHONAX

Sunrise is upon us—how could I possibly be ready! I beg you for more time!

AGE

You have until eight o'clock. By then, Commander Toussaint will expect you to have boarded the frigate.

> *(Suddenly, the stage is emptied. Lights create the illusion of early morning. SOLDIERS take up positions on opposite sides of the stage. BLACKS and MULATTOES crowd in.*
>
> *SONTHONAX, accompanied by his MULATTO MISTRESS and the rest of his ENTOURAGE, including RAIMOND and OTHER OFFICERS loyal to him enter. A path is cleared through the ONLOOKERS to allow him passage.*
>
> *Silence reigns as the CROWD of BLACKS, charged sincerely with affectionate emotions, remove hats honoring him, and TROOPS salute him with*

raised swords. TOUSSAINT moves slowly towards SONTHONAX, then embraces him affectionately.)

TOUSSAINT

Commissioner Sonthonax, I express the sentiments of all San Domingo in wishing you a safe journey to Paris. We thank you for your dedication to the cause of our freedom and equality. We are forever indebted to you—and pray that you will continue to champion our rights in the Chambers of the French Assembly as devotedly as you have done here in San Domingo.

(SONTHONAX accepts TOUSSAINT's felicitations without comment—then turns and leads HIS ENTOURAGE upon the Wheel.

As the Wheel revolves slowly, a volley of guns fire in salute. At the last moment, just when the Wheel is about to disappear from view, a flag dips and the VOYAGERS are revolved from sight.

All along, African drums have mixed equally with LE MARSEILLAISE. Eventually, the drums prevail. TOUSSAINT begins to ascend the Wheel, slowly and alone. The CROWD turns to acknowledge his solitary supremacy. The pace quickens as SOLDIERS execute formations before him and WOMEN dance ecstatically.

The scene builds to a throbbing climax; with TOUSSAINT standing alone at the apex of power—everything freezes.

The WOMEN turn Downstage and deliver "THE BALLAD OF TOUSSAINT L'OUVERTURE.")

WOMEN'S CHORUS

Old Toussaint

From despised birth bound in chains
Was ready to answer history's claim

Black as pitch and ugly as sin
His mastery of men did begin

Eh, eh, Bomba, heu, heu
Canga bafio te
Old Toussaint
Six years off his master's farm
At last stood upon the pinnacle alone
Had soared above friend and foe alike

Eh, eh, Bomba, heu, heu
Canga bafio te

First African to become Head Potentate
In the New World's pantheon of Estates
Commander-in-Chief of the land
Soon to rival Napoleon

Quick of mind and shrewd in wit
A ready match for English Minister Pitt

Eloquent avec phrase and expert in expression

A twin equal to America's President Jefferson

Drab of dress, unsightly in staturality
Nevertheless outshone Spain's King regality

Eh, eh, Bomba, heu, heu
Canga bafio te

Canga moune de le
Canga do ki la
Canga do ki la
Canga Ti

Old Toussaint

To Blacks truly the Opening

L'Ouverture
First ruler of an Ebony domain
Outside the Banks of African terrain
L'Ouverture
The Opening!

L'Ouverture
The Opening!

(THEY freeze)

LAVEAUX'S VOICEOVER

There stands this Spartacus, the Black whose coming Raynal prophesied—whose destiny it is to avenge the outrage perpetuated against his race! This savior of constituted authority and protector of Blacks and Whites alike!

PLAY II: THE FALL OF TOUSSAINT L'OUVERTURE

Play II: The Fall of Toussaint L'Ouverture

CENTRAL CHARACTERS

CAST PRINCIPALS

WOMEN CHORUS
TOUSSAINT
MADAME TOUSSAINT (SUZANNE)
BAILLE (JAIL WARDEN)

HÉDOUVILLE
VOICEOVER PARTICIPANTS
AIDES
NUMEROUS OTHERS

FRENCH GENERALS

ROUME

VINCENT

TOUSSAINT'S GENERALS

CHRISTOPHE
DESSALINES
MOÏSE
MAUREPAS

JEAN PAUL
BELAIR
VERNET

MULATTO OFFICERS

RIGAUD
BEAUVAIS
PÉTION

PINCHANAT
(MULATTO LEADER)

IMPORTANT OTHERS

MAITLAND (BRITISH OFFICER)
DON GARCIA (SPANISH OFFICIAL)
CITIZEN CLARE
NAPOLEON BONAPARTE
GENERAL KERVERSEAU
ABBE COISSON
ISAAC L'OUVERTURE

PLACIDE L'OUVERTURE
GENERAL LE CLERC
CESAR
AIDE-DE-CAMP FERRARI
MARS
GENERAL CAFFERELI
AMIOT

ACT ONE

(African drumming announces the beginning of the play. Lights rise revealing the WHEEL, considerably adjusted to serve new demands. It dominates the stage, a high top-level platform ranging across stage right to stage-left with steps and ramps giving access to the floor when necessary. The WHEEL is surrounded by different-height platforms extending in all directions, creating separate playing space areas connecting if the action requires. Stage Center, extending from the middle of the WHEEL is the most prominent playing area—a tunnel-like space representing a cell. It extends almost past the center-line of the stage and is bordered by platforms backed upstage by a wall with three small horizontal glass-paned windows covered by a fine-meshed screen. Within the cell are a curtainless bed, a chest of drawers, a table, two chairs and a small fireplace. There is an indication downstage of the area that it has access to another small room. Illumination in the cell is minimal and cheerless.

When lights have risen, the WOMEN'S CHORUS is arranged across the top of the WHEEL. The DRUMS back them as they open.)

WOMEN'S CHORUS

Ahyti, Ahyti
Land of Mountains
Realm of the Scorpion Claw Between the Atlantic
Above The Caribbean Below
Called the Isle of San Domingo
Ahyti, Ahyti
Land of the Scorpion Claw
The Upper Arm pointed at Cuba
The Lower prong aimed at Jamaica
Alpine-Like Spine Hump-Backed tight
Upon the Body of San-Toe Domingo
Completing one earthly terrain
Ahyti, Ahyti
Land of the Scorpion Claw
Between the Atlantic Above
The Caribbean Below
Spain clutched the Body
France gripped the Claw
Of the Island of San Domingo

(As they finish, the DRUMMNG is succeeded by strains of the MARSELLAISE. Lights outline the dim form of someone lying in the cell cot below. A VOICEOVER tops the MARSEILLAISE.)

VOICEOVER

Men are so inclined to envy the reputation of others—are so jealous of the good they themselves have not done—that a man often makes enemies by the simple fact that he has rendered great service....

(The VOICE is connected to the dim figure on the cot whom we can see turning and turning. The WOMEN'S CHORUS resumes with the MARSEILLAISE remaining under.)

WOMEN'S CHORUS

In France the Revolution was like a
wheel of fortune
Each turn of its bloody occasion
Thrust into prominence peoples of
different persuasions
All had a stab at posterity's pretensions
One faction's up, another faction down
Betwixt liberals, rebels and secret supporters
of the Crown
Life was slippery
Fame was risky
When so many had a stake in victory
One two three four five six seven eight nine …

(The WOMEN'S CHORUS ends and the MARSEILLAISE fades abruptly. A VOICEOVER—VAUBLANC jumps in.)

VAUBLANC VOICEOVER

Witnesses describe the most shocking disorder! San Domingo groans under misrule! Governed by gross, ignorant Negroes incapable of distinguishing between licentiousness and responsible liberty! Animals who profess a fierce hatred of Whites upon whom they heap nothing but cruelties and indignities! Barbarians who outrage human sentiments by selling their own children!

TOUSSAINT VOICEOVER

If because some Blacks commit cruelties—it means that you can often accuse all Blacks of being cruel, then it would be fair to call Whites of all nations 'barbarians'...

SONTHONAX VOICEOVER

Throughout my stay I was deceived by him, who cleverly masked his ambition. It was only when he demanded that I Sonthonax vacate the Colony that I became aware of his overweening desire, his obsessive goal to rule San Domingo alone!

TOUSSAINT VOICEOVER

How could anyone believe that I wanted to seize power when it was Sonthonax who I expelled for proposing to massacre all Europeans and sever all ties with the Mother country. How can anyone slander me with not wishing to obey any higher authority above me when I had already served devotedly under General Laveaux. I did not attack authority when I expelled Commissioner Sonthonax—I restored it!

> (*TOUSSAINT L'OUVERTURE upon his last VOICEOVER Phrase which repeats over and over, awakes and sits up abruptly on his cell cot. After a few beats, he moves to the fireplace and attempts to warm himself. The WOMEN'S CHORUS resumes.*)

WOMEN'S CHORUS

Old Toussaint
First African to become head potentate
In the New World's pantheon of Estates
Commander-in-Chief of the land
Prior to the reign of Napoleon
Old Toussaint

The Opening
The Opening
The Opening
The Opening

(The WOMEN'S CHORUS repeats "The Opening" as they file out, exiting. Meanwhile, TOUSSAINT mutters in disgust at being unable to gain warmth. Shivering he takes his mug and drinks from it, coughing. He retires to one of the chairs, takes out his watch and checks the time. He sits remembering. MADAME TOUSSAINT enters into the cell from the front, indicating a flashback scene from the past. TOUSSAINT rises and embraces her.)

TOUSSAINT

How is the coffee?

MADAME

It blooms.

TOUSSAINT

Bien ... and my roses?

MADAME

They manage.

TOUSSAINT

They would flourish if I had more time.

MADAME

As long as there is war, you will be chief gardener to your troops. Your flowers must survive your neglect.

TOUSSAINT

When hostilities cease, I will return to my gardens.

MADAME

I won't lose any sleep.

TOUSSAINT

How is everyone else?

MADAME

Très bien.

TOUSSAINT

Papa Bois?

MADAME

He will outlive us all.

TOUSSAINT

That I won't begrudge him . . . And Little Rose?

MADAME

Upset that I wouldn't bring her. She misses you most. She still can't believe her good fortune.

TOUSSAINT

Chasing my horse . . . "Papa, Papa, take me with you!"

MADAME

I am glad that you adopted her. She is a good child . . . Should I fetch Issac and Placide?

TOUSSAINT

Not yet. We must talk about them going to France. The time has come for a definite answer.

MADAME

I never believed you intended for them to go.

TOUSSAINT

I didn't wish it, but now they must.

MADAME

Why so?!

TOUSSAINT

San Domingo needs educated men to overcome the deficiencies caused by centuries of bondage. Issac and Placide will be beneficiaries of France's official offer to educate them.

MADAME

You are not being frank with me, my husband—your decision has something to do with Msieur Sonthonax's slander doesn't it?

TOUSSAINT

What better proof of my loyalty than entrusting my sons to be educated in France herself?

> (Abruptly, TOUSSAINT is startled out of his reverie by the entrance of his jail-keeper, BAILLE, through the upstage locked door, MADAME TOUSSAINT vanishes.)

BAILLE

Bonjour Gener—

(He stops himself)

Bonjour, Msieur Toussaint.

TOUSSAINT

What...!!!

(Pulling himself together, having been surprised out of his memory.)

TOUSSAINT (CONT'D)

Why 'bonjour'?... The day is not "good." I freeze one more night and dawn brings no relief. The chill weather of this dungeon does not dissipate with the onset of morning.

(He searches for something to relieve the cold.)

BAILLE

I sympathize, Msieur.

TOUSSAINT

Then why keep me in this cell where sunlight dares not enter? I suffer headaches, upset stomach, cough with ague. My teeth throb with pain

BAILLE

...I do all I can, Msieur.

TOUSSAINT

To degrade me?! Even the humblest soldier on the battlefield is treated better! No debased foe suffers more humiliation! I prefer death to this torture!

BAILLE

Msieur—from my own pantry I provide you goods far in excess of the rations allowed you—sugar, coffee—neck collars—

TOUSSAINT

Not the right kind!

BAILLE

—madras headpieces—

TOUSSAINT

Of inferior quality! Only four when I requested six!

BAILLE

I can do no more, General—I am your jailer. I follow orders. Whenever possible, I temper the severity of those orders. But I am restricted.

TOUSSAINT

The First Consul must be informed about my treatment!

BAILLE

That is beyond my capacity, Msieur.

TOUSSAINT

Among your superiors who would know . . . ? I see no one else except you and Mars.

BAILLE

Please understand, General—I am merely your keeper,—your equal. Jailer, prisoner?—what's the difference? You in your cell, me with my rules. Trapped like you. Neither you or I can reach beyond our bounds.

TOUSSAINT

You chose your circumstance. I did not.

BAILLE

In my years as prison-keeper, I have guarded many as esteemed as yourself, Msieur Toussaint. They did not choose their berth in this dungeon, but outside they did attempt to scale the heights. The plummet down was merely the hazard of their ambition.

TOUSSAINT

I was a slave, Commandant. My upward climb was not choice but necessity.

BAILLE

Nevertheless, Msieur—summits are where the trail narrows—the footing slipperier and the down plunge more severe . . . I cling upon a safer ledge, General—a lower plateau content to not risk blocking the path of more eager attainers. I stay out of the way. Yes, I admire you, General. You more than any other earned your right to the heights you conquered.

TOUSSAINT

Then help me get word to the First Consul of my disgraceful treatment.

BAILLE

That is not within my power, General!

TOUSSANT

All you need do is see that my message is delivered!

BAILLE

Non, General!

TOUSSAINT

I beg you, Msieur Baille. The First Consul is a soldier, too. I am certain he does not know of my plight.

BAILLE

Mon dieu.

(After a long pause)

Alright . . . I will give you writing material, Msieur. I can't promise that your message will find its destination.

TOUSSAINT

I will take my chances, Commandant. Merci . . . And since I am far more skilled at voicing my thoughts, could you be so kind as to bring me someone to scribble them down adequately?

BAILLE

Im-po-see-bul! I cannot do it!!!

TOUSSAINT

Please—please, Msieur Baille . . . I intend to relate the facts of my case with the simplicity and frankness of an old soldier. I will furnish the First Consul with the truth—only the truth—even if it is unfavorable about myself. The contents of my letter will cause you no harm . . .

BAILLE

Bien . . . bien—I will send my own secretary to scribble your 'thoughts.'

TOUSSAINT

Merci, bien, Commandant, I am indebted to you.

(BAILLE starts to exit)

TOUSSAINT (CONT'D)

Also, Commandant I would appreciate it if you could replace this madras headpiece with some of at least a little better quality...

(BAILLE just stares at TOUSSAINT without replying, exiting in silent frustration. TOUSSAINT returns to his chair and resumes his reminiscences.)

TOUSSAINT (CONT'D)

What better proof of my loyalty than entrusting my sons to be educated in France, herself?

(WOMEN'S CHORUS appears)

WOMEN'S CHORUS

One two three four five six seven eight nine...
The Wheel had spun another turn
And cast diehards of reaction
Once more from its highest rung
Vaublanc, Marbe de Marbois, Villaret-Joyeuse,
Delahaye, Bourbon, Dumas and Rochambeau
All reaction's pets
Now shipped to the Guianias
At the Directory's behest
This reversal of command was a
remarkable turnaround
Once again cheating the guillotine
Of ami Sonthonax's date with renown

For the thousandth time
Sonthonax snubbed his nose at fate
And newly targeted L'Ouverture
With his barbs of hate

SONTHONAX

It was only then that I realized the extent of his grasping intention. He had already deceived two kings, now he was determined to betray the Republic.

TOUSSAINT

General Laveaux, my dearest friend, ami, I must say to you with customary frankness that I was astonished that you are one of the people most eager to welcome the monster Sonthonax. You do me great injury when I learn that you believe Sonthonax more honest than me when he denies that he sought to make the Colony independent. Why has no one questioned this assassin of liberty to ask him in the name of what power have I deceived two kings? His answer to that accusation would confirm my love for liberty and underscore his infamy.

(Lights rise on a downstage platform where GENERAL HÉDOUVILLE and his AIDES are meeting with COMMISSIONER ROUME. One of the AIDES holds up a picture of TOUSSAINT matching the real article who peers on from his jail cell. The AIDES are laughing sarcastically at the picture.)

1ST AIDE

Look! Just look—that headpiece! He looks like a baboon in linen head-rag!

2ND AIDE

A ridiculous monkey!

ROUME

Mes amis—that "ridiculous monkey" is destroying the largest colonial army Great Britain has ever assembled.

3RD AIDE

They surrender because of his outlandish appearance—

4TH AIDE

—paralyzed by his voodoo chants—!

1ST AIDE

How could anyone take such a foolish figure seriously—?!

2ND AIDE

Just we four could take him into custody!

ROUME

It is a mistake to underestimate Commander L'Ouverture—or his generals.

HÉDOUVILLE

"With him, you can do everything—without him, nothing," says General Kerveseau...

ROUME

Recent events confirm that observation, General Hédouville.

HÉDOUVILLE

(Reads from a letter of Toussaint)

..."I will assist you to the best of my abilities—which are bereft of qualities shaped by the brilliance of education but consist of such talents it pleases the Supreme Being to endow me with—

qualities founded upon love of country, unshakable loyalty to France, obedience to her laws and gratitude for the blessings bestowed upon us."—From Toussaint . . .

AIDE

Is he always so sanctimonious?

ROUME

Commander L'Ouverture is a very pious man.

HÉDOUVILLE

Yes, I do not question his piety . . . I am concerned about his veracity . . .

ROUME

Pardon?

HÉDOUVILLE

Obviously, Commander Toussaint presents many different guises. Saint to some—Satan to others . . . Who am I to believe?

ROUME

Contrarily, his enemies' venom stem from the depths of their frustration.

HÉDOUVILLE

Sonthonax was not his enemy, but a proven friend. Msieur Vaublanc and his reactionary crowd detested Sonthonax even more than Toussaint. Yet Toussaint expelled his ally Sonthonax.

ROUME

For proposing independence.

HÉDOUVILLE

The same accusation Sonthonax lodges against him.

ROUME

I cannot fathom the truth of either claim, General. I value Commissioner Sonthonax's devotion—likewise Commander Toussaint's fealty to the Republic. General Hédouville, you must understand how upset Commander Toussaint and his Blacks have been. Nothing troubles Blacks more than talk of re-enslavement. It unites them like a closed fist.

> *(Scene shifts to another platform downstage, where Generals DESSALINES, CHRISTOPHE, MOÏSE, MAUREPAS and JEAN-PAUL are congregated. They are in high spirits.)*

CHRISTOPHE

Maitland's lines are stretched to breaking point!

DESSALINES

King Tom and his pudding faces will soon feast on San Domingo dirt!

> *(TOUSSAINT moves into the scene)*

TOUSSAINT

Maitland seeks to negotiate.

> *(The GENERALS are stunned momentarily, then drop their dignified composure and shout joyously.)*

MOÏSE

Why negotiate?

TOUSSAINT

He offers to evacuate Port au Prince, Croix de Bouquets, L'Archayle and St. Marc in return for an Armistice.

ALL

? ARMISTICE...?!

DESSALINES

Armistice!... Nothing can stitch his arms back together after the licking he took!

CHRISTOPHE

Commander, Je ne comprends pas... armistice? What does he expect to gain?

MAUREPAS

...A dignified exit from San Domingo, perhaps?

DESSALINES

I don't believe it! Temps upon temps, we beat the limey chiens and they pour more soldiers in to fight. The Spanish read the writing on the dung-pen, but not the British, stupide. I don't trust them!

TOUSSAINT

Dessalines, San Domingo is but one sector in Britain's war with France. Already she has lost more men ici than Wellington lost in Europe... cost millions of pounds. She couldn't seduce Rigaud over by offering Mulattoes equal privileges with Whites. Finally, she faces total humiliation at our hands.

JEAN-PAUL

What if Maitland's offer is a trick to gain time?

TOUSSAINT

I don't put it past the British to engage in trickery . . . But they will always always fail because they underestimate us. Slavery not only handicaps those suffering its constraints, it deludes those holding the whip—who can't conceive of victims as equals even when contrary evidence piles up in their casualty count, soaked in the blood of their fallen soldiers . . . If Maitland tries to negotiate avec foolish attitude, he will regret his delusion.

DESSALINES

I say crush Maitland!

MOÏSE

"Give no quarters, take no prisoners"—commands the British issue about us. Yes, finish him!

CHRISTOPHE

What do we gain that way if the British are willing to surrender without resistance?

TOUSSAINT

A humane policy, amnesty for those who collaborated will serve us better than acrimony and revenge.

MAUREPAS

And France, Commander—will she approve an Armistice? While she still contends with England?

JEAN-PAUL

France should have thanked us for saving the Colony!

MOÏSE

It should be our terms to make!

TOUSSAINT

The Republic has been listening to the slanders of traitor Sonthonax.

DESSALINES

Sacre bleu, if Sonthonax had landed in Paris sooner, he would be without neck to give ear now!

CHRISTOPHE

What great luck for him headed to his doom under the blade, only to have his executioners sail by the other way transported to exile in the Guianias.

TOUSSAINT

Meanwhile, France sends another representative, General Hédouville, hero of the Vendée.

MOÏSE

What does he say, Uncle?

TOUSSIANT

He went directly to Spanish Domingo to confer with Commissioner Roume.

MAUREPAS

Not come first to you, Commander? To Spanish Domingo first, Merdes!

DESSALINES

What do the French hold up their sleeves maintenant?!

TOUSSAINT

We too are French, Dessalines.

DESSALINES

Pardonnez-moi, Commander. I speak out of loyalty to you. It is the Mother Country who disrespect you not sending her representative to meet you first. You, who risk everything for her!

TOUSSAINT

She is possibly disconcerted. Sonthonax spread rumors . . . maybe General Hédouville is unsure of his reception . . . It is up to me to put him at ease.

> *(Scene shifts to a platform where Hédouville waits. TOUSSAINT goes to meet him.)*

TOUSSAINT

We are honored that France sends a representative of your heroic stature, General Hédouville.

HÉDOUVILLE

The Republic appreciates your efforts on her behalf, Commander. You . . . my only concern . . . have been more than fair in your negotiations with Maitland. An amnesty for all San Domingo planters and soldiers who fight for the British—is quite generous.

TOUSSAINT

I aim to restore San Domingo to its former prosperity, Msieur Hédouville. There's no room in my heart for pettiness or retribution.

HÉDOUVILLE

Remarkable, Commander. Since the British exhibit less restraint destroying weapons, slaying animals and setting plantations on fire as they evacuate. Such behavior could easily justify your retaliation.

TOUSSAINT

Despite those provocations, my officers have strict orders to not commit a single act of violence or pillage. The British alone will have to answer for breaking agreements...Yet, to you, my policy should not be too unusual, Msieur Hédouville. To have merited the title, "Pacifier of the Vendée" must have required similar concessions.

HÉDOUVILLE

C'est vrai, Commander. But, you face one problem that I did not have—General Rigaud. Shouldn't you take him into custody?

TOUSSAINT

Arrest Rigaud?... I would as soon think of arresting myself, Msieur. He is a most zealous defender of our cause!

HÉDOUVILLE

Not if Commissioner Sonthonax is to be believed.

TOUSSAINT

Msieur, Hédouville... Sonthonax's opinion of General Rigaud—like most of his views—is a construct of slanders and untruths. The division between General Rigaud and Commissioner Sonthonax was caused solely by the provocative actions of Commissioner Sonthonax himself—and further exacerbated by the atrocities of his decadent officials. I assure you that General Rigaud and his colleagues are true defenders of France. Britain sought to woo Rigaud. He rejected them, saying that he would fight them to the last man. No, Rigaud is not a traitor to France, but her worthy son.

HÉDOUVILLE

The enthusiasm and sagacity of your defense convinces me, Commander. Such magnanimity is a positive omen for the future of the Colony.

TOUSSAINT

As is your appointment, General. I am relieved that France has sent someone who can enlighten her with unprejudiced views about events ici—the glorious hero of Vendée. I intend to supply further proof of my obedience to the superior authority of France.

(Hédouville exits as TOUSSAINT moves to another platform where RIGAUD waits.)

RIGAUD

We meet face to face, Commander.

TOUSSAINT

Comrades—united by conflict but separated so many years by duty.

RIGAUD

I yearned to embrace the Commander-in-Chief who has done so much for our land.

TOUSSAINT

Without your contribution, General, we could never have prevailed against the British. Distinguishing yourself by disdaining all their enticements for your defection

RIGAUD

Rejection was not hard, très dure, Commander. Devotion to France made it very easy. Despite quarrels with agents of the Republic, our loyalty never wavered.

TOUSSAINT

Your troubles with Msieur Sonthonax weren't unique. His mischief harmed us all.

RIGAUD

And now we have a new official from France. What is your opinion of Msieur Hédouville, Commander?

TOUSSAINT

I'm pleased that France has sent an agent of his reputation.

RIGAUD

Pinchinat in Paris praises him. But I wonder if he will pursue the vendetta against we men-of color. I worry that Sonthonax's insidious propaganda may have corrupted attitudes towards us permanently.

TOUSSAINT

C'est vrai. Being truthful, Msieur Hédouville does express doubts about you and your colleagues.

RIGAUD

I suspected it . . .! Sacre bleu! What must we do to dispel unfair suspicion? Our sacrifices for France are consecrated in rivers of blood! What more does she want . . .?!

TOUSSAINT

Take heart, mon ami. Inevitably France views us like a mistrustful father looking at his children—doubting that they can resist straying from the path he has charted. We must erase such doubts. I have already spoken in your defense and received a cautious but favorable response from Msieur Hédouville.

RIGAUD

Merci beaucoup, mon frère! I owe you another debt of gratitude, Commander.

TOUSSAINT

You owe no debt, General. I acted out of self-interest. It is clear to me that no matter how sincere French officials assigned to San Domingo may be—it is our own unity which ensures the safety of our Colony. Without mutual support, without loyalty, the unity of Blacks, Mulattoes and Whites, our island, our sacred cause is subject to the catastrophe of renewed subjugation.

RIGAUD

Thanks to God, your wisdom matches your virtue, Commander. I will follow your lead.

(RIGAUD moves to Scene with Hédouville as TOUSSAINT returns to watch from his cell area.)

HÉDOUVILLE

What a pleasure, General Rigaud. Did you have a pleasant trip from Port-Républicain?

RIGAUD

Commander Toussaint and I traveled together. He was gracious enough to accompany me in my carriage.

HÉDOUVILLE

It must have been good for you two to renew acquaintance?

RIGAUD

I had never met Commander Toussaint.

HÉDOUVILLE

Really? I assumed that San Domingo's greatest leaders would have met long before now?

RIGAUD

Our only contact was through correspondences or messengers.

HÉDOUVILLE

Then your encounter must have given you fresh impressions.

RIGAUD

Commander Toussaint is a remarkable man, Msieur.

HÉDOUVILLE

I was similarly impressed ... However, I would say he is no more remarkable than you. The Republic is grateful with all you have done and intends to reward you.

RIGAUD

Pardon, Msieur Hédouville ... I sigh with relief ... I must confess, Msieur Hédouville, that I awaited your arrival in San Domingo with concern. Quite uncertain as to what conclusions the Republic had reached about us. You are probably aware that we have had our difficulties—not with France—but with her authorized representatives. We men of color are thankful that you and the Directory have not been influenced by those misunderstandings.

HÉDOUVILLE

The Republic is quite clear about your contributions, General. I have specific instructions to commend you, and acknowledge your contributions with adequate repayment. France views your authority as subordinate to no one, not even Commander Toussaint.

RIGAUD

I am his subordinate and content to be so, Msieur Hédouville. It never occurred to me or my people to consider any other future other than with France, Msieur.

HÉDOUVILLE

You have given fervent evidence of that, General. Now it is our turn to provide palpable proof of our regard.

RIGAUD

You have provided enough already, Msieur.

HÉDOUVILLE

Confidentially, General, I feel that all is not harmonious in the Colony. Of course, much that disturbs can be attributed to the natural dislocations of war, the colonial treasury empty, government officials and soldiers behind in pay. Ultimately, those particular conditions can be rectified, but there are other things which go beyond the necessary state of affairs—potentially more damaging matters... You are aware of the increasing return of émigrés into the Colony and their restoration to positions of influence? What do you think of this?

RIGAUD

Msieur, Hédouville, my opinion about San Domingo's former owners and officials is well-known. I don't welcome their presence in my district and I do not permit them to wield power or influence. However, I don't quarrel with decisions made by superior French authority.

HÉDOUVILLE

Further proof of your responsible attitude, General ... Even more troublesome to me are negotiations with General Maitland. France is content with what Commander Toussaint and you have achieved in thwarting British ambitions. But I'm disturbed by the exclusivity of the Maitland negotiations. I trust Commander Toussaint but I question whether such complex discussions should remain in his hands alone. As magnificent as he is in military matters—with all due respect—I doubt whether he is sufficiently schooled in the field of diplomacy to conduct solitary negotiations with an English foe of much more privileged background in such affairs.

RIGAUD

I didn't know that you personally were not part of the negotiations, Msieur Hédouville?

HÉDOUVILLE

I am not sure Commander Toussaint would welcome my participation, General. Which brings me to the most important reason for my uneasiness ... Although Commander Toussaint denies it strenuously, the suspicions which the Republic harbors about his ultimate aims remain—fears that he aspires to an independent San Domingo. If there is any truth in this, it forebodes disaster for San Domingo and its inhabitants. I'm willing to accept Commander Toussaint's disavowal at face value, but duty dictates that I remain ever alert. You understand that, General?

RIGAUD

Certainly, Msieur.

HÉDOUVILLE

What is your opinion about the matter? Rest assured that your confidence will be kept by me.

RIGAUD

Msieur Hédouville—the history of my relations with my distinguished Black compatriot has been very complex. As you stated, my loyalty to France has been constant, even when France ignored it and too often chose to indict me and my clan... Commander Toussaint has also been constant—constant in pursuing whatever course with which to assure his dominance. When it has served his purpose, he warred against France. When no longer advantageous, he returned to her side. I don't know if Commander Toussaint proposed an independent San Domingo, but from my recent conversation with him, I am convinced that he intends to occupy no position of leadership other than his own supremacy for which he sought my cooperation. I think Commander Toussaint will pursue that which assures unchallenged sovereignty whether it is with France or without her.

HÉDOUVILLE

And if it leads to hostilities, where will your own loyalty be, General?

RIGAUD

As demonstrated before, General Hédouville, my loyalty is with France. I will never betray her.

HÉDOUVILLE

I assure you France will never abandon you, General. I hold you responsible to no one but myself and the supreme authority of the Republic.

(After observing the scene, TOUSSAINT leaves his cell area and moves to a platform where DESSALINES, CHRISTOPHE and MOÏSE wait.)

TOUSSAINT

Why?! . . . Pourquoi?

DESSALINES

Because the merde hate us.

TOUSSAINT

The warmth of our embrace still lingers and he betrays me.

DESSALINES

Sloppy kisses can't stop a dog from piss-ass habits! Yellow mongrels never change.

MOÏSE

Merde, so, with Count Hédouville we are back where we started, with French tactics like before! Did Hédouville know that you were eavesdropping in the antechamber of the Government Palace when he met with Rigaud, Uncle?

TOUSSAINT

Whether he did or not, his attitude changed. No more the complimenting afterwards, conciliating Hédouville, but now a criticizer—quarreling and prodding—baiting me. But his insults must be ignored maintenant—A more pressing matter confronts us. Maitland stalls—his British comrade Governor

Balcarres of Jamaica pressures him not to evacuate Môle St. Nicolas.

MOÏSE

We'll drive him out!

TOUSSAINT

It would be better to obtain Môle St. Nicolas without blood being shed. We need it for trade with America. If we don't achieve an amicable withdrawal with Maitland, Britain will blockade the port ... I will send a message to The Earl of Balcarres and remind him that Jamaica is but a short swim stroke away from San Domingo and we could easily row troops across, burn his plantations and incite a revolt among his slaves. And address to Maitland—

(Lights isolate upon MAITLAND as TOUSSAINT addresses him.)

TOUSSAINT

I expect you to evacuate all the territory occupied by the British in our Republic. Jérémie is very strong, but I promise you that I will march on you and overwhelm you.

MAITLAND

I wish to negotiate. However, I must inform you that special arrangements have been made by Count Hédouville with my subordinate Colonel Spencer for the transfer of Môle St. Nicolas and Tiburon into his jurisdiction, contradicting agreements that you and I have already ratified. I apologize if these unapproved negotiations distress you.

(TOUSSAINT confronts Hédouville)

TOUSSAINT

My frankness, Citizen Agent, prevents me from suppressing my outrage at your lack of confidence. In direct opposition, without regard to my position as Commander-in-Chief of the Army of San Domingo—without reflecting, without even thinking it necessary to inform me—you send junior officers to negotiate with the British—I would have preferred that you told me openly that you did not think me capable of dealing with the British. It would have saved me from the disagreeable necessity of contradicting written agreements and squandering my word of honor uselessly.

HÉDOUVILLE

Commander Toussaint, I don't need you to teach me my duty! As Special Agent of the Supreme ruling body of France, the Directory, I act to protect the Republic and defend this Colony. I'm perfectly willing to approve your agreements with General Maitland if they benefit San Domingo. It was not my personal intention to cause difficulties in your negotiations—but to strengthen the bargaining.

(CHORUS enters)

WOMEN'S CHORUS

> The Cat-and-Mouse stabs of their early attempts
> at Complimenting accommodations
> Gave way quickly to furious contestations

TOUSSAINT

You treat me with less courtesies than my foes who even in the midst of conflict treat me as befits my rank.

HÉDOUVILLE

Don't be seduced by British flattery, Commander. They only use it to gain advantage!

TOUSSAINT

You don't have to caution me about flattery, Msieur. I am not susceptible to its appeals!

HÉDOUVILLE

I would be even less sarcastic about the honor accorded you if I was not convinced that Maitland was duping you!

TOUSSAINT

Duping me, Msieur...? Duping me?! How could Maitland dupe me when it is he who prepares to evacuate San Domingo after sacrificing one-hundred thousand men to my forces—depleting Britain's treasury, her influence in all of Europe diminished, her power curbed without one remaining foothold on our soil—while I inherit her fortifications and even some of her troops!

HÉDOUVILLE

And your trade agreements? Are they not beneficial to the English in her war with France?

TOUSSAINT

Whatever terms I have accepted are crucial to the survival of this Colony. With her blockade, Britain controls the sea. France cannot supply us. We are not at the mercy of the British Army, but we are at the mercy of British ships. Trade concessions to the British are not evidence of betrayal, Msieur Hédouville—but the necessities of survival!

WOMEN'S CHORUS

All pretense was dropped
As each one stopped
To charge the other with
The worst they could concoct
Like a tug-of-war between two gents who
had rose so far
Beyond other men's 'accomplishments
Hédouville and Toussaint
Strained their differences
To the Breaking length
Each instant of ready discontent
Became the occasion
For savage denouncements

HÉDOUVILLE VOICEOVER

You invite sworn enemies of the Republic to return to the Colony . . .

TOUSSAINT VOICEOVER

Their talents are needed for the restoration of the Colony.

HÉDOUVILLE VOICEOVER

You have broken Republican law which forbids association with religion

TOUSSAINT VOICEOVER

I am a devout Catholic who sees no harm in strengthening civil oaths with the support of God's edicts . . .

HÉDOUVILLE

Once again, I must remind you of my superior authority . . .

TOUSSAINT

You need not remind me...

HÉDOUVILLE

Once again I must remind you of my superior authority...

TOUSSAINT

You need not remind me...

HÉDOUVILLE

Once again, I must remind you of my superior authority...

TOUSSAINT

I bow to your superior authority and since I do not wish to bicker with you, I think it politic that I resign my position as Commander-in-Chief of the Armies of San Domingo... If I ask to resign, it is because having served my country honorably, having rescued it from the hands of powerful enemies, having a cherished family to whom I have become a stranger—I wish now to protect my old age from insult and shame which I have not deserved and surely will not survive... An honorable and peaceable retreat in the bosom of my family is my sole desire. It is only there that I shall find happiness...

> (*MOÏSE, DESSALINES and CHRISTOPHE, who were present during his last peroration, address him*)

MOÏSE

You can't mean this, Uncle?!

DESSALINES

Certainment, non.

TOUSSAINT

I do mean it, Dessalines.

CHRISTOPHE

It isn't necessary!

TOUSSAINT

Necessity pour moi, Christophe.

DESSALINES

We will break Hédouville and his popinjays like twigs—

TOUSSAINT

Civil war is too high a price to pay.

DESSALINES

Hédouville has no soldiers of his own. Our people will not get his support!

TOUSSAINT

He has Rigaud, and behind him—the Republic of France. I want no more conflict with France. I have no quarrel with the Directory. I have already sent my secretary to discuss terms of my retirement.

(THEY exit as Lights pinpoint HÉDOUVILLE)

HÉDOUVILLE

The Army will be reduced to three contingents spread among three departments. The Black Generals are to withdraw, with their coast commands assumed by Europeans. The post of Commander-in-Chief is to be abolished and all commanders made directly responsible to me...Toussaint L'Ouverture and his sooty henchmen will cease to be a factor in the affairs of San Domingo . . .

> *(Lights expand as an AIDE rushes in)*

AIDE

Unrest spreads! Revolts are threatened in the Army and uprising among the laborers! Without General Toussaint, we are helpless!

HÉDOUVILLE

Gain his support, appeal to him, cajole him, flatter him. I must re-establish civil authority.

AIDE

He declines to intervene. Moïse, his nephew, is even more defiant. He refuses to withdraw his regiment at Fort Liberté where he threatens the Mulatto and free Black population there.

HÉDOUVILLE

Dispatch Toussaint to Fort Liberté to ensure his nephew's obedience!

AIDE

Toussaint already makes excuses not to go!

HÉDOUVILLE

Have General Moïse arrested. Have another Black to replace him!

> *(Gunfire and the sounds of warfare are heard; MOÏSE is seen fleeing across the upper level of the WHEEL. HE exits, an AIDE enters.)*

AIDE

General Moïse, your replacement, fought Manigat! Now he's agitating the Black laborers of the plain to march upon Le Cap!

HÉDOUVILLE

What?!

AIDE

Thousands flock to him. His agents manipulate sentiment—shouting that you are disbanding the
Black armies and plan to restore slavery!

HÉDOUVILLE

Colonel Vincent is a close friend of Toussaint. Enlist his help and send a message to Mulatto General Rigaud to hurry to our defense.

(Sounds indicate a passage of time.)

AIDE

General Moïse captured Colonel Vincent and imprisoned him. Our emissaries to Rigaud were intercepted, slaughtered when they resisted. Dessalines's troops have already reached the outskirts of the city—and Commander Toussaint is marching upon Le Cap from his headquarters at Gonaïves!

HÉDOUVILLE

Toussaint is defying the authority of the French Republic—opposing me its supreme representative! He is a traitor to France!

AIDE

What are your orders, General?

HÉDOUVILLE

He will pay for his traitorous acts under the guillotine! Prepare a ship for my departure to France!

3RD AIDE

Local officials panicked, Sir, they will certainly not stay here in your absence!

HÉDOUVILLE

We will take as many as we can. Prepare a proclamation declaring Toussaint L'Ouverture a traitor to France! Deliver this message to General Rigaud... "As a result of the ambition and perfidy of General Toussaint, who has sold himself to the British, turncoat émigrés and the Americans—I find myself obliged to leave the Colony. I hereby relieve you, Citizen General, of the duty to recognize Toussaint as your Commander-in-Chief and instruct you to assume command of the Department of the South in addition to your other districts"... Quickly gather my belongings for leaving this hell forsaken island!

> *(Sounds indicate the triumphant reactions of TOUSSAINT's victory. He addresses an unseen Audience.)*

TOUSSAINT

At the very minute that I succeeded in driving the British from the Colony—just as San Domingo was about to enjoy the fruits of so much struggle—agent Hédouville found a Manigat! Yes, a Manigat—yes, this Manigat! Hédouville, this expert plotter, chose him, a Negro, to destroy General Moïse and the great 5th Regiment.

... I reinstate Moise to his former position. Remember henceforth that neither a Manigat nor a Hédouville have the right to dismiss a general—that he who draws the sword shall perish by the sword! Hédouville told you that I am an enemy of liberty. But who is it that should love liberty more? Toussaint L'Ouverture, slave of the Breda plantation, or General Hédouville, former Marquis and Chevalier of the Order of Saint Louis? ... If I had wished to surrender to the English, would I have chased them out? ... Remember that there is only one Toussaint L'Ouverture in San Domingo—and that at the mention of his name, everybody must tremble!

> *(Ecstatic chants follow thunderously: "Papa Toussaint! Papa Toussaint! Never leave us!" ... Lights fade as Scene changes back to cell.)*

END OF ACT ONE

ACT TWO

(TOUSSAINT is in his cell asleep on his cot—twisting and turning, shuddering in discomfort and cold. We hear his VOICE muttering)

TOUSSAINT

—my color—my color—my color? Does the color of my skin tarnish my honor, my valor...? My honor, my valor...?

(A WHITE WOMAN enters in a scene out of the past. TOUSSAINT rises to address her.)

Why Madame? Why do you wish me to be your son's godfather? Is it because you'd like me to give your husband the position he seeks?

WOMAN

General! My husband loves you, as do all Whites!

TOUSSAINT

Madame, I know Whites. I am Black and I know Blancs' distaste for us. Have you thought about what you ask? If I accept your offer, how do you know that when your son grows up, he won't reproach you for giving him a Negro godfather...?

WOMAN

But, General—

(MOÏSE enters as another memory intrudes upon the previous one, dissolving it. The WOMAN vanishes as HE enters, MOÏSE alludes to a different woman.)

MOÏSE

Another hopeful coquettish White beauty, Uncle? You will need a regiment to guard you. That is—if you wish to be protected!

TOUSSAINT

Your one eye does not cloud your vision on the battlefield, Moïse. But it certainly blurs your recognition of feminine beauty. Accommodating as her physical form may be, she hardly qualifies as beautiful...

MOÏSE

Your perception is enhanced by better sampling, Uncle. I am not besieged by dozens of Nordic mademoiselles prostrating themselves along my traveling routes.

TOUSSAINT

You do well enough, Moïse.

MOÏSE

But a drop in the bucket compared to you, Uncle. I wouldn't have the strength to discourage damsels trying to crash through my chamber door—as you are reported to do.

TOUSSAINT

Age equips one not with strength, Moïse—but discretion. When I was younger, I was known to lay upon much softer matter than duty. Habits are hard to banish into nostalgia, especially when one is constantly showered with locks of hair and many-colored tufts from more private body parts, sent to tempt me into private inspection. But Toussaint is not mischievous. Toussaint is discreet. Flamboyance is not his style.

MOÏSE

An opener, nevertheless!

TOUSSAINT

Pleasuring respite is needed from strife. Your aunt Suzanne's pillows are mostly unavailable during the appointments of war, but her sister's fleshy cushions abound everywhere. Sinners as men are, we snatch comfort wherever recess from turmoil allows it.

MOÏSE

What discretion rejects, Uncle, my flamboyance will accommodate. I put in my bid for castoffs.

TOUSSAINT

I will keep it in mind, Nephew.

MOÏSE

I hope my frivolity doesn't offend you, Uncle?

TOUSSAINT

No, Moïse. Levity uplifts... especially when State matters offer such depressing portents.

(Scene shifts to RIGAUD and BEAUVAIS. RIGAUD dictates)

RIGAUD

Roume will consult you as to my successor. Once again, Citizen General, I assure you of my loyalty, respect and undiminished personal regard.

BEAUVAIS

What do you accomplish by resigning, Rigaud?!

RIGAUD

It will settle all doubts about my commitment to France and dispel all talk about my hunger for power.

BEAUVAIS

Who can succeed you?

RIGAUD

You, Beauvais.

BEAUVAIS

Me?!

RIGAUD

General Toussaint looks upon you with great favor.

BEAUVAIS

I do not wish to succeed you. I deplore the fact that you and General Toussaint cannot be united. San Domingo benefits when you cooperate. Division reaps a bitter harvest.

RIGAUD

It is not I who cause division!

BEAUVAIS

What if Commissioner Roume does not accept your resignation?

RIGAUD

I will bow to his wishes as if I was obeying the Directory itself. Then what follows will be Toussaint's responsibility.

> (Scene shifts to cell area where TOUSSAINT has just received news which infuriates him.)

TOUSSAINT

Sacre bleu! It is barbaric!

AIDE

What, Commander?

TOUSSAINT

Thirty men—twenty-nine Blacks and one White discovered dead, piled up like rats—all suffocated in a windowless shed! Jailed by General Rigaud for rioting.

AIDE

(After reading the report TOUSSAINT had handed him)

He claims they must have perished from poisonous fumes. The room had been newly whitewashed.

TOUSSAINT

Roume should have accepted Rigaud's resignation! Why must it always be Blacks who pay the penalty for allegations. Always dying conveniently from accidents. Violence follows in the wake of Rigaud's command!

(Lights pinpoint RIGAUD and TOUSSAINT upon separate platforms confronting each other.)

RIGAUD

How dare you accuse me of your own abominations!

TOUSSAINT

You always sought to subjugate Blacks and exterminate Whites! You conspired in the deportation and massacre of the Swiss who had fought for you so heroically! Why? Because they were Black! You refuse to obey me because I am Black! . . . But you are lost, Rigaud! I see you to the bottom of your soul! Remember that even if my entire army was to vacate your Western department—my eye and arm will stay—my eye to seek you and my arm to apprehend you!

RIGAUD

If I was conceited enough to refuse to obey a Black, on what grounds could I claim obedience from Whites? There is no significant difference between your color and mine. Is it a shade of color, which bestows principles or confers merit upon an individual? If one man is less dark than another, does it follow that he must be obeyed in everything? . . .

Not willing to obey a Black? Hah!—why all my life, from the cradle, I have been obedient to Blacks. My birth was the same as yours? Wasn't the mother who brought me into this world a Negro? My older brother whom I respect and always obeyed, Black? . . . My teacher in Les Cayes who first inculcated lasting principles, was he not a Negro? . . . I am too dedicated a believer in the Rights of Man to think that there is one color in nature superior to another. I know a man is only a man.

(Lights fade on TOUSSAINT and remain on RIGAUD, who is joined by BEAUVAIS and PÉTION.)

RIGAUD

. . . Is that all? . . . Is his contention accurate enough to contain the truth? Is the division within our mixed blood father significant to my actions?

BEAUVAIS

It is not all, but such a noxious fever lurks within us like some hidden distemper ready to leap into view whenever motion prompts it.

RIGAUD

You fought under Toussaint, Pétion. Did your color interfere with taking his commands?

PÉTION

General, I didn't ask for my complexion. Color only imparts a particular status, peculiar, unique conditions and fraternal self-interest among others resembling me. When Commander

Toussaint's aims coincided with mine, I found his color of no importance in commanding my obedience.

BEAUVAIS

Toussaint is right in claiming that we follow him only when it suits us.

RIGAUD

We owe him no debt. We are not his subalterns! The South and Western provinces are ours to administer, as authorized by France through General Hédouville!

PÉTION

If we stubbornly cling to that position, I'm afraid civil war is inevitable, General.

> *(Simultaneously, we hear the same question posed by CHRISTOPHE to TOUSSAINT. MOÏSE, DESSALINES and possibly others are present.)*

RIGAUD & TOUSSAINT

As much as I wish it not so, there is no other course.

DESSALINES

Yellow merdes be cursed by all the saints! They'll lay dead avec my boots up they Mulatto butts!

TOUSSAINT

Our quarrel is only with Rigaud, Dessalines. Their beloved General Beauvais—does not share Rigaud's maladie. I will praise Beauvais and urge him to avoid this folly of civil war.

MOÏSE

He will not side with us, Uncle. We will have to fight him just like we fight Rigaud.

DESSALINES

No Mulatto chien will change his yellow spot for one blacker one. The first mongrel recruit in our ranks who hesitate, we should shoot him!

TOUSSAINT

Mistrust will be agent of the deed, Dessalines.

CHRISTOPHE

I can't believe Rigaud thinks he can beat us!

TOUSSAINT

He expects France to send troops. He is unawares that the Directory has already sent messages supporting me.

DESSALINES

The fucking two-face French probably sent Rigaud the same message!

TOUSSAINT

Dessalines! Arrête!

DESSALINES

My lips can't help speaking what my heart suggest, Commander. Forgive me... Mine is the rantings of an uncouth slave past refinement. You know I back your judgment with all that passes for my brain. You must be patient avec moi while you forgive me...

TOUSSAINT

(*Smiling slightly*)

You need no forgiveness.—Dessalines—but patience is very much demanded.

Now listen closely ... France is occupied in Europe. She is in no position to commit men ici. If civil war must be fought, it will be a combat between brothers. Between our divided race ... Time will tell whether San Domingo is the ultimate loser.

> (WOMEN'S CHORUS, *dressed completely in black, appear atop the* WHEEL. *Unisonal, they will, while assuming the* VOICE *of* AIDES, *provide reports to* TOUSSAINT *and* RIGAUD, *distanced at separate locales. Appropriate battle sounds and atmospheric music backgrounds the sequence, along with a verisimilitude of Lights.*)

(RIGAUD'S *headquarters*)

WOMEN'S CHORUS

Your strategy succeeds, General.
Commander Toussaint's forces are scattered thin
North and West
La Plume has been driven from Petit-Goâve.
Should we press on?

RIGAUD

No. Toussaint faces revolts throughout the Colony—his own Negroes will seal his fate. We will wait. Meanwhile, seek out his damn White lackeys and shoot them all.

(Scene shifts to TOUSSAINT'S headquarters)

Mulattoes in our armies revolt. Dessalines and Moïse were greater prophets than me. What about Rigaud?

WOMEN'S CHORUS

He stalls after driving La Plume out of Petit-Goâve.

TOUSSAINT

Is La Plume mortally afflicted?

WOMEN'S CHORUS

No, he is considerably weakened
But most of his army is still intact

TOUSSAINT

Not attack? Why does Rigaud hesitate? . . . Passive when he has most to gain being aggressive . . . While he dawdles, I will move . . . Order Dessalines to head South. Once the Mulattoes at Port-au-Prince are subdued, attack the Maroons to the east. While LaPlume keeps Rigaud occupied, I will head North, arouse the laborers and take St. Marc. From there I will relieve Port de Paix. Moïse and Clairveaux must unite and recapture Môle St. Nicolas and Jean Rubel at all cost. Christophe should subdue the traitorous garrison at Pierre Michel. Order all commanders to treat traitors ruthlessly—in front of the firing squads.

(Scene shifts to RIGAUD as he emerges disheveled with a disarrayed WOMAN in tow. The WOMAN exits as a single AIDE awaits.)

AIDE

Pardon General, but I have important news to report. General Toussaint has regained control of all his Northern territories and has already reached Port-au-Prince West...

RIGAUD

(Almost distractedly)

We control Port-au-Prince...

AIDE

General Dessalines drove the Maroons back into the mountains and disarmed our sympathizers within the city. Commander Toussaint caught up with him there after miraculously escaping two ambushes where almost all his comrades around him were killed.

RIGAUD

Maybe the Gods preserve him for me... Let him invade the South, ici, and he will suffer the destiny that fate has saved him for.

AIDE

Your orders to our troops, Sir?

RIGAUD

... Beauvais will know what to do.

>   *(Scene shifts to TOUSSAINT'S headquarters where he looks at a huge map. DESSAILINES and CHRISTOPHE are present. Muffled drumming is heard. An AIDE enters.)*

Play II: The Fall of Toussaint L'Ouverture

AIDE

General Beauvais swears loyalty to Rigaud.

TOUSSAINT

Moïse was right. He won't betray his kin. How sad for him, them—and us... It is foolish to assault Jacmel with General Beauvais' garrison intact. He has five thousand men—The place is a fortress perfectly protected by natural surroundings, mountains and low lands, also barricaded with heavy fortifications, blockhouses, redoubts and hidden barriers. We don't have the naval means to invade it by sea. Our only course is to lay ground siege to it... God forgive us ....

> *(Lights fade and rise again as the WOMEN'S CHORUS files back in and narrates "The Siege of Jacmel" accompanied by drums and discordantly eerie music suggesting the enormous horror and severity of the event.)*

WOMEN'S CHORUS

Jacmel, Jacmel
Another name for Hell
Blacks and Men of Color
Prepare for the ultimate quest in
A town that would be known
Famed as the site of death
Jacmel, Jacmel
Une autre name for Hell
With Dessalines a ferocious tiger of
destructive sentiments
Of awesome military skill to match
his temperament
And Christophe of earlier Granadan birth
Who took second place to no man in
warrior's worth Toussaint made suit for this

decisive campaign
The premier struggle was at hand
Over which class would rule the land
Blacks the overwhelming teeming mass
Mulattoes long superior and more powerful caste
Outcome to be settled at this modest clump of
earth Sandwiched between mountains and the sea
beyond the turf Jacmel
A shaded town of no particular ground
Soon to be enshrined as a city of brutal renown

Jacmel, Jacmel
Another name for Hell
Toussaint dragged big guns
Over a hundred miles of unpassable terrain
Over trails and streams and mountain drops
And aimed them at Jacmel's chimney tops
As Jacmel dug in
It's kind and gentlemanly Commander Beauvais
Appalled by this conflict of divided kin
Resolved his worrisome rift within
Removing himself from the fray
Abandoning his post he sneaked by night
Aboard a ship for France
Guided by moonbeams of light
Soon after successor Fontane
A fearful man
Fled his burdensome demand
And crept away as well
Furtively borne on waves of ocean swells

Stranded by their ranking chiefs and left undone
Jacmel found its fate in the arms of a favorite son
In the grasp of General Pétion

Pétion once member of Toussaint's band
Now defected in loyalty to his natural bloodclan
Pitted against his former Commander-in-Chief
In a battle to decide San Domingo's brief
Though destiny had not worked according to plan
Jacmel could not have been entrusted to
a better man
If anyone could grapple with Toussaint
Genius of military tactics and strategy
Pétion was that most capable enemy

Jacmel, Jacmel
Another name for Hell
Presto
The Siege looms
Big Cannons boomed
Showering a lethal
Rain down upon the town
The population bracing to fight
The strength of their morale
Contradicting fright
Women and children shudder in shelters
Men fire back fusillades of lead pelters

Jacmel, Jacmel
Another name for Hell
Time dwells
Battle swells
Pétion harangues his troops for
stauncher resistance
And counseled the inhabitants for
stricter subsistence
Blacks in no hurry could wait
Ravages of hunger their bait
Nothing could get in

Nor something sneak out
From the peep of dawn
To the pit of night
The vise is kept ever tight
Jacmel must survive on provisions already in store
Toussaint made sure they don't get any more
Avec Rigaud preoccupied at Les Cayes
No rescue in sight with the passage of days
Toussaint brought new cannons to
belabor the town
His infantry kept pressure daily round
Shot and shell fell
Like molten flakes from a bottomless pit

Jacmel, Jacmel
Another name for Hell
Toussaint eager to speed his triumph
And proceed toward Rigaud's base
Appealed to John Adams of good old USA
To help shove Jacmel out of history's way
But Britain frightened of a threat to Jamaica
Intercept the big US artillery cargo
And dry-dock it as auction embargo
Without giant siege-guns trained upon them
Jacmel held out even longer
But for all its bravery Jacmel's future was dim

Bullets, shot and shell they could withstand
But not Hunger's squeezing hand
Citizens cling to hope that hostilities will cease
But death did not slake its appetite
And refused to offer respite
Their store of supplies exhausted
They sought sustenance in the unlikeliest of
nourishments
Horses, dogs, cats and fellow animal

Play II: The Fall of Toussaint L'Ouverture

Inhabitants
Found their way to the dinner table
Rats and lizards considered delicacies
When totally gobbled up
Old leather was chewed as food
The grass in the street became the
Staple for meat
Leaves on trees a special treat
But even these were in short supply

And soon vanished as means to keep alive
Still
Jacmel Held
Barely
A shroud of death covers the town
Corpses pile up draped in its pallid gown
Bloated bellies mock death's stare
With the illusion of being well-fed
But the joke was really on them
For they were truly dead
Brilliant but vacant eyes
Stare sightless at the sky
Limbs scraped down to skeletons
And skulls scooped into hollows
Rampart witness to Jacmel sorrows
Starving stomachs are fed

Solely on a diet of Toussaint's withering lead
Even thirst is mocked
By azure waters lapping behind the dock of the
city's Back hip
Tempting to swallow
But too brackish to offer a quenching sip

Jacmel, Jacmel
Une autre name for Hell
Almost two-hundred days of heroic defiance
Still no relief from Rigaud stuck South
No columns from France to bail him out
Pétion barraged even more by Toussaint's lethal
guns Decided further stay in Jacmel was done

Trusting in Toussaint's humane repute
He sued the Black Commander for safe
passage route
Of all women, children and aged survivors
Out of Jacmel's infernal battle environs
Toussaint complied
And streams of mothers,
Grannies and babes
Straggled through his lines safely
But others filing out a different exit aisle
Were met with the murderous courtesy
Of Death's final welcome
A hail of spitting bullets from
Christophe's unaware weaponry
Another sneering gesture of Death's
insatiable gluttony
With women and children gone
Pétion and his battalion fought on
At last resort he primed his Mulatto fighting squad
For a final breakout
Feinting an escaping thrust to the East
He furtively crept towards the West
Just to be met by the fatal crossfire of
Dessalines' unfooled artillery
Only Pétion and a paltry few
Lived to expect another rendezvous

Play II: The Fall of Toussaint L'Ouverture

Jacmel, Jacmel
Another name for Hell
After six months
Jacmel
Fell
Sing no praise for victors
Heap no scorn upon the vanquished
Only remember the details of this
Extraordinary
Adventure

(Scene shifts to RIGAUD, who is raging)

RIGAUD

...Ungrateful wretch...! Bloodthirsty monster—destroyer of San Domingo! Executioner of Jacmel!—If he is mad enough to invade ici South, he and his army will be buried!

(Scene shifts to TOUSSAINT.)

TOUSSAINT

Citizens of the South, why do you pay heed to Rigaud? My quarrel is not with you but strictly with Rigaud! He does not value his color but sacrifices it to his pride and ambition. He did everything to seduce you into being his accomplices. Most of those misled have already perished in battle or upon the scaffold. Must others expect a similar fate...? Yet I am humane. I stretch my fatherly arms to you. But if contrary to reason, you continue to revolt, you trust in vain upon the defenses erected by Rigaud. The army of Toussaint L'Ouverture will overwhelm you and you will be vanquished...

(Lights expand with COLONEL VINCENT present.)

VINCENT

I have been instructed to place myself at your disposal, Commander. To mediate between you and General Rigaud in the best interest of the Republic.

TOUSSAINT

I don't need the Republic's office, Vincent. Such efforts always lead to stirring the fire rather than dousing it.

VINCENT

Toussaint, mon ami, it is I—not Sonthonax or Hédouville. If my presence embarrasses you, I am willing to withdraw.

TOUSSAINT

No Vincent—I welcome you. I wish to heal wounds, not exacerbate their festering. Go, tell Rigaud he must surrender. After surrendering, he must leave the Colony and remain abroad until the situation in San Domingo is stabilized. Then, he may return.

RIGAUD

Ingrate! Fool! Betrayer! How dare you come to me proposing my surrender to this murderer! This savage barbarian who should be chopped into pieces and fed to wild dogs! How dare you stand in front of me! You, Vincent, have always been his lackey, his ass-kisser! You dare face me?! I will have you shot! I will punish those ici who let you in!

VINCENT

I come as a representative of the French Republic, General.

RIGAUD

Who betrays me to her traitor—I who fought for her while he was defecating on her!

VINCENT

France only wishes that you and Commander Toussaint resolve your differences for the good of all.

RIGAUD

France asks me to fight him, now begs me to give in to him?! After thousands of my people have been killed!?!... No! I will fight him to the end!

VINCENT

Your people are weary of fighting, General.

RIGAUD

Weary?!... Weary?! How dare you malign my people! They are loyal to me and will fight as long as I tell them! I will have your head for slandering them!

VINCENT

I don't wish to argue, General. Only to resolve this conflict. I have brought something for you.

RIGAUD

What is it? Another lying parchment to stab me?

VINCENT

No, General. It was entrusted to me by your son.

RIGAUD

My son?... My son?

VINCENT

Yes, General. I met with him before I left Paris.

RIGAUD

You met my son?!

VINCENT

I took the liberty to visit him at his school.

RIGAUD

How is he?!

VINCENT

Read the letter, General. Although ignorant of its contents, I'm certain it will inform you about his well-being.

RIGAUD

(Breaking down despondently after reading the letter.)

...He says you were very kind to him, Msieur... Merci. Thank you... My son, my beloved son... I thought I would never hear from him again... I am so grateful, Colonel Vincent. I'm indebted to you for your thoughtfulness... If only there were more like you... Then I would not be the victim of betrayals... naive enough to listen to the advice of those who claimed to be my friends, only to have them betray me—left in to disgrace—my honor, my name, my good reputation taken from me! Nothing left but to take my life!—regain my honor!... I would do it now, Colonel, if I didn't have to think of my people who still look to me for leadership—who obeyed me when I promised them deliverance... Look at them now—heroic defenders of Jacmel brutally massacred by savages... fighting months, waiting for France to rescue them... I promised them relief if they remained loyal to France... poor unfortunate babes... females, the flower of womanhood... old grannies... all sacrificed to the blood-thirsty animals of the wretched monster who calls himself Toussaint L'Ouverture...

VINCENT

I sympathize with you, General, and assure you that Commander Toussaint wants to put an end to strife. I came because he would like to come to terms before the conflict extends into your Southern district.

RIGAUD

...Let him come! Let him dare advance into my homeland and I will hand him his head and you, too!... Yes, Vincent, I will destroy you!... servant of Toussaint! I will not surrender to the likes of an old darkie pretender. We deserve to rule San Domingo! If France had supported us early on, the Colony would already be at peace!... No, they elevate a slave—a Black, an ignorant savage, above me! I will make her regret. I will kill myself, but before, I'll show her who is supreme! Let him attack me. This is not Jacmel. I will tear the repulsive old postillion apart limb by limb! Get out!... Go tell your master that I will destroy him if he dares set foot upon my soil!

(As SOUNDS-OF-WARFARE erupts, we hear TOUSSAINT's VOICE.)

TOUSSAINT VOICEOVER

"I gave him his chance—give orders to invade the South..."

DESSALINES VOICEOVER

"We are met with little resistance. Instead, the people welcome us..."

RIGAUD VOICEOVER

Tar paint all the houses, then set them on fire! The niggers will conquer ruins! I will blow up the arsenal myself.

AIDE VOICEOVER

No, mon Général, we must not do these things...

(Lights rise on TOUSSAINT as DESSALINES enters.)

DESSALINES

General Rigaud and his family skip off to France. General, give me a petit ship avec one cannon and I will blast the Yellow fuck out the water!

TOUSSAINT

Let him escape, Dessalines... It's an appointment—he possibly sought at birth... Maybe it was too much to ask him to back our cause to the end... I suspect that his strategic indecision had to do with his troubled conscience all along. He fought half-heartedly. As if the Black within struggled with the White and conflicted his judgment.

(WOMEN'S CHORUS enters.)

WOMEN'S CHORUS

> Once more in victory Commander Toussaint
> Proved a generous man
> Content that his Mulatto nemeses'
> Were pacified beyond further mischievousness
> He applied gentle punishment
> And sparse reprimand
> Even appointed a son of their own
> General Clairveaux

Over Sud department to command
Toussaint's actions were remarkable
In their own right
But appeared even better
Upon second sight
When once again
Sacre bleu
He faced an ominous blight arriving
From another direction
Once more to bring on sleepless nights

(TOUSSAINT appears downstage with ROUME.)

ROUME

I will not approve it, Commander!

TOUSSAINT

You condone the Spaniards stealing Blacks from French territory and selling them off the island, Commissioner Roume?

ROUME

I deplore it as much as you, Commander, but it is not within my power to interfere with treaty agreements between France and Spain!

TOUSSAINT

My people are not stolen under treaties, Roume. This thievery is illegal even if it is winked at by corrupt officials.

ROUME

Register your complaints with the proper authorities, General. I cannot sign a decree giving you the right to place Spanish Saint Domingo under your jurisdiction!

TOUSSAINT

Roume, you have the right as governor of Saint Domingo. Spain defaults by her monstrous acts. I merely ask you to sign a decree empowering me, France's highest-ranking military officer in the Colony, to enforce the laws of France. Already, the First Consul has reaffirmed my appointment as Commander-in-Chief—certainly you can authorize my actions here in Saint Domingo.

ROUME

I cannot do it!

TOUSSAINT

Then you must have other reasons not to do so?

ROUME

Commander, cut me to pieces but I will not sign such a decree!

TOUSSAINT

Roume. Remember that!—when you are faced with the spontaneous anger of the people upon discovering their brothers being stolen and sold.

ROUME

Their wrath won't be spontaneous, Toussaint!

(TOUSSAINT exits as crowd-noise clamors outside.)

AIDE

Officials beg you to give in before the crowd gets out of hand!

ROUME

Non, I will not yield! I have explicit orders from Paris not to let Toussaint gain control of the only remaining territory not under his rule! Let them strike me with their swords but I will not yield!

(Scene shifts to TOUSSAINT, MOÏSE enters.)

MOÏSE

General Age, your envoy has been thrown out of Saint Domingo and Governor Don Garcia, on Commissioner Roume's advice, insists that he cannot step down unless he receives orders from both Spain and France jointly. Roume rejected the decree you asked him to sign. He delivers a message from the First Consul's Minister of Marine that reads: "The person who stains himself with the blood of his fellow citizens will bring down curses upon himself from his fellow man, and also Heaven; therefore, the First Consul expects to be informed immediately that you have made your peace with Roume and restored order."

TOUSSAINT

No matter. . . .Arrest Roume. Take him and his family to Dondon and keep him under surveillance. Prepare to march on Saint Domingo. Send this message to the First Consul: "Having decided to take possession of Saint Domingo by force of arms, I find myself obliged to invite Citizen Roume to desist from performing his duties and retire to Dondon until further orders. He is at your sovereign disposal. When you want him, I will ship him to you."

(The thunderous sound of warfare is heard as TOUSSAINT moves to another platform where SPANISH OFFICIALS wait gathered at a table. A ring of keys lies on the table. As battle-

sounds subside, TOUSSAINT approaches. The OFFICIALS wait for him to lift the keys. HE waits for them to be given to him.)

TOUSSAINT

I didn't come to Saint Domingo as your enemy, Msieurs, but as the emissary of a friendly nation, to seek the observance of a treaty solemnly agreed upon. To pick-up the keys myself would be the act of a usurper. Therefore, I ask your lordship to be good enough to hand them to me.

GARCIA

(After hesitating)

... Do you swear by the Holy Trinity that you will govern justly and righteously?

TOUSSAINT

That oath would be appropriate for a servant of his Catholic Majesty. I am the servant of the Republic, Msieurs. However, I solemnly swear to make the people, new French citizens maintenant, happy and contented.

(The keys are handed to TOUSSAINT. He takes them.)

TOUSSAINT (CONT'D)

Your lordship knew Count d'Hermona well, did you not?

GARCIA

Yes, an excellent officer.

TOUSSAINT

I served under him. He defended his sovereign with courage and ability. His majesty is to be congratulated if he has many like him in service.

GARCIA

I agree.

TOUSSAINT

Perhaps your lordship remembers a plan submitted to you years ago for the conquest of the French half of the Island...? I flatter myself on having contributed to that plan.

GARCIA

I remember it well.

TOUSSAINT

If back then your lordship had evaluated the plan accurately and allowed the Count to carry it out, I might still be in the service of Spain. The entire Island would now belong to Spain and your lordship would have been spared the painful necessity of handing over the keys of the Colony.

GARCIA

Are you familiar with Ozana, Commander?

TOUSSAINT

???... Oh, oui, yes—it is a bank ici, isn't it?

GARCÍA

Previously—it was the palace of Christopher Columbus, who was sent back to Spain in chains for wishing to make himself independent.

TOUSSAINT

Msieur, I know as well as you that Spain rewarded Columbus with ingratitude. Such is the lot of most men who serve their country. They attract powerful enemies who sooner or later undermine them. I do not doubt that there are many who reserve the same fate for me.

(As lights dim, KERSERVEAU's VOICE is heard.)

KERSERVEAU VOICEOVER

It is up to the Republic to consider whether, after having given laws to all the monarchs of Europe—whether it suits the measure of its dignity to allow a rebellious Negro to exist in its Colony.

END OF ACT TWO

ACT THREE

(BALL MUSIC *is heard. A string of well-dressed people stretches across the Stage as if in a waiting line. They are multi-racial—Blacks, Whites, Mulattoes; multi-national and multi-classed.*

TOUSSAINT is seen in the background looking on. Soon a fanfare of trumpets cuts through the dance music and TOUSSAINT moves from his cell area, crossing Downstage into the Scene. As he appears, officers salute, gentlemen bow and ladies curtsy. A beautiful woman steps forward and places a laurel wreath upon his head. He rewards her with a kiss to the enthusiastic applause of the room. The music resumes as a series of vignettes follow—various people step forward from the waiting line to address TOUSSAINT. Each exchange of dialogue is drowned out by the music until TOUSSAINT's reply takes place—at that point everybody freezes except TOUSSAINT and his addressers. The pattern repeats after each individual episode with the participants stepping back in line when their turn is completed.

While this occurs, VOICEOVERs from various observers are heard above the music.)

STEVENS

Perfect tranquility has been restored to the Colony...

LACROIX

Progress increases every day. In Le Cap and throughout the North buildings sprout up like toadstools after rain...

STEVENS

So rapid is the progress in agriculture that the island's next crop promises to match two-thirds of the sugar and coffee output yielded in its most prosperous year before conflict...

MADIOUX

Bickering among caste groups fade. Races melt at Toussaint's embrace...

POYEN

Toussaint L'Ouverture restores and embellishes the cities, builds bridges, administers justice, visits schools, hospitals and barracks. It is difficult to measure the activity of this extraordinary Negro who sleeps only two hours out of twenty-four...

(1ST SEQUENCE: A Black Man steps forward. Talks unheard. Freeze)

TOUSSAINT

So you want to be a magistrate ... You know how to speak and read Latin?

NEGRO MAN

Non, non, mon Général.

TOUSSAINT

You don't know Latin?! How can you be a judge without knowing Latin! Vade retro!

> (The Man steps back.)

> (2ND SEQUENCE: An officer steps forward and points out a lady to TOUSSAINT and talks briefly unheard. Freeze)

TOUSSAINT

See that the wife of my old rogue-enemy Biassou is treated honorably. Give her an ample life pension ... Do likewise with the Mulatto martyr Chavannes' widow.

> (3RD SEQUENCE: A White Woman presents her daughter to TOUSSAINT. He notices the Young Woman's too-low décolletage, takes out his handkerchief and covers the exposed area, then motions for the mother to take her daughter away without rejoining the line. No dialogue was heard during this encounter.)

> (4TH SEQUENCE: TOUSSAINT is approached by his former master, the Bayou de Libertat, who starts to clasp him warmly. TOUSSAINT eludes the embrace. Freeze)

TOUSSAINT

Not so fast, not so fast, former master, Manager Bayou de Libertat. Remember that the distance between you and I is now far greater than the gap that once existed between you and I. Return to your plantation. Be conscientious and just. See to it that the cultivators work well, so that the State profits as well as you may benefit.

> *(After the last SEQUENCE, the BALL-MUSIC rises and the stage participants spread out in natural party behavior.*
>
> *At this juncture, the crowd has drifted offstage and TOUSSAINT has ended up on a platform where he is speaking with DESSALINES. DESSALINES' WOMAN is present. She listens briefly then starts to leave the Men alone.)*

TOUSSAINT

Ah, don't leave, Citizen.

CITIZEN CLARE

I leave you men to weightier matters.

TOUSSAINT

Such matters will seem drab without your radiance. I am at a loss to see how Dessalines could have been so favored by fortune.

CITIZEN CLARE

It is I who have been favored, Commander.

DESSALINES

Commander Toussaint speak truths. A bullfrog don't deserve a princess. Every night I wake up beside her, squeezing myself to make sure I am not dreaming.

CITIZEN CLARE

Shame, Dessalines! You should not reveal that we comport in sin. Commander Toussaint is shocked!

TOUSSAINT

Citizen, I would be shocked if Dessalines pretends otherwise. While our supreme deity might not approve, He will surely forgive you as long as matrimony is planned. Dessalines can scarcely be expected to curb his passion during the wait.

CITIZEN CLARE

Nor, I, Commander.

TOUSSAINT

You do plan vows? They are expected.

CITIZEN CLARE

If he will have me, Commander.

DESSALINES

Say when, Commander. Your orders are not to be disobeyed!

TOUSSAINT

Oui, but you often execute them extremely, Dessalines. For example, your treatment of the Mulattoes after Rigaud's defeat.

DESSALINES

I purged them as instructed, Commander.

TOUSSAINT

I said to prune the tree, not uproot it . . . However, Citizen, do what you can to curtail our impulsive brave bull. Temper his ferocity. If he remains slave to passion, let it be confined to bedroom chambers.

CITIZEN CLARE

If boudoir confinement is sufficient, Commander, I assure you that beyond its border he will behave as a lamb.

(SHE *exits.*)

TOUSSAINT

Bien, she is a good woman.

DESSALINES

Much too good pour moi . . .

TOUSSAINT

Still many claim, because of infamy, she too is not worthy of someone of your rank.

DESSALINES

Merde on them!!! . . . If I can be general, she should be empress! A ex-slave have no rights to look down on a ex whore! She is more qualified for high station than ugly hags ici, White, Mulatto or Black. Her Blanche mistress-keeper saw to it that she got the best education on the island. She is a hundred times more intelligent than me and as for her beauty—mon dieu!—even though she is no longer young, her face and form is still the glory of San Domingo!

TOUSSAINT

That's what I suspect infuriates her detractors. Have no doubts you couldn't find a better mate. Leave go after her. Our concerns will wait.

(DESSALINES exits. TOUSSAINT approaches MOISE and CHARLES BELAIR.)

TOUSSAINT

Ah, my nephews. Are you enjoying yourselves?

MOÏSE

Sumptuous attractions entice me greatly, Uncle.

TOUSSAINT

Away from the battlefield, Moïse, I think most of your thoughts center on a banquet to fleshy enticements.

MOÏSE

I confess, Uncle. Womanly wiles are impossible to resist.

TOUSSAINT

My directive for my generals to attend mass once a week suits you. You have a heavy load of penance to undertake.

MOÏSE

I admit to a lapsed condition, Uncle.

TOUSSAINT

Don't be too neglectful, Moïse or God's chastisement will overtake you.

MOÏSE

I intend to outpace his punishment, Uncle.

TOUSSAINT

And you, Charles? Why such frowns?

BELAIR

I am not at ease among so many Whites, Uncle.

TOUSSAINT

Then you must overcome your discomfort, Charles... Look how we depend on the United States of America—whitest of all. We need her. Our armies, our economy. Despite her slavery, she keeps us from being re-enslaved.

BELAIR

I realize it, Uncle, but it galls me. My wife, Sanite, is even more unforgiving.

TOUSSAINT

Then you must not let Sanite influence you. A woman's fury is implacable, but men must adjust feelings to reality, Charles... You have fought beside me heroically—risen to general's rank at the tender age of 23. San Domingo's future is in your hands—yours and Moïse, when he can loosen his grip on more seductive pursuits. We lay foundations for a strong colony—must even abandon our present system of fermage.

MOÏSE

Why so, Uncle!

TOUSSAINT

The cultivation of small plots is not sufficiently productive, Moïse. Our people produce only what they need for immediate upkeep.

MOÏSE

Having their own plots, Uncle, rewards them for their past sacrifice.

TOUSSAINT

Their liberty is endangered if the colony is weak. No. No sale of tracts less than fifty acres is to be permitted and no one will be allowed to purchase land if he doesn't have resources to develop it. Former owners will be invited back to operate their big plantations.

MOÏSE

How will this differ from slavery, Uncle?

TOUSSAINT

Supervision of the plantations will fall to you and your comrades. Under our firm control I expect my officers to resist the temptation to abuse our people or grow fat with riches upon the backs of cultivators under their jurisdiction. Yet to prevent men from indulging their penchant for injustice, strict accountability will be enforced. Blacks will prove to be inferior to no one in deportment, morality or cultivated demeanor. Just as my sons now acquire the graces of the most cultured Frenchmen, I will send many other children to France so that they can rule after us and no longer need White or Mulatto secretaries to transcribe their every thought into the familiar written discourses of civilized communications . . .

(The Scene dissolves with MOÏSE and BELAIR vanishing, as TOUSSAINT continues, with VINCENT present.)

TOUSSAINT (CONT'D)

Slavery is forever abolished. Every municipality is to be governed by a mayor and four administrators selected every two years by me from a list of sixteen names submitted. The Catholic religion is confirmed as the State religion and the Church is strictly subordinate to the State, with the Clergy forbidden under any pretext to form associations within the colony. All departments of administration, finance, police, army, are under my direct control. All issues relating to the Colony and the Mother Country will be handled by me. The content of all proclamations and other printed matter is subject to my approval. All laws are to be prefixed with the formulation; as proposed by the Governor. The Central Assembly has the right to accept or propose laws, but that Assembly is to be elected by principal officials nominated by me. The Constitution appoints me for life and gives me the right to appoint my successor. The Constitution encourages and welcomes increased immigration of Blacks from Africa.

VINCENT

This is madness, Commander!

TOUSSAINT

Do the cheers of our people sound like madness, Vincent? . . .

(Scene shifts to a downstage platform where VINCENT joins BONAPARTE and KERVERSEAU. TOUSSAINT returns to his cell and lies down in bed.)

BONAPARTE

How dare this impudent, gilded African test me! I will not leave an epaulette on the shoulder of a single nigger in San Domingo! Not only does he fashion treason, he is brash enough to present the traitorous deed to my face!

VINCENT

He doesn't think the document treasonous, Sir. If you communicate with him, I'm certain that he will moderate his position. No doubt there are clauses in his constitution which can be interpreted as usurping France's control of the Colony, but I know that is not what General Toussaint wishes.

BONAPARTE

Con-sti-tu-tion!!?? This is blatant treason! How dare you defend this revolted slave! This preening blackamoor who flaunts before me this offense of a "constitution"! He has charted a defiant course for years. Why should I reply to him?! I'm not a lover of Blacks! Especially one who fancies himself another Bonaparte! When he sights my ships, he will know that he is still just an upstart nigger!

VINCENT

Sir, I beg you! A positive word from you and he will rescind his provocation.

BONAPARTE

I once considered consulting him. I even drafted a letter. I never sent it.

VINCENT

Why not, sir?

BONAPARTE

Because I was uneasy about conferring praise upon a possible ingrate! . . . I was right! And your "constitution" proves it! So now, instead of receiving my blessings, he will be destroyed. I had hoped for his cooperation in my North American conquests. But now he will suffer the wrath of my disapproval instead!

VINCENT

Sir, if you proceed according to your first instinct you will indeed gain an ally, who will assure you triumphs in the New World. Engage him in battle—you risk an opposite result.

BONAPARTE

The old Black has taken possession of your judgment. I don't underestimate your gilded nigger, Vincent. My expedition will include my best officers. How could they who have no fear? Why should they fear being repelled by a bunch of revolted slaves?

VINCENT

Because they will confront not only one of the fiercest armies they have ever met, but because commanding that army - pardonnez-moi—is this man of uncanny abilities. Sir, I do not exaggerate when I say that Toussaint is most fearsome when faced with great danger. He is amazing in making sound judgments when attacked. Possessed with the unusual faculty of being able to function without rest, exhausting everyone around him.

The talent to cajole and beguile everybody, even to the point of deceit. Those who fear him may be dismayed about his aims but are powerless to act.

BONAPARTE

Do you describe Bonaparte, Vincent, or some fictitious nigger?

VINCENT

In his own bailiwick, I would dare to measure him as remindful of the great Bonaparte.

BONAPARTE

And such a unique specimen will be content to rule San Domingo subordinate to French authority?

VINCENT

I stake my honor on it—that if you assure him and his people that they will never be re-enslaved—he will repay his gratitude in wondrous ways.

BONAPARTE

Do you conquer, General Kerverseau?

KERVERSEAU

Let there be no mistake, Consul—as long as Toussaint remains in the colony, he will be omnipotent. He may rule in the name of France, but only so long as France is willing to bow to his will. There will be order, but it will be his kind of order. Authority there will no doubt be, but it will be his authority. If he deigns to receive the representatives of France, they will be like the pashas of the Porte in Egypt—honored captives without a trace of power. The moment they incur the displeasure of this easily-offended and distrustful man, they will be driven out ignominiously.

BONAPARTE

You see, Vincent, your optimism about your impudent blackamoor is not shared.

VINCENT

Sir, I believe that you will regret confronting him when you can accomplish so much more by enlisting his cooperation.

BONAPARTE

I will regret nothing! Rien! Setting sail from France and other ports of Europe will be the greatest overseas expeditions ever assembled. Eighty-six war and transport vessels will embark from—Brest, Orient, Rochefort, Toulon, Havre, Cadiz and Flushing—under the command of Admiral Villaret-Joyeuse. Chief of the expedition army will be my brother-in-law, General Le Clerc, distinguished hero of our campaigns in Italy, the Rhine and Portugal. His staff will include thirteen generals of division and twenty-seven brigadier generals—men of proven valor throughout the world—like Rochambeau, hero of Martinique and the Tyrol—Dagua, hero of the Pyramids—Humbert of Ireland—Boudet, victor of Marengo—Lacroix, Hardy, Debelle, Claparde and autres... As a special treat for Toussaint, his old Mulatto amis Rigaud, Villate, Pétion, Boyer, and many more will sail along to remake his acquaintance... And as final pièce de résistance, Toussaint's sons whose return he begs for will accompany the expedition. So considerate am I of our sooty postillion that I have convinced my brother-in-law to take his wife, my dearest sister, Pauline. She may resent absenting herself from the dazzling joie-de-vive and social contretemps of Paris, but she will certainly bring culture, taste and vivacity to San Domingo.

She will, I'm sure, take an enormous staff along to accomplish the purpose. As for you, Vincent, I think it best that you serve the Republic in new surroundings—I'm assigning you to the Island of Elba.

VINCENT

Where I will faithfully serve you as always, Sir. But I would not be worthy of your trust if I didn't repeat once more, Consul, that the expedition you plan, if carried out, will someday give you cause for remorse.

(Scene shifts to TOUSSAINT jumping from his bed in an agitated state.)

TOUSSAINT

Regret! Regret?! Regret?! No! It had to be done!

(He moves to confront MOÏSE on another platform.)

TOUSSAINT (CONT'D)

Traitor! You want to overthrow me!

MOÏSE

That's not true, Uncle!

TOUSSAINT

Cultivators revolt with your name on their tongues! "Long live Moïse! Long live Moïse!"

MOÏSE

I have come ici after quelling a rebellion at Dondon!

TOUSSAINT

Only after your scheme was doomed! Thanks to the alertness of Christophe and Dessalines!

MOÏSE

Uncle, cultivators object to labor edicts you have imposed. I, too, disagree about some of those policies. Yet I have carried them out dutifully. Rioters shout my name but not with my consent. I punish them severely, many before the firing squad and many others I bring to you to be dealt with!

TOUSSAINT

Those rebels massacred more than a hundred Whites!

MOÏSE

Without my complicity, Uncle.

TOUSSAINT

You lie! It is your own antipathy that encourages them. "My uncle is an old fool! He thinks he is king of San Domingo. He always talks about the interest of the Mother Country, but those are the interests of the Whites, and I shall never love Whites until they give me back the eye that they made me lose ... Whatever my old uncle does, I am not prepared to persecute my own color ..." What kind of talk is that except incitement to rebellion?!

MOÏSE

Uncle, I disapprove favoring untrustworthy Whites—Whites who still look on us as slaves—but I have no hatred for those who are committed to our well-being. When General Age turned traitor at Port-Républicain, even you told us not to trust Whites. "Whatever you do to them will be well done," you said.

TOUSSAINT

That gives you no excuse to lead laborers in murderous rebellion against my policies.

MOÏSE

Uncle, those Northern cultivators fought and sacrificed more for liberty than anyone else on this island. If they are discontented, they feel they are not reaping the fruits of their efforts. Instead of leisure they are driven harder—more and more by the same owners whom they once ousted.

TOUSSAINT

There is no leisure! They must be as conscientious in work-precincts as they were on the battlefield! They must produce more yield from the earth than their harvest of valor in conflict!

MOÏSE

I only try to alert you to the source of their discontent, Uncle.

TOUSSAINT

A discontent cultivated by you!

MOÏSE

Uncle. Listen. I implore you. I'm innocent.

TOUSSAINT

Evidence convicts you!

MOÏSE

Enemies bribe witnesses to falsely accuse me!

TOUSSAINT

You broke my trust and sacrificed the cause of our people to your own selfish desire for power!

MOÏSE

Then put me on trial, try me! I am prepared to face a tribunal. Uncle, I am confident that I will be exonerated.

(TOUSSAINT turns to address the Audience.)

TOUSSAINT

For slander, defamation and murderous actions, my nephew, General Moïse, will pay for conspiring against France! Any man who takes up arms against the Mother Country, even if it is my own son, will suffer the fate of traitors!

(A MILITARY OFFICIAL appears above.)

OFFICIAL

This hearing finds insufficient evidence against General Moïse and thereby acquits him.

TOUSSAINT

Ignore the findings! Documents are evidence enough! Convene a new Commission, restudy the documents.

COMMISSION

"After further examination, General Moïse is found guilty of neglect of duty and hereby sentenced to death."

(MOÏSE appears. He marches briskly and confidently to a spot Onstage; he stands fearlessly facing an unseen firing squad and gives the order himself.)

MOÏSE

Fire, mes amis, fire . . .

(MOÏSE falls under the execution fusillade. TOUSSAINT is even more agitated, pacing his cell, ranting almost incoherently. MADAME TOUSSAINT listens)

TOUSSAINT

Ambition corrupts. It had to be done—loose living...nothing but women and...and pleasure...and loose living...drink and dancing the Chica...Life is more than...debauchery...didn't go to church...blasphemy...couldn't wait his turn...first served me then went astray...guilty...Treachery cannot be tolerated...Guilty...No favorites...When I assembled the rebels and ordered every tenth man shot...not one begged for mercy...all stepped forward, saluted and died obediently...they knew...guilty. Had shamed me, our race, jeopardized our freedom...Moïse, I had to do it...he died bravely...he had to be shot...I did what I had to...why, he was brave to the end...he knew it, too...I...I am right...! It had to be done! I had to do it. Had to! I hear them—hear them. There can be no rivals to my power...calumny.

MADAME

Yes, my husband...But what about others now? Will they be trusting...? Or as trustworthy...?

ACT FOUR

(CHRISTOPHE listens to a letter from LE CLERC read by his AIDE.)

AIDE

"Citizen General, I am indignant that you refuse to accommodate my forces. I warn you that if you fail to turn over forts Picolet and Belair and all coastal batteries, fifteen thousand men anchored in your harbors will debark. Four thousand land this very minute at Fort-Liberté and eight thousand at Port-Républicain. I value highly past services you have given but will now hold you responsible for what follows."

CHRISTOPHE

Tell General Le Clerc that I await orders from Commander Toussaint who, because he didn't expect to see dozens of ships arrive ici without warning, is not in Le Cap. Until he orders it, I can't permit you to land. If you attempt to force your way ashore, you will enter a city reduced to ashes. It will disappoint you as a place to stop, much less rule from. And even in the midst of smoking ashes I will continue to fight you. As for troops that you say have already landed, you have erected a house of cards that will be torn apart and scattered to the winds.

> (HE turns to his own AIDE after LE CLERC's has exited.)

Prepare for the immediate evacuation of Le Cap. Shoot all who object. Take this message to our commander of Fort Picolet. "Watch the French fleet. If any hostile move is made, fire. Your salvo will be our signal to reduce Le Cap to ashes."

> (A thunderous explosion follows and the entire stage is bathed in fiery red, accompanied by the sound of flames crackling. WOMEN'S CHORUS appears. Two singular voices speak up, too.)

WOMEN'S CHORUS

A spectacular greeting to a momentous expedition
Le Cap so magnificently risen from the
embers of 1793
In 1802 was once more a horrific sight to see
That amazing earlier transformation—

L VOICE

Imposing houses of stone, streets crowded
with prosperous Citizens, fountains gushing in
expansive squares,
Impressive public buildings, handsome
private residences—
An awesome Government Palace of stunning
proportions With neat landscaped gardens
Spacious rooms hung with gold brocades,
Tasteful furnishings, liveried servants
And smart-dressed soldiers in attendance—

WOMEN'S CHORUS

Incinerating itself maintenant to
catastrophic devastation
As for the invading fleet,
Every eye on deck
Looked at what no one did expect
A city blazing speck by speck
Into a total wreck
In a matter of hours
Well-lit torches
Burning the city backwards
To a Dark-Age municipality
Regressing by fire
To Back-Water provinciality

WW VOICE

A town in ruins, streets piled with animal and
human corpses And debris, choked with rubbish,
only fifty-nine out of
Two thousand houses fit to live in,
All public buildings demolished, property damage
worth One hundred thousand francs—

WOMEN'S CHORUS

When Mistress Pauline Le Clerc's wife and
Napoleon's sister Now Le Cap's visitor
Stepped ashore
To establish a
Parisian Esprit-de-Corps
Instead of elegant Haut-du-Monde
She and her entourage
Had to survive
With a life-style more fitting for
The less-fortunate poor

A dire fate to deplore
All fancy dreams faced detour
Soon French soldiers would be
Begging door-to-door

The fleeing citizens of Le Cap
Were no better off
If anything,
Hardship burdened them
With an even greater cross
Many thousand-file
They streamed out on horseback
In coaches, by foot with sacks

Rich and poor and
Blacks and Whites and Mulattoes
Mixed in fright
Creole ladies in carriages
Atop their salvaged boxes
Negro femmes balancing
Their possessions upon their heads
Miraculously free from dropsy
The whole gaggle of them
Equal in dread
Everyone suddenly plunged from the heights of
Well-being and productive routines
To the depths of chaos and threatening lack of
means Dislocated, disoriented, demoralized
with despair
Refugees
Huddled at the foot of Haut du Cap mountain's lair

And there
Suffered an even crueler fate

**When the Arsenal blew with a thunderous shake
Unloosing boulders from the mountain top
Rolling along in a menacing quake
Crashing down upon their heads
Crushing thousands dead**

(While the flames still flicker and the sounds of artillery shells boom intermittently, TOUSSAINT and CHRISTOPHE look down from the upper Wheel.)

TOUSSAINT

With all you commanded, why didn't you try to hold out until I returned?

CHRISTOPHE

General, your directive ordered me to torch the city!

TOUSSAINT

Yes—but only if necessary. I was less than a day away.

CHRISTOPHE

General - mounting pressure—threats from Le Clerc—I was forced to act—I had no choice!

TOUSSAINT

Christophe, relax, you acted understandably. Christophe, I do not blame you . . . it's only that it grieves me to see what we accomplished with so much effort vanish into flames once again . . . Yet the deed is done. We move on. Withdraw to Grande-Rivière. I will move my headquarters to Gonaïves.

(CHRISTOPHE exits; TOUSSAINT returns to the cell area where he relates to his AIDES and his GENERALS at different locales and possibly time periods.)

AIDE

General Rochambeau captured Fort Dauphin and massacred all the prisoners who resisted.

TOUSSAINT

We will soon avenge these brave martyrs!

DESSALINES

Port-Républicain is surrendered to foes by that sniveling White bastard coward Chief-of-Staff, General Age. He disobeyed your orders and without a pistol-shot welcomed the French merdes!

TOUSSAINT

Don't despair, Dessalines. You may still be able to torch the city. It is built of wood. Watch for the time when the French have been weakened by their expeditions into the plains and then take the city by surprise. While we wait for the rainy season, fire and destruction are our only resources. The soil bathed with our sweat must not furnish the enemy with any subsistence. Make the roads impassable. Throw dead corpses of men and horses into the wells so that those who have come to enslave us have before their eyes the image of hell they so richly deserve.

LE CLERC

Toussaint's scorched-earth policy will leave France with nothing to govern. Like Le Cap, every city will be burned to dust. How can we make him bow to our will?

(ABBÉ COISSON, followed by ISSAC and PLACIDE, enter the cell area.)

ABBÉ

Is this Toussaint—ami and servant of France? . . . We have waited impatiently for your arrival home!

TOUSSAINT

And I have been as anxious—when I learned of what to expect!

ABBÉ

Here they are, Citizen. The moment they yearned for.

(PLACIDE and ISSAC approach their father and the three embrace, overwhelmed with emotion: "Mon père . . . Mes chéris . . . Mon fils . . ." etc. TOUSSAINT finally disengages from his sons and addresses the ABBÉ.)

TOUSSAINT

I am grateful to you, ami Coisson, for being my children's guardian. The only solace I had was knowing that they were with you.

ABBÉ

France treated them well, Commander. And they have turned out splendidly—more than justifying your decision to suffer their absence for the great good of their education and refinement.

TOUSSAINT

The only outcome which could mitigate the loneliness I suffered these many years, mon ami.

ABBÉ

And to enrich fortune, I bring you another gift, Commander, an item of extreme importance. I suspect it will give you great comfort and bode well for the future of San Domingo.

> *(HE hands TOUSSAINT a gold-enameled box. TOUSSAINT, after opening the box, breaks the seal of a letter which is contained within.)*

ABBÉ (CONT'D)

It is from the First Consul himself.

ISSAC

Let me read it to you, father?

> *(After reading a few lines silently, TOUSSAINT hands it to him.)*

"I am pleased to recognize the great services you have rendered to the people of France. If the French flag floats over San Domingo, you and your valiant Blacks deserve the credit. You persevered in circumstances, surrounded by enemies, while the Mother Country could neither help nor send provisions. During that time, it is understandable that you had to rule alone and to even propose a Constitution containing extraordinary powers. But happily, today when circumstances have changed, you can render homage to the sovereignty of the nation which counts you its most illustrious citizen..."

> *(At this point, BONAPARTE appears above upon the WHEEL enunciating his Secret Instructions. His dialogue alternates with ISSAC's.)*

BONAPARTE

In the first of the three stages—promise him whatever he asks in order to establish yourself in key points of the Island...

ISSAC

"What is it you want? Freedom of the Blacks?... You know that in all countries where we appear, we have brought liberty to everyone who didn't previously enjoy it...."

BONAPARTE

As soon as this is done, get firmer. Order him to answer the proclamation and the letter I sent to him through Abbé Coisson which includes my warning that contrary courses of actions against the Republic will bring misery to valiant Blacks whose courage we admire and would hate to punish as rebels.

ISSAC

"Is it respect you wish? Honors, fortune..."

BONAPARTE

He must swear loyalty to the Republic. On that same day, he and his followers are to be taken into custody and shipped to France...

ISSAC

"Considering the high regard we have for you, can you doubt that you will not be rewarded in full measure...?

"I'm restoring—"

    (TOUSSAINT *stops him*)

TOUSSAINT

Abbé Coisson, when you left Le Cap, did General Le Clerc send any message to me?

ABBÉ

No, Commander, but I know that he would welcome your visit.

ISSAC

Yes, Papa—he told Placide and me that he is anxious to come to an understanding with you. He considers the war a grave misunderstanding.

TOUSSAINT

Abbé, you are my children's tutor and also France's envoy—It seems the First Consul's letter contradicts General Le Clerc's conduct. One speaks to me of peace while the other wages war. I am open to any reasonable agreement with Le Clerc, but he must cease all hostile acts against us and reveal any confidential orders to him from the First Consul, which goes counter to this communication to me.

ABBÉ

Commander, General Le Clerc and the French army are here as friends of San Domingo.

TOUSSAINT

Friends, Abbé...? Friends?!... What manner of "friends" shows up in a surprise visit twenty thousand strong? What sort of "friends" bring enemies like Rigaud, Vilatte, Pétion, Boyer and others of their ilk...? No! Too late, le temps has passed for the "friends." The war's begun. The battle of rage is in everybody's blood. However, if General Le Clerc will cease fire, I will do the same. With my sons, return to him that message.

(ABBÉ, ISSAC and PLACIDE exit as TOUSSAINT listens to LE CLERC'S reply. ISSAC and PLACIDE re-enter immediately.)

LE CLERC'S VOICE

The unfortunate chain of events upon our early attempt to enter San Domingo, are the sole responsibility of General Christophe. The solemn declaration contained in the First Consul's proclamation which Christophe refused to distribute and now reiterated in the letter sent to you—should remove further anxiety about the liberty of you and your fellow citizens ... Come meet with me General, I promise that during the next four days, my division covering the Cape will not conduct any hostile actions ...

TOUSSAINT

But are given rien to attack everywhere else!

ISSAC

Father, before we left Paris, the First Consul met with us himself—he promised he would never enslave us. His wife, Mme. Josephine, often entertained Placide and me at her castle! And General Le Clerc held a big dinner for us just before sailing. I believe General Le Clerc can be trusted. He wants to promote you to Lieutenant Governor!

TOUSSAINT

I remain loyal to France. But we have no choice but to show her how mistaken she is in attempting to suppress our liberty ... Mon cher fils, I respect your love and devotion to the mother country, which has bestowed upon you her best education and courtesy. I will not influence you in choosing between San Domingo and France. And remember—no matter your decision, I will always love you dearly.

ISSAC

I won't bear arms against France!

(HE *rushes out*)

PLACIDE

I am with you, mon père. I am older than Issac. I fear the future. I fear slavery. I am ready to fight so that it will never happen again. If need be—I will renounce France!

TOUSSAINT

It is not France you must renounce, my son, but men whose policies betray her. I am humbled by your loyalty to me and your people. I appoint you my aide-de-camp to command a battalion attached to my own guards.

(THEY *embrace. ISSAC is brought back on stage by his mother.*)

MADAME

Issac also stays ici. He does not have to bear arms, but ici he will stay!

(LE CLERC'S VOICE *is heard.*)

LE CLERC'S VOICE

Generals Toussaint, Dessalines and Christophe are declared outlaws. All citizens are ordered to hunt them down as rebels against the French Republic!

(*Battle Sounds erupt . . . WOMEN'S CHORUS appears above.*)

WOMEN'S CHORUS

Only Maurepas and Dessalines
Early-on won outright victories clean

Instead of fading into the interior
Others tried to fight pitched battles to
Prove who was superior
Or not wanting to cede command
Surrendered easily upon French demand
Even Toussaint's brother Jean-Paul

Gave up Spanish Domingo overnight
Upon receiving Toussaint's misguided message
not to fight
Although the letter was authentic
It was never meant to be presented
Intended only to be intercepted en route to deflect
French Attention
The messenger was killed
His purpose discovered
The French delivered the letter
And reversed the black schemes' chutzpah
Now Toussaint faced a threat
That would put him to the test
Without doubt it would require
His greatest effort yet

LE CLERC'S VOICE

I am master of the North but almost all of it has been burnt and I can expect no life support from it. Unable to surround Toussaint at Gonaïves, I intend to attack and occupy the interior....

TOUSSAINT

Le Clerc's drive inland will be obstructed at the opening into the mountains of Cahos—at Crête-à-Pierrot. With Dessalines overall chief of operations, we will station twelve thousand fighters inside the fort commanded by General Magny, head of my dragoons, and Lamartinière, second in command... You must not submit my children no matter what. Yes, you are my children—from Lamartinière who is as White as Whites but who glories in the Negro blood-flow in his veins, to Monpoint, whose skin is as soot-black as mine.

LE CLERC'S VOICE

General Debelle, the fort must be taken at all cost!

WOMEN'S CHORUS

>Blacks broke Le Clerc's back
>At fortress Crête-à-Pierrot
>With a plan so simple
>It seemed almost laughable
>Dig a ditch in front of your house
>That people outside don't know about
>When they follow you home
>Trying to break open the door
>Let them stay close
>Then suddenly dive down below
>Exposing them to sniper fire
>From hidden supporters inside

>"Jump in the Ditch"
>First to snap at the bait
>Was Commander Debelle
>Who met a small
>Group of Blacks outside
>The fortress gate
>Hastily they retreated for safety
>With him in hot pursuit
>Suddenly—Surprise! Surprise!

"Jump in the Ditch" Shell-fire crackled
In an instant
Four hundred French dead or wounded
Debelle hisself seriously injured
"Jump in the Ditch"
Next to take the bait was General Boudet
Who sought to Capture the prize

Avec Dessalines now inside
Like before
Boudet lit out after a Bunch of rebels fleeing
Lickety-split
And close to catching up
When Presto
"Jump in the Ditch"
Rapid volley couldn't miss five hundred
men of Boudet
Hit Hisself got
More than nicked

"Jump in the Ditch"
Next on the hook Chief of Staff Dagua
Avec General Le Clerc an observer
That day
They were suckered along
To the same old song
Could you believe it

"Jump in the Ditch"
Three hundred more fell
Dagua wounded twice
And Le Clerc slightly as well
"Jump in the Ditch"
Le Clerc's original plan ineffective

He issued a new directive
Using most of his best effectives
Twelve thousand men would besiege the fort
To overpower stubborn Negra Billy-Goat

Dessalines snuck out to raise support
After getting his troops sworn to never let
Em cross the moat

"Take courage. The French chiens will
Soon be few.
If they set foot ici blow
Everything up!"

With turncoat Pétion maintenant
Giving France orders
The Fort took a
Fearful bombardment
Both sides boosting their morale
Hoping to better their case
By singing the Marseillaise
After three days of constant shelling
Making the edifice impossible to dwell in

It was Rochambeau's cocky turn
To attempt a new invasion
By now you would think
Veteran men so skilled at Victory
Would catch on to le Black's slick trickery
But no dice
Once more and thrice
His attempt at another assault
Ended with the same
Damn result

"Jump in the Ditch"
three thousand fresh casualties attach to the list

"Jump in the Ditch"
Finally, when it was plain to Blacks
They had nothing to gain
The French now mortally drained
Restrained from upholding their oath

Upon secret orders from Dessalines
Eight hundred crossed the moat
Avec guile passed enemy lines
Caught Rochambeau by surprise
And just missed capturing him alive
Abandoning the Fort
Thus, making Le Clerc the silly Goat
So distraught with how he got caught
Le Clerc Le Jerk only reported a quarter of
Casualties to Napoleon Bonaparte
No wonder
When the sum of his victory was estimated
All he netted totally was unremovable
Sick and wounded
Left behind
Avec
A spiked cannon
Toussaint's musician bandsmen
And a few scattered pieces of Dessalines' luggage

LE CLERC'S VOICE

The rainy season has come. My troops are exhausted, fatigued and sickened. I tried to make Toussaint and his generals surrender, but Citizen Minister, even if I were to succeed, I would not be able to enforce strict measures unless I had twenty-five thousand European soldiers here.

(TOUSSAINT moves to a platform area where his GENERALS wait along with an AIDE.)

TOUSSAINT

Our Maroon chiefs are in position. Macaya at Linoe, Scylla in the mountains of Plaisance, Sans Souci at Ste. Suzanne and Vaillière.

AIDE

Citizens in the North attack the French everywhere. Hit-run ambushes, heavy stones dropped from above, avalanches of rocks from mountains and precipices, trail paths blocked with thorn bushes and heavy trees.

TOUSSAINT

Spies in General Le Clerc's camp say that after almost eight weeks—of some seventeen thousand veteran French soldiers, five thousand are already dead and eight thousand in the hospital. Le Clerc can't depend on our defected troops in his ranks. We will go on the offensive. Attack at strategic points. Dessalines, at Marmelade and then Charles you will link up with him to take Crête-à-Pierrot, sealing off the interior. Vernet and I will capture Plaisance and Limbe. Moïse and Jean Paul will—

(HE pauses as the others look on puzzledly.)

BELAIR

There . . . is . . . there is no Moïse, Uncle . . .

DESSALINES

And Jean-Paul is trapped in Spanish Domingo, after he give up to the French, Commander.

TOUSSAINT

There is always a Moïse aussi mon cher frère. I outwitted myself sending him an order to submit never meant to be obeyed. I forgot...—I just didn't remember... Anyway—Christophe, keep pressure on Le Cap so that the French there stay pinned down.

VERNET

My Mulatto kinsmen in Le Cap are reported to be disillusioned with Le Clerc. He miscalculated. On some flimsy pretense, Le Clerc deported General Rigaud and his family back to France. Pétion is said to be extremely bitter.

They brought Rigaud ici back against me; but it is not for me they now deport him. I feel sorry for him.

DESSALINES

Pour moi! Good riddance!!

TOUSSAINT

You are dismissed. Mon Dieu be with you... Christophe stay. I wish to consult with you.

CHRISTOPHE

Oui, Commander!

(The OTHERS EXIT.)

TOUSSAINT

Le Clerc must realize the position he is in. Search for any signs that he might wish to negotiate.

CHRISTOPHE

With the French on the brink of defeat, should we accept anything other than total capitulation, Commander?

TOUSSAINT

And what would a campaign to the death mean for us . . . and for France?

CHRISTOPHE

I will keep you informed, Commander.

> *(CHRISTOPHE exits as TOUSSAINT returns to cell area.)*

LE CLERC'S VOICE

Rebels recapture many towns and districts. More troops must be sent from France.

VILTON

Mon cher compère, Christophe, I have been asked by General Hardy to invite you to a meeting at Vaudreuill Plantation in order to discuss matters of mutual concern that could affect the future of San Domingo. . . .

> *(CHRISTOPHE is seen handing the letter to TOUSSAINT.)*

HARDY

For twelve years, General, we have fought for liberty. Can you believe that after such great sacrifices we would make ourselves so vile as to reintroduce slavery? Malicious persons aroused in you a distrust for the French Government and its representatives, but the treatment of generals who have bowed to French authority—including Commander Toussaint's brother himself, is proof that your suspicions were unfounded.

> *(CHRISTOPHE presents this letter to TOUSSAINT.)*

LE CLERC'S VOICE

Citizen General, trust in everything Citizen Vilton has written you in the name of General Hardy. If you do decide to submit to the Republic, think of the great service you can render by enabling us to apprehend the person of Toussaint L'Ouverture.

CHRISTOPHE

This degrading proposal demonstrates your inability to attribute any feelings of honor and fair play to me. Commander Toussaint is not only my chief but my friend. Do you think friendship is compatible with such monstrous, cowardly conduct? ... General Hardy, we, too, fought twelve years for liberty, for those same rights which, like you, we bought with our blood.

I have always been unwilling to believe that Frenchmen, after making such great sacrifices to obtain freedom for themselves, would one day come to take it away from a people who gloried in being part of such a great nation. We need more than assurances that our freedom will be protected. We need laws. In my country's name, I demand these unbreachable laws—once laws prevail, San Domingo will be saved.

LE CLERC'S VOICE

Heretofore, the First Consul was unable to draw up a code for a country which he was unfamiliar with and about which he had received contradictory reports. Come to Haut-au-Cap tomorrow. I assure you that after an hour's discussion if we have not come to an agreement, you may return safely to your troops. As General-in-Chief, I give you my word.

> (TOUSSAINT *indicates for* CHRISTOPHE *to go. After he exits,* HE *goes to start a fire. After it is aflame, his* AIDE *enters.*)

AIDE

Officer Christophe says that he will visit if circumstances allow.

TOUSSAINT

... He won't come.

AIDE

Citizens berate him, Sir. People congregate in your yard to assure you of their loyalty and resolve.

TOUSSAINT

Take this message to Le Clerc. Although you offer to bargain in good faith, I don't believe it. If I'm right—let me remind you that the mischief I have already done is proof of the mischief I am still capable of doing. I am still strong enough to lay waste to the Colony and sacrifice a life that has been often useful to the Mother Country.

(TOUSSAINT moves to DESSALINES.)

TOUSSAINT

Christophe has betrayed us!

DESSALINES

Pardonnez-moi, General—I know Christophe well, I can't believe that he would go to Le Cap without your approval. Why didn't you arrest him!

TOUSSAINT

I did give him permission. But to keep me informed. He even brought this letter from Le Clerc. But he did not tell me he had struck a personal agreement with Le Clerc to submit to the French with all his army. I only discovered his treachery after the Commander at Dondon refused to turn the town over to the French and after many of Christophe's soldiers escaped into my ranks.

DESSALINES

What does Le Clerc's letter say, Commander?

TOUSSAINT

I haven't bothered to read it.

DESSALINES

Be honest with me, Commander. You know what's in it . . . You, too, mean to treat with the French. c'est vrai . . . ? It puzzles me, also. We are close to wiping the French out altogether, so whatever happens if you join Christophe will be on your shoulders.

> (DESSALINES exits. TOUSSAINT moves to a downstage platform as a VOICEOVER intones the terms of agreement.)

VOICE

The liberty of Negroes and Mulattoes of San Domingo is assured. Their rights as citizens are to be respected. General Toussaint is confirmed as Lieutenant-General and is to retire from active service, his staff intact, and may live wherever he chooses. All Negro and Mulatto officers will retain their rank and continue in active service.

> (TOUSSAINT crosses downstage from left to right, walking alone. Cheers are heard from Blacks and Mulattoes; then boos from a group of White men.)

TOUSSAINT

I have seen them crawl at my feet—these same White men who now insult me . . . they may yet live with regret for this.

> (TOUSSAINT *goes to stoke the fire. His* TRANSCRIBER *speaks.*)

TRANSCRIBER

Why, General, why? Our officers in San Domingo were stunned by their good fortune. Rumors had spread that our mission in San Domingo was collapsing in the face of your resistance.

TOUSSAINT

For the good of the Republic! What greater proof of loyalty than my voluntary submission when Le Clerc was most vulnerable to defeat? Through General Boudet, I had already sent a letter to the First Consul offering to cease hostilities if he recalled Le Clerc. Why continue warfare which could only devastate the colony. My surrender to Le Clerc was final proof of my sincerity. I was not fooled by Le Clerc! Despite the warmth of his greeting, I did not trust him. His lavish banquet in my honor, I stayed aloof, hardly touching the feast except a thin bite of cheese and a small glass of water. And him? He was primarily concerned about whether Dessalines would submit and obey his orders. I assured him that Dessalines had his faults, like any man, but that he was a disciplined soldier. Almost at the end of the feast, he turned to me and asked, "General, tell me if the war had continued, where would you have gotten your arms and supplies?" "From you. I would have taken them from you!" I replied.

> (TOUSSAINT *moves from the cell area to a platform which will serve as the setting for an outdoor field and garden.*)

LE CLERC'S VOICE

If circumstances force me sometimes, Citizen Minister Bonaparte, to appear to deviate from your instructions, believe me I do not lose sight of them—and if I bow to circumstances, it is only to master them and afterwards make them serve in the execution of our ultimate master plan. General Toussaint has surrendered. He left here perfectly satisfied and ready to carry out my orders....

(MADAME TOUSSAINT *approaches him while he is working steadily in the garden.*)

MADAME

Many others can do that work, my husband. Why do you insist on doing it?

TOUSSAINT

You always doubted if I would ever find time for such chores.

MADAME

Non!—I meant your flower gardens. In these plantation rows, your labor reminds me of your exercise in command of your armies. Is field sweat a substitute for the toil of battle?

TOUSSAINT

Non, the soil is less obedient. It has too greater a mind of its own. Yet—I confess to temptation. In any event, I also wish to bend nature to my will... I must set an example for my officers and soldiers who show up every day after being dismissed by Le Clerc for insubordination.

LE CLERC'S VOICE

Articles you publish in France also happen to appear in newspapers here. It is politically damaging to print anything that would disparage ideas of liberty and equality, principles that drip from everybody's lips ici. I beg you, suppress any jokes about Blacks, it prejudices my operations ici. If I have not executed your secret instructions, it is because a suitable moment has not occurred. When the time comes, I will act, but I must first have the reinforcements I have requested....

(A group of BLACK LABORERS approach TOUSSAINT.)

LABORER I

Papa Toussaint, have you forsaken us?

TOUSSAIINT

Hand me that bottle you carry.

(The bottle is handed to him. HE fills it with white and black maize, considerably more of the latter, then shakes the bottle.)

TOUSSAINT (CONT'D)

Now tell me which color dominates? No, do not fear, mes amis. Your brothers are still armed, our officers of all ranks are at their posts.

LE CLERC'S VOICE

Sickness causes frightening havoc in my army. Thirty-six hundred men are in the hospital. For fifteen days I have been losing thirty to fifty men a day and no day passes without two hundred to two hundred and fifty men being stricken, while not more than fifty survive. To be master of San Domingo, I need twenty-five thousand European troops. I have only half that number. There is not a moment to lose in sending me the twelve thousand men I request.

(PLACIDE enters)

TOUSSAINT

What new news, Placide?

PLACIDE

General Dessalines has been appointed commander over the St. Marc district where Maroon rebels are holed up in the mountains. Msieur Le Clerc's attempt to confiscate weapons from the laborers has been very disappointing. He estimates that for every musket turned in, four others remain in their possession. He protests to the American envoy about their selling you so many arms. More than thirty-two thousand he claims.

LE CLERC'S VOICE

Here is a list of more prominent people who have died since my last dispatch, among them thirteen soldiers who lived in General Hardy's house and all of General Legodin's secretaries. This sickness approaches with symptoms of slight pains or bowel pangs or shivering called Yellow fever or Siamese disease. In some, the sickness affects them suddenly and kills within two or three days. Of those afflicted, not one fifth have escaped death.,—The Blacks are mostly unaffected. . . .

TOUSSAINT

So many trips to La Fossette Hospital each night! . . . The hospital is a henchman of providence.

PLACIDE

Oui, French soldiers die like flies!

TOUSSAINT

As well I knew they would... Through Issac, send Le Clerc a message, that I protest the behavior of his troops in this district. He has increased his garrison here from fifty to five hundred men. These soldiers commit outrages among the people and disrupt work on the plantations.

LE CLERC

My position grows worse by the day. Toussaint is untrustworthy, as I had expected.

(ISSAC enters)

ISSAC

Mon père, General Le Clerc says that if you think the troops stationed here in Ennery are frightening to the laborers, he is instructing General Brunet to confer with you regarding the transfer of these troops to Gonaïves and Plaisance.

(PLACIDE enters along with MADAME TOUSSAINT, CÉSAR, his aide, and MARS, his valet.)

PLACIDE

A letter from General Brunet, mon père.

TOUSSAINT

Read it Placide.

PLACIDE

"We have, my dear General, to reach an understanding—impossible by correspondence, but Which an hour's chat would settle. If I were not worn out by work and petty cares, I would have visited today instead of writing to you. But, since I am unable to leave, come to me . . . ? If you have recovered from your indisposition, come tomorrow. When good is to be done, there should be no delay. You will not find in my house all the comforts I should like to put at your disposal, but you will find me a frank and honest man, whose only ambition is to improve your happiness and the welfare of the colony. If Madame Toussaint, whose acquaintance I am very anxious to make, wishes to accompany you, it will give me pleasure. If she needs horses to travel. I will send her mine. . . . I repeat, General, you will never find a more sincere friend than you have in me . . . Your servant on his way to Port-Républicain called here this morning. He has continued his journey with his pass in order. I saw to it.

CESAR

Don't go, sir.

PLACIDE

I agree, mon père!

MADAME

So do I! Besides, you are not well!

CÉSAR

We have received word from your brother, Jean Paul, also Vernet, our Mulatto general, that Le Clerc intends to arrest you—a plot confirmed by the boasting of a French officer passing through Ennery.

TOUSSAINT

The wish is Le Clerc's desire, but he fears its repercussion. He is no fool. My nephew Charles, Dessalines, and yes—even Christophe—still command their armies and the laborers have their weapons.

ISSAC

General Le Clerc claims to have a letter from General Dessalines accusing you of plotting with Maroon chief Scylla to revolt.

TOUSSAINT

Le Clerc is a master of forged letters.

MADAME

I beg you not to go my husband! The French have a constant record of deceit and chicanery. I implore you.

TOUSSAINT

Dear Suzanne, there are no grounds for fear. During enslavement, a decade of war with shifting alliances helped perfect my talent for detecting the deceit and chicanery of plotters and deceivers—I can readily spot a man of truth—of candor. Brunet is honest. I will accept his invitation.

CÉSAR

Sir, take a contingent of your dragoons with you!

ISSAC

Yes, father!

PLACIDE

Do it, father!

TOUSSAINT

Mes cher amis et familles, an escort would suggest that I have less than good faith in my host. No, I will journey only with two companions, you César and Placide.

(HE embraces MADAME.)

TOUSSANT (CONT'D)

I will apologize for you, Suzanne, explaining that you are taken up with domestic duties. However, if Brunet ever has the occasion to pass through Ennery—you will be pleased to receive him.

> (TOUSSAINT, followed by CÉSAR and PLACIDE, moves to a downstage platform. The latter two wait offstage as TOUSSAINT meets with GENERAL BRUNET, who greets him effusively. The two men mime dialogue between them until finally BRUNET excuses himself and exits. TOUSSAINT is left waiting alone for an inordinate length of time. Suddenly a squadron of soldiers with fixed bayonets, led by LE CLERC's AIDE-DE CAMP, FERRARI, pistol in hand, rushes in. TOUSSAINT draws his sword. FERRARI lowers his own sword which he carries in his other hand.)

FERRARI

General, Captain General Le Clerc orders your arrest. Your aide and son are already in custody. Our men are everywhere. If you resist, you are a dead man. Your rule in San Domingo ends. Hand over your sword.

TOUSSAINT

> (Sheathing his sword)

General Brunet gave me his word of honor!

> (Soldiers pounce upon him, taking his sword and tying his hands.)

TOUSSAINT (CONT'D)

I have surrendered—this outrage is uncalled for!

> (HE is hustled towards his cell of imprisonment as LE CLERC'S VOICE is heard)

LE CLERC'S VOICE

After separating him from Christophe and Dessalines, I ordered his arrest. I think I can trust Dessalines in whose mind I have made myself the master. I acted, Citizen Consul, to show strength. But if I don't receive reinforcements, my position will worsen. I beg you to send ten thousand more men immediately ... My own health is unsteady. This climate is extremely unfavorable to me....

TOUSSAINT

> (Centerstage, turns out front to address an invisible presence.)

By overthrowing me, you have cut down only the trunk of the tree of liberty. It will spring up by the roots again because those roots are many and they are deep.

LE CLERC'S VOICE

Along with his family, I send to France this man who is a grave danger to San Domingo. Lock him up in a safe, impregnable place in the center of France's countryside so that he may never escape and return to San Domingo. If he reappears here, he would destroy all that France has done ... You cannot keep him at too great a distance. He has raised the country to such a fever pitch, it would explode again in flames at his presence....

TOUSSAINT

I have suffered every imaginable hardship during my voyage and my wife and children subjected to shameless treatment from which her sex and their youth should have sheltered them ... My wife is not involved in my affairs. Nor my staff. I alone am responsible—whatever they have done, they did by my orders.

> *(TOUSSAINT says good-bye to his family, SUZANNE, PLACIDE, ISSAC, BERNARD and LOUISE CHANCY.)*

TOUSSANT (CONT'D)

Soon I will see you all. I am innocent. I will be vindicated.

> *(THEY depart as MARS remains; TOUSSAINT and MARS enter the cell.)*

TOUSSANT (CONT'D)

What news, Mars?

MARS

According to General Dessalines, General Le Clerc issued a proclamation claiming that you, according to General Dessalines, never did lay down your arms in good faith. Msieur Le Clerc published a letter you wrote to an aide to back up his contention, as proof that you meant to overthrow him.

TOUSSAINT

I will have all my correspondence brought to France. It will prove my innocence and expose Le Clerc as the forger he is.

LE CLERC'S VOICE

Sickness continues to make frightening inroads among us. General Hardy is the latest to perish. I shall be very fortunate myself if my health permits me to carry out all that I plan. . . .

TOUSSAINT

(*Addressing COMMANDANT BAILLE*)

Why, Commandant? Why take away my servant? He is as much a prisoner as me!

BAILLE

It is a decision, from high-up, Msieur.

TOUSSAINT

I am forbidden visits from my family scattered throughout France and now deprived of my Servant's company! I'm no criminal! I can address you, but you are not allowed to respond to me!

(*MARS enters with his belongings*)

TOUSSAINT (CONT'D)

Thank you, Mars, for your service and devotion to me and my family these many years. I look forward to a future when I can repay you.

MARS

I have already been rewarded, Commander. Someday we will be reunited and I will tell you how much.

TOUSSAINT

If you see my family, tell them I love them dearly.

(MARS exits; TOUSSAINT begins to shiver with cold, then lies down upon his cot. Time forwards, HIS TRANSCRIBER appears and TOUSSAINT dictates)

TOUSSAINT (CONT'D)

I have important revelations to make. I will relate the facts with all the simplicity and frankness of an old soldier. I will assert the truth, though it be against myself. . . .

(Once again, TOUSSAINT retires to his cot in a coughing fit. His TRANSCRIBER exits as BAILLE enters with GENERAL CAFFARELLI, Bonaparte's aide de Camp. CAFFARELLI, appalled upon seeing the shocking physical condition of his renowned prisoner, turns to BAILLE)

CAFFARELLI

Why has he not been attended to?

BAILLE

General, the Negro is constructed differently from us. I had a doctor attend him at first, but since then dispensed with his services since it would be useless.

CAFFARELLI

Leave me with him, Commandant . . . Sir, I am General Caffarelli, aide-de-camp to First Consul, Napoléon Bonaparte. I have been sent by him in answer to your request. I am pleased to meet a man of such renown, who has lived so extraordinarily and accomplished so much. I am anxious to listen to what you have to say.

(TOUSSAINT presents him with a written position. CAFFARELLI looks it over for a moment.)

This is very striking. Commander, but I am afraid it is not dealing with what would interest the First Consul and promote your own suit favorably. Speak to me directly.

(CAFFARELLI and TOUSSAINT mime their conversation; simultaneously, CAFFARELLI'S VOICEOVER delivers a summary of its content.)

CAFFERELLI'S VOICEOVER

This man, yes . . . willfully deceitful and secretive, self-possessed, adroit and subtle, confiding with a great show of sincerity—had his theme all prepared and said nothing except what he wanted to say . . . What were the terms of your secret treaty with Britain? . . . Since there was nothing of any surprise, he chose to list them all . . . Where is your reputed treasure hidden? . . . He said he was rich in land and cattle, but not in money—I tend to believe him—Seeking sovereignty hadn't he been influenced by General Washington of America? . . . He stubbornly denied it. He admitted that it was a mistake to introduce the Constitution before submitting it for approval, but nothing more . . . I told him that what he had said to me so far was unworthy of a man of his race, and although he was now broken without hope of ever regaining his former status—there was another kind of glory to which he might aspire. He could earn that glory by having the courage to step from behind the shield of negation of denial he had built around himself and boldly declare that he had driven out the agents of the Republic because they had interfered with his plans—that he had organized an army and civil administration, had negotiated treaties, created a treasury, stocked the arsenals and powder magazines—all with the single purpose of achieving independence . . . By taking such a stand he would gain a glory only attained by genuine courage, from which many things would be forgiven him. For a long time, he remained silent, then spoke—only to declare that he had been a faithful servant of the First Consul. Then he picked up his pen—

TOUSSAINT

"Citizen Consul, I have had the misfortune to incur your anger. I was one of your soldiers, first servant of the Republic in San Domingo. Today I am wretched and ruined, a dishonored victim of my own fidelity. Let yourself be touched by my circumstances. You are too sensitive and too just to not pronounce on my destiny. A man more unfortunate than guilty awaits your verdict. Cure my wounds, which are deep. You are the physician. You alone can apply the healing potion that will keep them from festering. I count on your sense of fairness and justice and salute you respectfully . . ."

(CAFFARELLI is handed the letter. TOUSSAINT returns to his bed. CAFFARELLI turns downstage and moves to leave.)

CAFFARELLI

The prisoner is patiently resigned and adamantly expects from the First Consul the justice he feels is due him.

(CAFFARELLI exits. Time passes. Suddenly BAILLE rushes into the cell with two subordinates. THEY rouse TOUSSAINT and begin rummaging through his possessions and the room.)

BAILLE

You must hand over everything brought in when you entered this prison!

TOUSSAINT

Non, I will not! What is your reason for this intrusion?

BAILLE

I will have you put in irons!

TOUSSAINT

What is it, Commandant? You—who have treated me with a little humanity, why debase me now?

BAILLE

Les Hommes—That visitor who claimed he was a doctor, who, contrary to instructions, I allowed to see you has been discovered to be fake—an ex-priest, seminary teacher. Onetime Mayor of Dijon. The First Consul learned of his visit and now threatens my life!

TOUSSAINT

(Handing over his possessions—several gold pieces, two letters, etc.)

His visit, I'm sure he meant no harm. Although sympathetic, he was mostly curious.

BAILLE

Your nice watch, too! You can count the castle-clocks striking every quarter-hour. From now on, I must be more strict. No one is allowed to see you. I will bring your food myself and even carry out the slop pail. I alone must hold the keys and padlocks to your cell. You understand, General? I can no longer be lenient—my life is at risk.

(THEY exit. TOUSSAINT addresses BONAPARTE)

TOUSSAINT

Nothing can compare with the humiliation you caused me today Consul Bonaparte. You have taken both my watch and the coins in my pocket. I hereby serve notice that these objects are my personal property and that I will call you to account for them on the day I am executed—when I shall expect you to return them to my wife and children.

(BAILLE *enters*)

BAILLE

Commander, the onus of being your jailer, your janitor and your hotel-keeper bore too heavily...I asked for help only, but they have seen fit to replace me. I have come to say good-bye.

(TOUSSAINT *merely looks at him without answering.*)

BAILLE (CONT'D)

Amiot, an officer, a young battalion Chief from Minister of War Berthier's staff, will be your jailer...Before I depart, General, I leave you with this news and pray that you will never disclose knowledge of it to another soul... General Le Clerc is dead, mort ----last month, November eighteen oh trois. Your colony is once again in full-scale revolt. Laborers rise up throughout the Island, led mainly by bandit chiefs whom your own generals fail to conquer... I have said enough, Msieur Toussaint L'Ouverture, respectfully I bid Adieu.

LE CLERC'S VOICE

Let the Government send me ten thousand men in addition to reinforcements already assigned.

Dispatch them at once by ships of state and not by merchant vessels whose arrival is too slow... send me two million francs in coin and not in paper... Or let the Republic prepare for a cruel and interminable war in San Domingo and perhaps the eventual loss of the Colony. It is my duty to tell you the whole truth. I tell it to you... News of slavery being re-established in Guadeloupe has dissipated the greater part of my influence on the Blacks... Also keep in mind the question of my successor for I think seriously of quitting this country... I leave now to return to my bed where I am hoping not to stay long. I wish you better health and more pleasant thoughts than mine. Since I have been in this devilish country, I have not had a moment's peace.

> *(The castle clock strikes continuously, indicating a passage of time. Finally, AMIOT, followed by a subordinate with a lantern, enters, forces TOUSSAINT from bed and leaves him shivering as his bed and room are searched. While the search proceeds, AMIOT recites a litany of TOUSSAINT'S complaints.)*

AMIOT

He complains of pains in different parts of his body, I notice he has a dry cough.

> *(As the clock strikes, THEY exit; immediately swirl around and repeat the same procedure.)*

AMIOT (CONT'D)

He complains a great deal about stomach pains and does not eat as before.

> *(Once again)*

AMIOT (CONT'D)

He has vomited a number of times. For several days I have noticed his face is swollen.

(Once more)

AMIOT (CONT'D)

His face is swollen. He complains continually about pains in the stomach. He has a bad cough.

(Ditto)

AMIOT (CONT'D)

He coughs incessantly. He wears his arm in a sling because it hurts him. Three days I have noticed that his voice has changed. He never asks for a doctor.

(Finally, AMIOT returns alone.)

AMIOT (CONT'D)

Toussaint, I will be gone for three or four days. I leave you food enough. Since you won't need anything, I'm taking the keys to your cell with me. I will look upon you when I return.

> *(HE exits. After he leaves, TOUSSAINT struggles to make a fire and brew tea in a little earthen pot. HE then sits sipping the brew and gazing at the flames. The castle-clock strikes at quarter-hour intervals. HE repeats his procedure three more times. After the final sequence, HE sits watching the flames. The clock strikes. HE remains upright. MADAME L'OUVERTURE appears before him. HE addresses HER.)*

TOUSSAINT

Why, Suzanne...?

MADAME

A man, un homme, can act right... and believe wrong, my husband.

(SHE disappears. HE remains still, stationary, his right arm already hanging limp. He is dead... The wind howls in the chimney, the flames flicker. The clock strikes its final ring.)

WOMEN'S CHORUS

Old Toussaint
Although his mortal life undone
In April 1803
Had climbed history's highest rung
Once free
forty-five years in slavery twelve years of war
How could one so lowly
Go so far?
Old Toussaint
Ugly as sin
Now Immortal's kin

Old Toussaint
The greatest of men
His loyalty to France
Did him in

L'Ouverture
The Opening
L'Ouverture
The Opening

His loyalty to France
Did him in
L'Ouverture
The Opening
His loyalty to France
Did him in
L'Ouverture
The Opening
His loyalty to France
Did him in
The Opening
The Opening
His loyalty to France
Did Him in
The Opening
The Opening
The Opening
The Opening

His loyalty to France
Did him in
The Opening ...

END OF PLAY II: THE FALL OF TOUSSAINT L'OUVERTURE

PLAY III: DESSALINES

ACT ONE

(LIGHTS rise on a largely bare stage. However, there are 'things' strewn throughout lying flat on different surface areas of the floor. These 'things' will be brought into view or utilized at appropriate moments, some remaining to eventually become part of the scenery and decor; for example—a hangman's gallows (maybe two) which ultimately gets pulled upright into view. In a sense, the set is created as the drama progresses.

The most numerous scene-pieces Onstage are rock-formations of various sizes and heights. They provide sitting and lying surfaces, also areas to store and hide 'things' behind. Two of these rock formations stand out. The first, positioned Downstage-Right or -Left, is a large boulder-size stone which ultimately is transformed into a Throne when sat upon. The second rock-formation dominates the set Centerstage. In actuality it is a multilevel platform cleverly shaped as a rock. Its lowest level starts Downstage—Center, circling upward, ascending finally to a smaller surface approximately six-feet high from the floor; about six platform levels altogether.

At the edge of the stage, steps or ramps on opposite sides give access back and forth from the audience floor to the onstage surface. A corridor fronting the first-row audience is almost as much a playing-area as the onstage space.

The overwhelming focus of the play is always upon the performer—his movements, his hand-held props and his changing costumes. These elements root us and clue us as to time and place.

The drama occurs in historical time, but 'time' is collapsed into 'then' and 'now' as much as the protagonist's typical collapsing of grammar-tenses during his spoken narrative. The theater audience is doubly addressed as contemporary presences and historical participants. Dessalines recognizes no separation.

House-Lights fade and remain. Soon, DESSALINES, dressed in resplendent military garb, rushes down a theater aisle (or stage wing). From the rear of the house, lashing out at the audience. Although he is moving on foot, imaginatively, he is actually, bestride his horse. Once in front of the 1st row, he paces side-to-side upon the floor corridor, singling out, freely attacking and berating all present.)

DESSALINES

Get back! Get back! Get back! I will kill you! . . . Dare lift arms against me! You don't know what you doing! . . .

(Baits the AUDIENCE)

Open fire? Open fire? . . . Why don't you, chiens?! Why don't you, merdes?! . . . Come on, come on!—Go head and shoot! . . . What's the matter? What's the matter?—Go on try! . . . You bastards can't do it?—Where's your courage?!—You don't have fucking nerve? Cochons too scared? Of me? . . . You oughta be! Fuck with me canailles and I'll have your heads! I'll make you all dead! . . . Why you think you can attack me? I am emperor! Invincible! Emperor is invincible! How I make myself one!

(Pauses to deal with an AUDIENCE attacker.)

Brute? . . . Barbarian? . . . How dare you! I give you your freedom! Without me you'd still be licking your master's spit! Cleaning up his shit! You still be groveling at the feet of Whites and Yellows of the earth! I make you independent! Not Toussaint! Me! No one but me! Dessalines, your worst nightmare come true and your dream . . .

(Shifts to confront accusations from other directions.)

Blood-soak betrayer . . . Amis des Blancs all the while? . . . You fucking lie! Après the invasion, coward niggers and traitor breeds go one by one over to the French chiens, but we three Honchos alone, seulement, is still just set to bust loose our nuts from French grip. Then for no reason, Christophe give up to Le Clerc!

(Bitterly)

Old Toussaint claim he didn't know, but he lie! He prove it giving up too! What was I to do? Fight the French and them, too? . . . I do the only thing I could! Quit.

(Remembering, moving Onstage)

. . . I am last to go, mais when I march into Le Cap to hand over my sword, they know in their heart who is first nigger to reckon with . . .

(Illustrating)

. . . I ride through the street, horse prancing high, looking the White jackals in they eyes till they force to turn away. It good they turn 'cause if they keep looking they see all you Nègres and even some breeds falling to your knees before my horse's feet . . . Dessalines, your worst nightmare come true and your dream . . . ???

(Hearing another interjection)

. . . Shoulda hold out like the others? What autres?! . . . Don't count! Little petits bandit chiefs! Brigands! No better than petty thiefs! They could never be a threat to the French! All most of them want is all they can pillage! . . . Useless! . . . Mais au meme temps aussi useful! Quoi so? You think Le Clerc trust me? Me, Dessalines, who had fight him like a tigre, squash his soldiers like ants, who give orders to shoot any of my own men who try to give up to him?

You think he going believe my surrender? He know where I stood. Now he need proof of my change of heart, le cœur. Evidence of my sincerity. I give him more proof than he can stomach avec the corpses of nigger bandit chieftains! At least now they serve a good cause!

(Sarcastically)

... Le Clerc brag he make hisself master of my mind. Hah! I keep him thinking that way. Soon he will run out of time to change his mind. Blanc soldiers already drop as quick as they step off the boat to sniff our island air. Siamese sickness grip they nostrils and fastly send them packing to the graveyard. In no time Le Clerc will have more niggers and breeds in his army than White men. Then who can he depend? Who is master of whose mind????

> (*Abruptly lashing another attacker as he descends into AUDIENCE again.*)

What?...That's a lie! I'll break your neck accusing me of disloyalty to Toussaint L'Ouverture! He is mon père, my father! He make me! Whatever I done, he make me become! Je l'aime, I love him. Without Toussaint, I would be rien—! You would be nothing! All Nègres would be rien! Papa Toussaint! I am as much his son as les enfants born from Mme. Suzanne's womb!...

> (*Begins to cry*)

... How dare you accuse me of disloyalty! I will slice the tongue from any mouth what dare say so!...??? Crocodile tear...? You ever see a crocodile cry?... Maman-Eater don't shed a tear in his life—lest you mistake that gleam in his eye when he ready to devour you. Too cold to cry! I make no excuse for what I do!

> (*Moves away, back on stage as he begins to reflect while half-addressing AUDIENCE.*)

Toussaint betray hisself! Who will go meet without his Grenadiers to protect hisself?... He shoulda die in his horse's stirrup—a death he cheat—a fate he escape so often we think the gods make him non-killable. He coulda die in bed next to his chéri wife—a jail cell instead! Merde!... mais arrête! Whatever happen backward is our own damn fault!...

(Almost to himself)

We fight the fucking French for ten years, beat they asses to a tatter, whip the British and Spanish till they shout "enough"— still we want to negotiate matters! Stick with Whites no telling what! Keep them as master! Basta mal! Up they go-go!

(Pauses and starts to change uniform; resuming)

... Deux months après Old Toussaint arrest, Le Clerc come down with fever hisself. Soon big desertions from his Island Army begin—first ordinary soldiers, then officers—Sans Souci, Capois—???

(Interrupted)

... Quoi? ... Oui! Toussaint nephew Charles Belair! Yes, Belair! I tell you I make no excuse for what I do! White man don't take nigger at his word. Know his word not worth breath he mouth it with!

Le Clerc still suspect me! When Charles defect avec droves of niggers joining him, I wasn't ready. I got no choice. I trick him and his wife Sanite to meet with me, seize them and turn them over ...

(Interrupted again)

??? ... Didn't matter whether I know Le Clerc was going to shoot them. What the fuck I care what happen to them! What was I going to do after I arrest them? Keep them as my guests?! ...

(Pauses)

Like Moïse, they die good. Stood hand-in-hand bien before the firing squad and order theyselves shot. Hail ma mère Mary full of grace, Damballah, too ... It calm Le Clerc's suspicion, but what the rogue didn't know is that all the while I been meeting with Pétion.

(*Reacting to a look of incredulity*)

Oui, Pétion. Pétion! Pétion the Yellow fuck who for Le Clerc and Napoleon Bonaparte almost shell us to dust at Crête-à-Pierrot. But after he see what General Rochambeau was doing to his precious Mulatto kin in the West—begun to believe that whatever the French had in store for us niggers, they plan the same for his breeds if not worser. He and me we meet in secret. Whatever I think of the bastard's color, the son-of-a-whore can fight . . . I know together we unbeatable . . .

(*Stops for another uniform change; resumes before completely done dressing.*)

Even after I turn Belair and Sanite over to him, Le Clerc still not full satisfied avec moi. But the more he complain, the more I beg him not to leave me on the island after he left back for France.

(*Begins to illustrate, mimicking himself and Le Clerc on his knees.*)

I don't know what will happen to me since I mistreat all mes autres nègres so terrible! . . . Almost fainting, sweat running down his face like a waterfall, he moan about being in the worst position a general could be. His soldiers, come only a month ago from France, is now all gone. "Hold out rebels attack bolder and bolder making it impossible for me to go on the offensive."

(*Rising*)

. . . Alors—shades of Baron Samedi—Just then the rooster neck get broke for good—a ship name the Cockade sail into Cap François! La nuit some niggers dive overboard and swim ashore. Le Cap Blacks fetch them out the water and they give a first-hand account of what already been rumored—how slavery again restore upon France Guadeloupe isle, even Mulattoes put up for sale.

The stupidest nigger and dumbest breed had to know—how long it take for us to be next? About as long as it took the fucking French to crush the holdout rebel bandits, next strip us of our own muskets and chop off us leaders' heads. Soon we will all be dead . . . The message took none too late. Pétion, first one, don't wait. Stationed at Haut du Cap, he had his breed troops spike the big guns useless, took weapons from Blanc artillerymen there, then he wake up Clervaux, his then superior, and tell him what he done. That stupide Mulatto fart Clervaux instead of taking Pétion's advice and attack Le Cap quick, jump on his horse and run off to the mountains for hours—to contemplate!
. . . Merde! . . . Gave Le Clerc time to pull together enough French troops backed by his National Guard. He took guns from all Blacks left in his own regiments and sent the niggers to be lockup in the holds of ships in the harbor. Uncertain further, Le Clerc, I hear, order his wife Pauline to stop switching her tail to get men's attention and board a ship to Paris, but she refuse . . .

Octobre sixteenth, Pétion maintenant in full-scale revolt, making a bold attempt to conquer the whole territory, mount a furious attack on Fort Jeantot. Mais après three brave days de lutte, get beat back in defeat. No artillery . . .

(Resumes redressing, finishing with coat and hat)

Things might have been different if Christophe nearby had join in. But he wait too long. Christophe only defect when he find out the one thousand two hundred Black troops lockup on ships in the harbor was all butchered to death by Le Clerc and dumped in the water.

(Moves to edge of stage)

Play III: Dessalines

Papa Legba open the gate. Le temps arr-ee-vay for the diable stake. Belair and Sanite celebrate. My turn. Dessalines, your worst nightmare come true and your dream. Time to realize the close-kept secret prophecy of the final scheme!

>   *(Moves down to AUDIENCE corridor; addressing spectators.)*

I tell you, take courage. The French will not be able to stay long in San Domingo. They do well at first, but soon fall sick and die like flies. If Dessalines surrender to them a hundred times he will fool them a hundred times. Take courage and you will see they will not be able to guard the country and they will have to leave. Then I will make you independent . . .

"Independent!" "Independent!" "Independent!" For ten years we accuse of it! And ten years we deny it! At last I break the taboo and say it out loud for the first time ever back then a few months ago at the siege of Crête-à-Pierrot! Now the guns I did not turn in is ready. The bandits I meet with lately is ready. Cultivators who hold the weapons I give them, that Sonthonax; long ago brought for them, that Toussaint made them keep is ready! To unloose Ogun Communion Damballah Redemption!

>   *(Moves back onstage center, eventually sitting on a rock-table where he demonstrates actions which follow.)*

Vite vite, soon as I hear Pétion defecting I leave Gonaïves; with a small squad set out for Petite Rivière. Travel toute la nuit. Ce matin I come to the mission church on the outskirts. The Blanc ici priest invite me to breakfast ignorantly. I sit down at the table and the Mulatto woman, Madame Pageot, the curé's servant bring me a bowl of water to wash my hands. Then I notice she keep staring, staring at me très dure, pressing her elbows to her side then backwards. She keep doing it over and over again and again! Suddenly it dawn on me she giving me a signal that they mean to tie me up and take me into custody! I leap up from the table and with the fucking two-face priest calling after, I run outside, climb on my horse and race off to the Artibonite, shouting to the laborers, as I ride: "Aux armes! Aux armes! Aux armes! To Arms! To Arms! To Arms!" ...

(Ends demonstration, then resumes narrative calmly.)

Sacre bleu! A close call. Captors had surround the priest house to snatch me ... Not yet! To they regret. Mon loa had un autre path set. Avec my whole army I overrun Fort Crête-à-Pierrot, conquering as I head North to link up with the others ...

(Begins to remove cockade hat)

Already said defectors run out of arms and supplies. Pétion beg the shitty bandit Colonel Sans Souci for gunpowder, but he refuse—say he is first to desert Le Clerc and risk his life and need all his ammunition maintenant to keep alive and healthy in one piece. Sans Souci still want to kill Christophe for pursuing him. Christophe—his side itch to finish up the pursuit. All shit get put to rest when I catch up to rescue them. They all recognize me as Commander-in-Chief. Toutes les hommes they must all answer to me! If the bandit canailles fail to cooperate, I will decorate they ingrate smelly carcasses! ...

Ogun be worship! Mon fetish replenish! The most important somebody already did answer—by not being able to answer at all! Le Clerc! Thank Jesus, Bless Satan—il mort—he dead! Hail Joseph's Mary full of grace, good things come to them that wait! Il mort. Mon plea be granted. He dead ... Not even a month after we desert the cuckold! Yellow fever all say. Shit! It's a lie! Musket to musket! He die like he was suppose to! We broke his dick and his spirit! ... He come enero thinking he would soon be doing the Chica in Le Cap! By Novembre he dead in bed ...

(Reflecting)

Old Toussaint tell us once that the Whites is doomed against us 'cause they underestimate us. Le Clerc's underestimate is costly. Thirty-four thousand French soldiers come ashore only a eye blink ago. Before the cock crow a whole year twenty-four thousand already dead avec eight thousand hospitalized and only two thousand left to barely tremble alive. Blessed be the vengeance of Damballah...

(Moves to again directly address the AUDIENCE.)

Napoléon's sister, Le Clerc's slutty wife, who only had fever for his officers since she come, took Le Clerc back to France, crying her petticoats loose after cutting off all her hair and laying it in his coffin. She shoulda wait till she got back to Paris and cut her brother's nuts off for sending her husband here to fuck with us! I'm Dessalines, your worst nightmare come true and your dream!...

(Startled by a statement from the AUDIENCE)

What?... To hell with you!

(HE fires his pistol at the AUDIENCE then rushes down to lambaste them.)

... Merde on you all!

(Furiously)

Didn't matter if Toussaint know this was going to happen! Even if it was why he waited for—he would still want to deal with the next master sent! We'd still be asking French consent! You don't know what the fuck you talk about!

(Pausing to regain composure; then begins a uniform change; half-through, he resumes)

Le Clerc is out the way, but we still got Rochambeau. First time that ugly bugger come to San Domingo, Msieur Sonthonax had to ship his tookus back to France for acting too vicious. Even more than he detest us, he hates Mulattoes, except pretty Yellow bitches he likes to fuck—keep harems of 'em in Port-au-Prince. We can expect no quarter from him. I almost capture his pecker at Crête-à-Pierrot. He had to hotfoot dive into woods to escape our ambush. But one thing for sure, the maman-fucker can mix it up. Soon as he take command, he stop our advance at Gorge de la Providence. Two days later, his rosary bead speak with favor and what Le Clerc long beg for 'peared in the nick of time por lui. Thousands of fresh overseas French troops land in San Domingo. Right away Rochambeau use them to retake Port-de-Paix and Fort Liberté and cheat me out of total victory. But I'm in no hurry. His lines is stretch thin. He can recapture towns but he has to hold them! . . .

(Downstage, takes a drink, then laughs, gets comfortable and relaxed; sits top of steps.)

While I play a hit-and-run game, I get news how Christophe take care of his old foe Sans Souci in a way that even make me proud. Sucker the dumb rascal to meeting at Grandpré, a deserted plantation. Christophe send a message he ready to listen to some advice from Sans Souci. The fuck Sans Souci show up with only a few men. He get off his horse and is walking through the empty rooms of the great house when Christophe jump them and bayonet through les cœurs everybody except one—and the one left breathing wasn't Sans Souci. Blessed be the trickery of Eshu, super duping hexster, I could'na done it better! . . .

(Rises, moves, and completes uniform change as he talks.)

There is more like Sans Souci, but they hafta wait till the French is finish with ... to cette purpose, I call a meeting of all my generals from every province. For four days we map out all assignments and strategies. All duties and responsibilities. Who is to fight and who is to wait. Who is to decoy and who is to keep straight. Then on the last day, on the last day—I say, "For more than ten years we fight under the same flag as our enemy. Our people never know who we really fight for. Even the French claim we still fight for France since we fight in the same uniforms and under the same flag, this tricolor."

> (HE picks up the tricolor and addresses real and imaginary AUDIENCE.)

... See this flag? See this flag ...

> (HE rips the flag and tears out the white section, throwing it to the floor and stomps on it.)

... This is the flag we fight under maintenant! It has no white in it! No white in it!

> (Begins to ascend the center platform again, continuing to talk.)

It is bleu et rouge—bleu et rouge—blue and red! Blue and red! Blue for how deep our flesh couleur and red for the blood we done spill! This flag is not sewn avec les lettres R and F—Republique of France! It will be stitched avec les mots 'Liberté ou Mort'—Liberty or Death! Liberty or Death! ...

> (At the top height of the platform where he anchors the flag upright.)

We know who we are! We know for who we fight! At last our people will know it clear forever! There will be no doubt no longer! ... A douzaine years and oceans of blood flow to end our dependency! To uncoil the blanc-pale serpent twist round our brains et memory and dash it away! To finally say for now and forevermore, we stand alone come what may be! . . . I'm Dessalines, your worst nightmare come true and your dream! . . .

> *(When the climax ends, HE descends the platform and moves downstage to address the AUDIENCE conversationally.)*

The tête-à-tête summit session knot us together and point sure-fire direction. Mais back North, Christophe find hisself worse off than before. Lacroix beat him bad at Fort Liberté. Sans Souci ex-soldiers ambush him constantly. Petit-Noël, an autre old bandit foe, then drove Christophe and Clervaux over the mountains in retreat all the way down to Gonaïves. Paul L'Ouverture went to plead with Petit-Noël for unity. Shit-Noël get so mad at him for making the plea he order his men to waylay Paul L'Ouverture on way back to his lines and cut his head off. They obey—exact-lee as he say, avec glee . . .

> *(Getting progressively angrier, while unsheathing his sword)*

But the maman-fuckers don't reckon on me. Knowing this bandit waste-manure can't go on much longer, I march North avec three columns on Dondon, where I know the turd-Noël is headquartered—swoop down on his rump, chase his tail into the mountains, catch his behind and pay him back for Paul chopping off his own maggoty head. I'm Dessalines, your worst nightmare come true and your dream! . . .

> *(Pausing to take a drink and get calm)*

After this all the autre little petits cheeky holdout rebel bandit chiens fall over they bootstraps rushing into my ranks to face up against Rochambeau . . .

> *(Takes a long thoughtful pause, begins to take off hat.)*

... Rochambeau ... Rochambeau ...

> *(Evoking HIS precise memory)*

Remember Maurepas, the great Noir General! He stayed with the French even after we all deserted. To show his gratitude, Rochambeau took Maurepas, his family and staff and row them for reward out to the warship Daguay-Trouin. Once aboard, drop the act, sprung the trap, strung Maurepas high-up full-dress and tie him to the ship's mast avec his cockade hat mashed ridiculous on his tête. Then Rochambeau's ship carpenter, hammer pounding, blood spurt like a fountain, nail Maurepas's epaulettes into his naked shoulders. Before they finish him, they bayonet his wife and children front his eyes and throw them overboard to sink slow under les eaux ...

> *(Moves, crossing back and forth downstage as HE describes Rochambeau and his actions.)*

...Rochambeau, crazy dung eater, one night he give a great big ball and invite a lot of Mulatto women. He halt the dancing in the middle and take the breed women to a room lit only by a candle. The room is jam-full with coffins and hymn music fill the air. The breed women stand bug-eyed, scared to death. Rochambeau smile, bow to the women, point to the coffins and thank the breed women for just attending they husbands and brothers' funerals ...

In Le Cap bay, Rochambeau drown so many bodies, town-people stop eating fish, afraid they might be chewing on they own Brown relatives fried up inside ...

Rochambeau ... he buy special dogs in Cuba to sniff out our ambushes. When the dogs show no talent for the task, he then

train them to recognize niggers by sight, and tear us apart limb by limb. Training take place at très grandes fêtes avec select guests, beaucoup many fancy White ladies in fine gowns. They drag out a hand-tie-up buck-naked nigger. The dogs is sic on him. They nip at him—but stop—won't go on . . . They untie the garçon, stick a riding crop in his hand, a bayonet in the back, and shove him once more on the dogs. The animals run away instead. You think Rochambeau give up? Non Msieurs! He move the show to a even bigger arena. Use his own servant as bait. The critters still won't cooperate, even though this bare-ass new nigger candidate is now tied to a post.

Boyer, Rochambeau's Chief-of-Staff, so embarrass at this disgraceful delay, jump into the arena and split the nigger's belly wide open with his sword so that the fresh blood and guts will give the dogs greedy appetite to bite and swallow. It work just right. Like welcome dessert, the dogs chew with delight . . .

(*Pauses, before illustrating the ensuing actions*)

It work for the dogs . . . but it don't impress us niggers sufficient—too insolent stubborn maybe to agree? . . .

(*In French accent:*)

Attention! Three Blacks is stood back to back over bagasse tied to each other by neck collars. The bagasse set on fire. Flames roast them. Two scream. The wind keep the fire away from the third. He shout to the other two: "You don't know how to die—watch how I die." He strain twist hisself into the flames and without a word let hisself burn crisp to death, sans a murmur, not even a groan . . . Une autre condemn Nègre femme comfort her daughter hung long wit her avec the advice: "Be glad that you will not be the mother of slaves" . . .

But the most stubborn lesson of all is the one I provide the cockculottes snots. Maman-Fucker Rochambeau dig a great big pit to bury alive five hundred niggers. La nuit, where everyone soon sure see I built five hundred hangman gallows . . .

(*Raises the prone gallows to its standing height*)

. . . up and down the hills outside Le Cap. Ce matin, soon as daylight rise, one by one, one après one another, I hung five hundred captured French officers each in his own private noose upon they own personal gallows!

(*Admiring his handiwork*)

They make good shadows as trees. A forest of skeleton leaves! I'm Dessalines, your worst nightmare come true and your dream! . . .

It is obvious Rochambeau and his boss Bonaparte did give up on San Domingo Nègres ici and hope to start over with a whole fresh new batch from Africa. But time was running out on them. Just like it finally done for Old Toussaint . . .

(*Moves even closer downstage to AUDIENCE*)

Toussaint L'Ouverture died in his oversea France jail cell sometime early Avril eighteen and three. We find out in May when news reach the Island . . .

Time also Le Clerc had rush Toussaint off the island so fast Blacks didn't get a chance to sound the drums or sacrifice a goat, not even sign of the cross over him—while his trick hoodwinkers expect quick burial they think. But instead of dying at they proper time, Toussaint managed to even outlive his old foe Le Clerc by almost six months. I wonder if he ever knew . . . Papa Toussaint . . .

(*Sits, confessing candidly with no remorse.*)

Yes, I had to get rid of him. Like he rid hisself of Moïse. He teach me to be thorough. But he can't follow his own teaching. The French could never be trusted. He knew it. But he couldn't accept it. I could. I risk my life for him a hundred times. I would die for him a thousand times. But in the end, he stand in the way of his own cause. He won't fight the French forever. What he start, his children has to finish without him. I won't betray him, but I did give him a push. I'll revenge him. I'm his real spirit . . .

(Moves to retrieve new tricolor flag.)

May eighteenth, eighteen and three, only a month from Toussaint death-date, the flag my wife Claire's god-daughter sewed together is first unrolled and took into battle. Old Toussaint die far away from his home and soil, but the flag of Independence lift up in his place.

(Hoisting flag)

That same day a senior officer of mine, Laporte, about to be captured aboard ship by a French cruiser, sank his own boat carrying him and his men, and he and the whole crew shout "Vive l'indépendance" while they disappear below the waves. Give thanks to Damballah when bravery pays . . .

(Putting flag into makeshift stand and putting on battle hat)

Les temps arrivay to show Rochambeau who is not only his match but his master. He take twelve thousand troops to Port-au-Prince for what he believe to be his final push, but his saint-sign blink, his loa frown, and war broke out between France and Britain pour un autre Europe round.

(Accelerating his delivery)

Suddenly the English got him blockaded without a fucking hope of reinforcements. Quick I negotiate with the British to sell me arms and ammunition. The slippery English don't much like the idea of backing us Blacks against Whites but they greedy—Americans, too—cash in pockets come before color preference...

Armed sufficient, we drive Rochambeau from his fortified positions, out trick him on land, on l'eau aussi. By early August we ready to take back coast cities, avec British ships anxious to collect retreating French soldiers as war booty... Throughout the field for we, victory continue to pile up on top of victory, key towns fall, one by one. Après two months, the only prize left is Le Cap. To take it, Christophe and Clervaux put twenty thousand men in the field against Rochambeau's two thousand.

 (Moves onto platform)

Done taming the West, I advance toward them through Limbé and stand on a hill overlooking the main front.

Novembre eleven the 'cisive battle begin, the outcome certain, no way the French can win. Mais eureka, we Afrique chiefs musta displease Shango, thinking victory a sure thing. To notre surprise we get chastise! The French stop us in our tracks. Mow us down entrench high up, again we got no artillery to match.

...Un Noir officer called Capois Death, because how brave he is, determine to snatch our advantage back, attack the French blockhouse of Breda and Champlin. Top his horse he lead his men up the hill again, then again and again and again. Each time French fire drive him back. Then a fifty-pound-six cannon ball blow his horse from under him. Frantic, he shake his leg out under his dead horse's stirrup, jump up and charge up the hill again, now on foot, waving his sword, shouting to his men, "Forward! Forward! Forward!" "Avant! Avant! Avant!" All at once from all over, all around, high up the hill, the French matching ours start to shout "Bravo! Bravo! Bravo!" Toutes les hommes they cease fire and beat they drums loud and long. They might've fight all over the world but they never see such stubborn determination like this nigger show . . .

(Begins to move off the platform)

Then I can see a French soldier ride down to where Capois stand puzzle. He get off his horse, click his heels, salute Capois and, as I learn later, say "Captain General Rochambeau send his congratulation to the officer who has just covered hisself with so much glory" . . . Whatever else Rochambeau the skunky ape-pisser is, he is first a soldier.

Not long, the fight resume, soon the earth did rumble, heavens thundered and rain pour down from high up the sky in blinding shower-sheets and stop the battle. Cold. The rainstorm up high is the final sigh of Le Cap's ill wind. Each waterdrop a bad mauvais omen for Blancs trap within city gates. Siege-starved French soldiers who already done ate up all they mules, horses and asses, at last found good use for Rochambeau's nigger-hunting dogs—they stew-cook them up and fast gulp them down to fill they stomachs and still their hunger . . .

(Downstage center)

Novembre twenty, eighteen and three, Rochambeau send a messenger to me ce matin bargaining to hand over all his forts and artillery if he and his men is allowed to evacuate in ten days. I tell him he had till the twenty-ninth to get him and the French fuck gone!—out of San Domingo all together! Hosannas to Damballah, good riddance eternally. I'm Dessalines, your worst nightmare come true and your dream. Destiny descend pour un curtain finale. Rochambeau pack up in defeat. Vite vite adieu!—joyeux to baissez avec a wet smack each Nègre back rear-end crack! Mais, while I wait his disappearance, I begin to suspect the sly vulture. Either the British drive a hard bargain to let his ships through they blockade—or could be the sneak got some fool idea to escape to Spanish Santo Domingo and later double back to attack us? All I know, the merde not moving. Novembre twenty-ninth deadline pass sans not a twitch of a Blanc ass. Bon dieu. Next day thirty. Everybody wake up surprise to see our bleu et rouge flag fly over Fort Picolet occupied by us sudden overnight. When Bligh the British sea captain come to find out what's going on, I tell him that if I don't see the French boat start to move out the bay right away, I'm going to sink every last one of them with red-hot shot already aimed at them from the Fort. Bligh say that won't be necessaire since Rochambeau just agree to surrender into his custody. That is fucking oui oui oui with me I say, just as long as they get the fuck away from San Domingo just as fast as ships can ferry them... That same day no more delay, the maman-fucker Rochambeau aboard three frigates, et seventeen more petites ships and about eight thousand piss-poor survivors set sail, slipping out the harbor firing a puny broadside and lowering they colors. They shoulda dipped the goddam ship flags down to the hell we bury them! Sixty thousand fresh Frenchmen dead in they graves in less than two years! Add on to they autres frères!—lost to us! To they ex-slaves! To niggers and breeds! To cheeky Congolese seeds! To Toussaint! To Moïse! To Boukman, et tu the ghost of Jeannot, et Jean-François, Biassou, Jean-Paul, et martyr Maurepas, breed Lamartinière, Sanite, and Belair. To me, to Dessalines! Savior from French tyranny clean. Napoléon master plan suck-up under Domingo quicksand! His nouveau world expansion up in flames!... Nobody but Dessalines to blame...

Avec France absent at last!... Maintenant, I can carry out Old Toussaint's dream even if it's not the same one he conjure up. Non... That's not accurate. It's not the same one he fancy in his day thoughts! But it is the one his nights had brought. The night one was better—if not better, it is the closest one what we can be true to. The same hope night bring him when his day wasn't foul up avec vapors of French education, culture and manners. The plain dream about us from scratch being Black with nothing rien but our own goddamn backs to depend on.

(Ascending the center platform)

And on the first day, the new year, on the first day of January eighteen and four at Gonaïves me and thirty-six generals and officers declare the first day of the independence of Haiti! Yes, Haiti! Ahyti! Ahyti! Ahyti!—land of mountains! What the first people call it before any White man ever set foot on it, before any Black man was drag off a boat on it, before any Yellow breed was yank out his Nègre mama's womb on it! Ahyti! Ahyti! We swear to posterity, to the heavens, to the universe, to each other, to our children and our children to come to renounce France forever and to die rather than give in to her, to fight till our last breath run out before living under her domination! Curses upon the French name, everlasting hate to France and her Dominion! I am Dessalines! Your worst nightmare come true and your dream!...

They all present put they name to our first document of Independence. While about me they vow, "In the name of the people of Haiti, we generals and chiefs of the Island of Haiti, grateful for the benefits received from Commander-in-Chief Jean-Jacques Dessalines, protector of the Liberty we now enjoy; in the name of Liberty, Independence and our thankful people, we proclaim him Governor-General of Haiti for life. We swear complete obedience to the laws he shall see fit to make, his authority being the only one we recognize." ... Jean-Jacques Dessalines, Governor-General of Haiti for life! Governor-General of Haiti pour la vie! Governor-General pour la vie! Pour la vie! Pour la vie! Pour la vie!

(Intones "Pour la vie" over and over while dancing a jig as lights dim to black.)

CURTAIN DESCENDS ON ACT ONE

Play III: Dessalines

ACT TWO

(House-Lights dim to half and remain. From the Wings offstage DESSALINES enters. He is essentially dressed as we last saw him, indicating a brief passage of time. He pauses; surveys the Set and Environment which will be referred to and utilized in this opening sequence. The Centerstage spiraling platform is actually configured in the shape of Haiti. He commences his dialogue.)

DESSALINES

Fortune top the wind, war destroy the land again. Bandits roam the South and the French still got a foothold in Spanish Domingo. Mais, more important for Haiti's safety, Christophe in control up North. Pétion in charge of the West and General Geffrard, un autre Mulatto, over the South, while my headquarters at Fort Marchand, where I will build Haiti's capitol and make my home as Governor-General. Pour la vie après seulement douzaine années...digest it, Jean-Jacques Dessalines!... Slave who's back is still a map of scars and welts as high and as long and as wide and as many as the mountains what crisscross this island from Nord to Sud, from East to West...

(Moves to AUDIENCE Floor-Aisle)

I remember every welt and feel each ache every day of my life. And every inch of each scar is earned. Because I make sure I cause every one of 'em by the way I behave!

(Picks up a stalk of sugar cane from Floor. Joints of the sugar cane will be chopped as he talks.)

Slave?! From the beginning I make clear anybody who own me know what a slave is like! A real slave is ME! Who could never be tamed! Not somebody obedient!... Somebody obedient was not a slave but a not-to-yet-be-born-ghost!... A true slave: the harder the beating, the stronger the disobedience!...

(Removes hat)

I was born like that. My people was Congos. From where exact I don't know since I didn't get to remember them. They die—or master kill them or sold them or some such. Don't matter. They birth me. Didn't even name me. Master did. Duclos, after himself. Just to make sure everybody know who I belong to. He never guess. He soon regret, 'cause nobody as troublesome contrary as me need be going round bearing some other body name.

All this take place at the Cormiers' plantation in the district of the Grande Rivière. Ma tante bring me up, as much as anybody can bring me anywhere. She did until she was sold and took away to the West. Then I bring myself up, making certain that whoever had to deal with me is sure to have that brought down! I wage a one-man war before any breed or Nègre ever think about war. The more I fight, the more I get sold down lower and lower on the ownership ladder until finally at the age of thirty-three, the age Catholics claim they lord Jesus die, I am sold to the lowest of the low, not even to another White man, not even to a Mulatto, but to a free Black Affranchi. Didn't matter. I don't care. A owner is a owner and they was all going to catch hell from me equally . . .

(Begins to collect cane joints which had fallen to Floor. He places them upon the Stage ledge.)

Best thing about my new owner is he did work that give me chance to move around. He is a jack-of-all-trades—carpenter, tiler, potter. I can move around and enjoy my main grande passion at the time—pussy! . . . Putain Hot! . . . Noir-boss got his licks in on my back, mind you. He also give me my name what took, but he was smart enough not to give me his name. He give me the name of some old Frenchman he use to work for—Des Salines! I figure he must give it to me because I remind him of the bad memories he kept about the White mackerel. "Bad" is what he say about me. "Bon ouvrier, mais mauvais chien!"— good worker but bad character! I try not to disappoint him . . . He always had to keep a close eye on me when we went to Le Cap—he was afraid I'd fly away to the mountains and become a Maroon. That he don't have to worry—even though in my blood the slave revolt hope to happen.

Non. My lonely war was waiting for a bigger battlefield. I spit on the stupide Mulattoes hung at Le Cap asking for liberty. I know way they going about it was foolish. Oge is a fucking imbecile to tell Whites what he plan to do to them. That's how he get hisself dead! . . . Ah, but Boukman! Boukman knew what to do and when he did it, I know sooner or later that this was that place I had to be! Fate, Damballah, et Jesus Christ see to it that I am put in the hands of Old Toussaint, who was building him an army to match all the fighters in them military Europe books he use to read.

(Begins to ascend onto Stage proper.)

I can't read and write, but I know how to fight. Avec my body! Now I learn to use ma tête. There was no better teacher than Toussaint de Breda, who set the world on fire when he turn hisself into Toussaint L'Ouverture—the Opening! . . . Jean-Jacques Dessalines, Governor-General! Pour la vie . . . Avec Christophe and Pétion beside me . . . !

(Moves Upstage and busies himself putting chaotic Set pieces in order while continuing his dialogue.)

. . . Christophe and Pétion . . . Christophe almost bad as old Toussaint trying to imitate Whites, but he is loyal—long as you keep him in line. . . . Pétion? Ah, Pétion! Toussaint and Christophe try to catch up with the White man but Pétion voilà. Pétion is just as White couleur hisself and much slicker since he is educated in France. Toussaint and Christophe in spite of they grande affaire d'amour avec la France, neither one never lay eye on it till Toussaint free to peep a lil piece her sky out his French jail window . . . Avec Rigaud long gone, breeds in the South and West look up to Pétion—even Blacks like him. Despite they mischief, Mulattoes is needed. Five hundred thousand Nègres is kept ever ignorant about everything except what they can handle with they hands and lug on they backs. Whites and Mulattoes hog the brain work for theyselves. Twelve years de la guerre prove we can outthink them all when opportunity present itself, but our smartness still must be put in shape by them, with long practice at it. Niggers too busy fighting and dying to master the tools of communicating!!

(Replies to a question)

Do I trust breeds? Fuck no! Trust don't have shit to do with it! Can I control them is the issue! Dessalines won't rule if Dessalines can't control! . . .

(Completes his business with Set pieces; then resumes as he puts hat back on.)

Everything in place but une old problem yet to be faced... Every time we rise on top, Whites grin, bow, and kiss our toes to live among us and prosper. Mais soon as a Blanc-hope-to-be-master show up to drag us under his feet, these same frères rush to help crush down the boot! Sure enough, Whites in the South support traitor bandits against me.

(Moves; steps on the Platform indicating locales)

Right away, I head out to Jérémie and wipe out all the Whites in the city. I sweep back through Port-au-Prince and finish them there, too. Then I march up to Cap François. My own generals, everyone plead with me. Fuck them! I kill, murder, execute, put to death, eliminate every White in Cap François except les foreigners and a few loyal Frenchmen who did fight in our cause. I comfort Blancs in hiding I might a missed, promise them my full protection if they come out and receive certificates of safety.

(Starts off Platform)

They come out, get they safety certificates and I shot them all, every last one of them, sans mercy! We repay these cannibals de la guerre crime for crime, outrage for outrage. I save my country! Cette vengeance before heaven and earth is mes pride and glory! What do I care about the opinion of mes contemporaries or future generations? I did do my duty; I approve of myself. That is sufficient to me; it is the only sufficiency I care about."

(Responds to interruption)

What about women and children?... What about les femmes and enfants of slavery, the whips and the lianes, the buried-in-sand-up-to-the-ears-till-the-ants-bit-your-brains-out, the drownings and roastings, the pregnant bellies ripped open...

    (Accelerating)

Treat 'em to the four-post... tie 'em to the ladder... hang 'em in the hammock... neck 'em with the collar... close they wounds with hot sealing wax... spice they cuts with brine and pepper... burn gunpowder in the arse of a nigger... Keep at it. Broil 'em in the furnace... singe 'em in the fire... dunk 'em in hot sugar-vat syrup... barrel-roll 'em down the mountain... cut they dick off clean... crucify 'em on the cross... stick a nigger head on the pike... make 'em eat they own shit!!!...

I wipe out a few thousand Whites and we Nègres wind up with almost a quarter-million men, women and children altogether dead and gone in not even a dozen years—one out of each two of us!!!... Monster?! I was teach by the best teachers....

    (Listens to another interjection)

Revenge? Revenge?... Non, non, non! Protection! Against future betrayers! Haiti have enough trouble with breeds around, but most of them hate Blancs as much as we do. They can't be trusted, but they prove worthy against the French...

    (Making himself more comfortable, pausing to eat and drink; then resumes.)

I trust Pétion so much I try to marry him up with one of my bastard daughters. He beg off—claim he already engage, but I know the Yellow merde turn her down 'cause she too Black...

Oui, it's my turn to teach! Time Whites learn the lesson. Shitty Blancs don't give a fuck about they dear blood brothers. Britain and America ones too busy selling us things to care about they close kin...

(Thinking reflectively)

Death...?... Death ordinary. Killing normal. All things die. Raise your eyebrow 'cause it happen violent?... Avez no fear? Don't you say everyone just only going to another place? Heaven, Purgatoryville, Damballahland, wherever? Then why complain? Life is hard—très dure. Them that has it easy just living on slack time—just waiting to get theirs later...

(Returning to his active narration, anticipating the next Crowning-beat.)

Bonaparte is not going to take Rochambeau's defeat without answer back. Why I forewarn him and tout le monde, Tremble tyrants who seek to conquer us. Any nation bold enough to attack me, let it come. I will gladly vacate the coast and torched out places where towns once existed, but woe to those who approach too closely to the mountains! It would be better that they be swallowed up in the depths of the sea than torn to pieces at the furious hands of the children of Haiti! Never, jamais, will a colon or a European ever set foot on this soil avec the title owner. This resolution is now the cornerstone of our Constitution... I am Dessalines, your worst nightmare come true and your dream...

(Starts to shed coat, hat, and weapons; moves to rock-throne where he retrieves emperor-garb from behind.)

Then I make certain I'm not outrank by that little petite pipsqueak wee-wee Napoléon Bonaparte.

(Begins to put on robe and crown)

I get crowned Octobre huit at Le Cap seven weeks before him. In Notre Dame church, same name as his coronation chapel in Paris. Mon crown from Philadelphia America. Ma coronation robe sent by the British from London, likewise my six-horse carriage that bring me to the church after parades everywhere and the entire country rejoicing! The whole world recognize me first, before our skimpy lil tiny dick pretender! They all on hand to celebrate. They know who is master.

(Sitting on [rock] throne.)

I get crowned emperor in style! Just me. There is no other rank. I am emperor and nobody but me has a title. Everybody else is equal, égal! Nobody can be jealous of nobody else 'cause all the blackguards have the same rank. Fuck all autres titles—comte and earl and baron and baroness and chevalier and crap. I am emperor and everybody else is they plain old self.

(Moving off throne, closer to AUDIENCE.)

And just to make sure nobody look down or up to nobody else, I wipe out all the ox ca-ca San Domingo is buried in over its head through all its history. It is writ in the Constitution from now on that all citizens of Haiti is Noirs, Blacks! No more griffe, marabou, mameluke crap! Bastards had carefully work up more than a hundred words to name theyselves by color shades of skin and mixtures of blood. Some fuck who prove he has two hundred-and-some-parts of White blood to somebody else's ninety-some-part nigger is supposed to be superior to some other fuck with only fifty-some-parts nigger and one hundred-some-part White.

(Building and intensifying to a stem climax)

This silly but fatal shit is outlawed. No matter how much the maman-fucker hate it, they is all niggers since that one drop of a nigger-part is all that count to make you Haitian! We really is going to be the equal right of man—the Black equal man right. White-sight is not going to have nothing to do with making you better. If you want to think so, you is welcome to it, but you damn sure not going to get it proven by how the fuck you get treated. Haiti is the land of the high place, but every maman-fucker except me is just as low as the next one he catch sight of... I'm Dessalines, your worst nightmare come true and your dream...

> *(Gathers himself; gets canteen of liquid to drink, with replenished energy; resumes)*

... As long as Britain blockade the sea I don't have to worry. But like I already told, France still got hold of half of Hispaniola under agreement with Spain. To say fini to France forever and join the island complete together, I strike avec three columns from the Sud. Christophe attack from the Northern coast. Only catch is—niggers in Spanish territory like old Biassou once said they been treated so lazy by Spanish pricks more interested in fucking bitches than stripping Black tails avec work-switches—these niggers don't display much joy in us coming to free them! Damn slave ghosts!...

Santo Domingo is well-fortified during our attack. Twenty-two days trying to break through, I get a message that a French warship is off the coast of Haiti ready to invade at Gonaïves. Interrupted, we withdraw quick, hurrying to Le Cap. But on the way back, I give the Spanish-pampered pissoirs memories to last they lifetime and carry over even in they hereafter. I burn every town in my path, taking everything we can lay hands on or lead out on four feet. If those sons-a-whores never don't become citizens of Haiti they damn sure won't ever be able to fuck with us!... Curses on the bastards and Madame Erzulie turn they backside to ashes!...

> *(Pauses to make a composed transition)*

Once at Le Cap, I find out the French invasion not true! Avec nobody to seduce and plenty of time to regroup, while I stay, Christophe treat me royal.

(Eats some fruit)

Not long after when I make him Commander-in-Chief... Not because he fawn on me but clearly he best man for the job. Pétion is not Black and nobody not sure Black can ever rule us, no matter how bien they feel about us. Only we can make you cockamamans obey! That's why I'm here ici to deal with chiens maintenant! Like Toussaint teach, without prosperity we can never be free. And that's the point! Niggers think slavery mean work and freedom mean not work—at least not so hard. And there's no way to get you to change your mind except to make you produce!

(Pausing for interruption)

Voluntary?! My ass!

(Once again)

??? Religious instruction? You full of holy communion du-du! Your only inspiration is fear of punishment—even death!—what the White man knew. Needed for stable, steady produce. Why his Catholic practice is calculate not to interfere with labor, while notre Nègre Voodoo is excuse for idleness. Why I outlaw it!...

(Pause)

??? Morale?... La bayonet is my morale! You got to be firm—coax before you 'dopt the habit all by yourself! You be punish if you idle! The whip is outlawed but lianes still sting your behind! Leave your plantation, you must have written permission!...

??? Slavery renew again?... Blasphemy! It's for your own good! Toussaint was right! Why he refuse to sell little petite acre plots of land. He knew you slackers would never produce more than your own upkeep. You got to be force to work hard and even harder for your own protection, for your own safety, for your own defense, like he teach. Time we revolt, not half of us is even born on this island. Fresh from all over Africa—didn't talk the same, didn't behave the same. Only thing we share the same is the White man, the Yellow man, few times a free Black Affranchi's whip and command! We show them all the mistake they make to bring us ici, but now we force to stay, we got to become Haitians—free, strong, independent, proud, productive and ready for combat! Only way to do that is work till we drop! . . .

??? For self-richment of me? . . . Non! For emperor-sake! For emperor need! Emperor can't live like nobody else. A emperor is nobody else! He got to have right things surround him. People got to look up to him special. Special demands is made on him. He take special risks. Got special appetite. He can't live like ordinary people . . .

??? . . . You goddamn right I'm more happy to fight! But combat suspend now. I need special attention to keep me interested! Not get restless . . .

> (*Ponders a suggestion*)

. . . Maybe so. But I can't read and write. It's too late for the rooster to go back and hatch itself as a chicken! Away from battle, I juice up my love for fucking and 'quire a new love, dancing!

> (*HE cuts a few steps; stops to deal with another offering.*)

. . . ??? More than twenty mistresses? . . . Spread throughout the island? Treat like queens? . . . Screw you! If I got a hundred, it's still lot fewer than I deserve! A emperor privilege! One pussy don't have a thing to do with another one. They all the same and different at the same time. They appreciated for being the same and being different, too! ... Temptation due. Putain to the rescue ..

(Takes out tafia flask and downs some stiff shots.)

Now, old Toussaint—he intend to improve our moral he say. Even skin-alive his officers for living 'in sin' avec femmes other than they wife. Say he don't believe in adultery—being strict Catholic—in public that is. Cause when Le Clerc get hold of all his private papers and so, he find tons of secret letters and other hidden stash—locks of hair—snippets from heads and pussies—bedroom keys, rings, anklets, bracelets, pendants, engraved lockets, tiny boxes avec curls from crotches, hundreds of fucking love letters and notes. Some sent out of just plain black-nosing and even true admiring, but most of the junk is so close and personal that the French lackey who find it want to burn it up so nobody can ever catch sight of it ...

Quoi? Save?

Who you think write that stuff? "I'm ready!"—"Come and get it!" ... Niggers didn't know how to write! Hell no! Must erase it! No white papa ever want it to leak out that his milk-bright wife and daughter is hot for black meat and dead set on getting her some on she own private invitation. Heavens no! Those limp pee-pee jackababoons want to keep pretending that we jungle brutes spread they women's legs open only by force. Them letters and trinkets of old Toussaint is too damaging evidence to the contrary. The truth in the fucking is too painful for them to deal with. Merde! Got to get rid of it! ...

But you ain't never, jamais, going to find no letters like that in my possessions! ... What?! Sent so my secretaries promised to translate them? My wife to read them? Fuck no! Let the hussies keep they hair on they head and stuck fast between they legs. I got plenty time to muss it up and pluck it out when I get there ...

Play III: Dessalines

> *(Moves close to AUDIENCE)*

But tending pussy is too blood-boiling. I need something more calming. Dancing. Not congo dancing! Somewheres down the line, that always gets too much like fucking. Anything done to the best of the drum can't be too soothing. Mais, European dancing!

> *(He starts to dance)*

... The minuet, the tippy-tippy-toe slide across the floor like you ready to keel over in a dead faint if you fast-speed-dance! Our congo-dance come out the drum, the beat in the feet and the hot flush below the belly and the itch in the dick et the fever in the pussy meant to get the God's attention—not show them how prissy we is in honoring him for creating us with how sedate we done become! I am Dessalines, your worst nightmare come true et your dream!

> *(Stops dancing; refreshes himself; starts to take off crown.)*

... My wife's too good for me. Don't care about another woman long as I don't parade her too open. But that's hard for me. Not my nature to hide things, cover up... Fucking. Even Ca-tholics do it. Even Adam and Eve in the garden had to do it, though forbidden. They couldn't help it—dick had to git, pussy has to have it! Can't fool me—know that snake shit tale? And the apple what had to be bit? What's shape like a snake and what else's juicy-fat tasty as the apple?...

> *(Underneath robe, strips down to dancing tights and puts on dancing slippers.)*

Oui, my wife understand. Man keep as many women as they can. Only reason to stick to one wife is you can't afford more. Pussy can't be carried wherever you go, so it's gotta be waiting door to door. Mistress and wife don't have anything to do with each other...

(Starts to dance)

...The minuet—so dainty, so in control, so elegant, so civilized. They laugh when I do it. Smart to not let me see them. They strain to not expose it. I don't give them away. I want to see how long they can keep theyself lying. Forever—if they know what's good for them. Even the goddamn instructors I sneak in from Paris. Everyone think they laugh safely in secret. I laugh at them all flirting with they lives! I dance their dance cause I want to see if I can beat them at they habit other than war—like I conquer them in battle. But it's too late! The martial temper is in my blood, the juju pulse in my veins and the congo tempo in my limbs. The minuet sooner or later always end in the chica!

They all look on, mimic Whites and call me a jumping jackass. Christophe whisper it and Pétion back him up even more insulting. But I don't caper wildly like they think. Without hint out mouth, I show them what's most natural and show up what they make artificial avec all they pretense to refinement. Yes, dance the minuet on top of slaves graves! I will rise out the tomb and dance the chica on your bones! My temper your own swan-song. I am Dessalines, your worst nightmare and your dream.

(HE concludes with a vigorous climactic Chica. Throughout the next section, he continually replenishes himself with food and steady hard drinking.)

???...Temper?...Wouldn't be me without it. Make me what I am. Take the bitter with the sweet, the fat with the meat... Oui, it très dangereux...Christophe almost get his when he oppose killing les Blancs. Pétion when I find out what the bastard say about my dancing. Old fart Télémaque almost lose his life defending Whites. I give him a choice avec his own hands to hang two Whites on the spot or get his own neck chop off. Guess what choice he pick? . . . I didn't poison that prick Geffrard though like rumor say. When he drop dead sudden, I was surprise like everybody else and told those who suspect me, "God wanted Geffrard sooner than I did." . . .

My anger don't keep. Look at Christophe. Just after I am ready to kill him, I make him Commander-in- Chief. I can't abide breeds but they is all secretaries and advisers to me. Look at all the Yellow pussies boost up by my dick support. Even let some of them birth me children. One White heifer I offer a deal to have her head lop off or climb in my bed. One jump she give me some best putain I ever have . . . gladly, even avec ecstasy . . . I'm Dessalines, your worst nightmare come true and your dream..

(*Drinks*)

Talk about pussy-loving me?—Catholics ici on the island every chance they get, buy cunt-favor according to what they money-pouch can cover. Only difference is they pretend it's a sin and hire full- time holy confessors to forgive them. Act like somebody other than theyself saddle them with out-of- control desires. But kings and emperors and autres in the head horse-seat don't have time for this fool-self shit or give a poot about whether the women they amour stick, even love, them.

They got too many more serious things to do and think. A king don't really give a fuck about who his queen is screwing on the side, except when what the flirty fly-trim is doing gets his authority question—his power undermine. He don't care about pussy shared, but control damage! A maman-sucker who might snicker about fucking your wife, or somebody who might just know she's being poked by some man other than you, just might get up the nerve to overthrow your ass. That's what mainly matter, not the adultery . . .

(Dancing)

I wonder what will happen if Whites ever hear the drumbeat? Will they still think me awkward or will they find out how stiff they use to be? ... Temper? It got its drawbacks, mais aussi its good points ...

???... Hope for balance?... No balance avec me you say?... ???... Great general, bad ruler?... How the fuck you know?! Three years ain't just pass! Since Haiti free! This island flat on its ass when I save her! Soon it will prosper. Thrive if we don't have to fight! That's why you bastards got to be made to do what's right!

Ever since Santo Domingo, nothing but catastrophe! Goddamn workers won't work, fucking Christophe talk against me even after debacle I make him Commander-in-Chief. Listening to the high mighty Whites and Mulattoes in Le Cap. He just as ignorant as me but needs these shits to give him class! I'm my own class! I need them seulement just to carry out orders! I make Christophe come to Marchand, where I mean to really kill him. He musta get wind of it and don't show up. Say he sick and never come. I remember one other time he say he sick and don't show up. When he defect to Le Clerc!

(Goes back to taking regular nips, often)

Mais! But like I say, I don't keep grudges.... Until worse brew up avec Pétion and Geffrard. A little bug warn me they plot to bring that bastard Rigaud back to San Domingo. Night of the Independence anniversary ball January I, I'm going to kill them both! ... Mais luck be they loa ... Christophe, Paul Roman, and Pierre Toussaint talk me out of it. Then these two sonsayellowbitches come to see me. "Why you so cold to us?" they ask. "Cause you trying to bring Rigaud back!" They swear on a stack of Catholic bibles, "That's not so. They wouldn't think of doing such a thing! How could I even dream they could ever—?" Arrête! I tell them, Arrête—I believe them, rest assured my trust in them don't falter. It's true, since I never trust them to start with! Soon après then's when Geffrard croak. Back to study my dancing and fuck Euphémie Daguilh, moi favorite mistress!

(Cuts a few more steps)

... Yes, mistress cost a fortune. You can't expect them to stay satisfy, content, for whenever you might drop in unless they well-provide for. It's expensive keeping them in a good mood waiting for you to get there. And there ain't nothing more useless than a bad-mood woman avec a pussy with a gripe. You not keeping a mistress-slit to argue with, to make excuses to. You going to get some stroking et some stoking, even if they put on a good act. That's they advantage. They can pretend but our dicks will show us up even with the best of intentions.

Pussy is like war—no matter how easy you go about it, the end got to get vigorous, eventually go at it hard and heavy. No man cums gently. No jissom is shot off lightly. Some friction is nécessaire. Got to rub constant and steady to get a blast. Even if you don't, when time is ripe you gon' lose hold and explode ... Woman stay in charge. Ever in control. Even fake the end. Dress up the outcome. That's why we envy them. Resent them. Mistrust them. With all our muscle they be like a flower and make us too weak to bother ...

(Pauses to retrieve his water gourd; drinks liquor and then water)

I need money! Money not coming in! The treasury almost empty! I order a checkup and find you South Mulattoes not paying your taxes, giving nothing but notes of promise!

(Moves upon the AUDIENCE)

Who the fuck you think you fooling with?! You don't think I don't know you don't have any intention to pay?! You think 'cause I can't read and write that I don't know how to count?! You trying some shit like this when I know you plan to bring that bastard Rigaud back from France?! I will kill you all!

First, I come to Les Cayes and do no more than order every ship search to chop off Rigaud's head if they find him. I go back home to Marchand. Not a month pass than before over army pay you bastards revolt and spread your sickness throughout the district! That is it! Before I let you twits interfere, I will have my horse walk in your blood up to his breastplate! I'm Dessalines, your worst nightmare come true and your dream . . .

(HE begins to change into the first uniform that he originally entered with.)

. . . Send a message to Christophe at Le Cap that I leave for Archaie, where to Port-au-Prince I will send three columns of light infantry and three companies of my Grenadiers, headed-up by Colonel Thomas Jean and Major Gédéon; avec my staff and personal guard I will follow and, behind us—two battalions of the 4th demi-brigade. Advance troops wait by Saint Martin plantation at Pont Rouge. I will join them in the morning after they have got a good night's rest.

(Pausing, deeper in thought)

Un aide of mine once say, "Our Constitution will be writ on the White man's skin for parchment, his skull the inkwell, his blood, the ink and a bayonet the quill to write with!" . . . I say Mulatto backs is the exact spot to carve everything else on top of. I am Dessalines, your worst nightmare come true and your dream! . . .

> (HE continues to dress combat-order resplendent)

Besides old Toussaint, the only one someone I worship is my wife Claire. The smartest most beautiful woman in Haiti. Her old slave-time White mistress-keeper know it and see to it that she get the best education a femme could get in San Domingo. After the revolt she free to have her pick of men, but she choose to try and tame me!

... What the fuck you talk about? "True to her"?—I'm ever true to her. Nobody else in my heart but her! The heat in my groin got nothing to do with her. She the wife tell me what to do—order me, advise me, teach me, chastise me—only she and Toussaint! I'll rip your bowels out for saying I don't respect her! I got nothing I want for—other women don't touch her and what happen between them and me got not a thing rien to do with her! ... Fuck you!

... Five o'clock. Time to move on to Pont Rouge. I'll add troops from the garrisons there before heading into Port-au-Prince and then later lay rebel Les Cayes to waste! When Pétion and his Port-au-Prince breeds see me and the strength of my army, they don't dare think about joining they bastard cousins down South! All need remember who I am: Emperor on the throne but terror upon-the battlefield. I'm General Dessalines! Votre Mauvais Hell-Fire Avenger!

> (Battle-dressed he crosses stage-left to right, subtly simulating riding astraddle his horse and addressing roadside attendees.)

That's right, c'est vrai, all you cultivators 'side the road, you remember. Oui, it's me! Your Supreme Chief! I make you free! I see you too tongue-tied at the sight of me. But you forget never. We fight close together, seem like forever. Remember how you swear to die with me at the siege of Crête-à-Pierrot when I shot the fucking French messenger they sent with a white flag and told 'em I'd blowup the goddamn Fort with the torch lit next to barrels of gunpowder!... Remember? How you fall to your knees in Le Cap like you doing now even though I had come to surrender?... They say you mad at me for making you work too hard, punish you too brutal, but you know since Toussaint that if you don't get a push, you'll wind up doing the chica round the clock without stop. Haiti can't afford that. Napoléon is coming again from 'cross the sea and where will you be if you too weak to stay free?...

???... Colonel Léger, quoi? Why you worry? Each horse-step more field hands come out to greet us, too in awe to talk. They my people—mes enfants, my children. I'm them. Talk like them. Screw like them! No manners like them! Mulatto mutts ici got traitor in them, but niggers true to each other. If anything wrong they'd warn me. Don't worry. Our soldiers 'll be waiting cross the bridge at Pont Rouge ready for inspection...

See, just ahead. What I tell you... See, right 'cross the bridge? There's Gédéon in front of my Grenadiers. Shit! Who can miss him—avec his roly-poly fat self and that red pantaloons of a uniform what make him look like a ship ready to set sail! I need to change that uniform just so he won't look so foolish...

???... Que?... what are you talking about, Léger?... You don't like the look—I know you serve with the fifteenth demi-brigade of Port-au-Prince!... ??? What?... Those troops is from the Sud?!...

What the fuck you talk about! Impossible! How could they be? South troops in revolt?! How could they be here?! Ici, among my men?!... "Halt"...? Who say that?!... Over in the bushes!... "Form a circle"?!... What?!... Who the fuck you bastards?"...

Creep out the bushes, Léger... now start to block the road on all sides!...

It's a ambush! Sacre bleu, it's a ambush! I been betrayed! I been betrayed! It's a ambush! Dogs betray me! . . .

"Open fire"?! "Open fire"! "Open fire"? . . . Why don't you chiens! Why don't you merdes?!

(He lashes out with his riding crop)

Take this! Why don't you? Take this! Can't raise muskets against me, huh? I'll show you how to 'open fire'!

(Fires HIS own pistol)

You still can't do it?! Even avec un bastard rascal dead! Still can't lift your arm against me! Hundred to one! Go ahead and shoot! Coward officers in the bush shout "Open fire"! "Open fire"! . . . What stop you?

Where's Pétion? He behind this, oui? Join his traitor mongrels South, oui? Trick or capture Gédéon and Thomas Jean, correct?! I never trust Mulatto curs!

But I will have you all dead! Mort! Destroy breeds once and for all! I am Dessalines, your worst nightmare come true and your dream!

You cannot kill me. Only in my own dream come real when I see loco-crazy Défilée squat on the ground crying beside the grave where she come each day to put flowers on top and weep. The grave got no mark, it just plain except for the wild flowers she bring. Only she come every day, alone, only by she-self, nobody else . . . and sit . . . But the dream lie! 'Cause you can't kill me. I am emperor! I am invincible! I am Dessalines! I make you forever free! Your nightmare and your dream! You can't kill me! Jamais!

(HE fires a shot)

Get out the way and let my horse through.

(Finally, a shot rings out from the AUDIENCE's direction. HE reacts as if his horse is about to topple over; locating the shooter.)

... Mon dieu, it's a boy ... un petit garçon ... A boy! Only a petit garçon can fire! Not aim straight. Can't shoot me, miss, hit the horse instead, buckling his legs ... Keel him over sur la tête ... Only a petit garçon avec the courage ... Only a boy have the nerve to shoot ... Dessalines ... his dream ...

(DESSALINES keels over slowly to the floor, trapped with one leg beneath the invisible animal. HE attempts vainly to dislodge his leg. During this effort he instinctively lets slip the utterance)

Cochons ... Aidez-moi ... HELP!

(Shortly, HIS body contorts in a MIME-DISPLAY as a fusillade of musket shots pierce his body. HIS physical response is grotesque and gruesome. Finally, after a gigantic, defiant, heroic resistance—at one point HE almost succeeds in overcoming HIS lethal attack, rising almost to HIS feet to take the offensive—HIS torso and limbs finally succumb. Once inert, HE remains still and silent for moments of eternity. LIGHTS then fade slowly.)

END OF PLAY III: DESSALINES

AFTERWORD

"David McCullough,
Martha's Vineyard, Massachusetts
December 6, 1977

Dear Doug,
　　The Haitian Chronicles, this incredible play of yours that you left for me to read, is such a brilliant, terrible assault on every nerve ending, it's such a monstrous and impossible and beautiful piece of work that I've had no idea how to tell you what I feel or think and so I've sat on it all these months and said nothing, and I feel perfectly rotten about that.
　　All I can say now in all honesty is the same as I felt when I first put it down. I'm overwhelmed by your talent. I admire much of the play in ways past describing; your writing, your pace, the gathering momentum of the play are so powerful that I forgot all about where I was or what was happening around me or that you were the writer. There are pages here that literally take your breath away. But oh my God, Doug, how could any audience withstand such an onslaught? How could they take it? I know I couldn't. I would go groping my way out of the theater not because I hated what I was seeing and hearing but because I was being torn to shreds, because I can't survive all that horror.
　　Can we talk about this some time?"

Noted author, historian, lecturer and biographer David McCullough's reaction in the above quoted portion of a letter to me sets the standard for spontaneous, critical assessments of the entire trilogy. His response occurred on Martha's Vineyard, a regular summer vacation destination for me and my family trio. David, and his family maintained a permanent home across from the Agricultural Hall on Music Street in West Tisbury. I sought his opinion upon finishing Play I, The Rise of Toussaint L'Ouverture.

From the moment stage director Michael Schultz implored me to write a play on the Haitian Revolution, I was aware of the many dramas that already existed on the subject, some very good. I thought it might be redundant to add another to the pile and I needed a motive to undertake the project. I first had to absorb what had already been written to convince myself to provide an addition. Once involved, it became important for me to disclose how my decision to proceed came about - a raison d'etre.

Every summer I proceeded to devour everything Michael gave me as well as all the materials I could find on the subject. But the most impressive treatment of the subject matter was CLR James's masterpiece, *The Black Jacobins*. Its Marxist, historical, political and philosophical depth was so superior to all other investigations that it became my touchstone and eventually inspired me to tackle the project in dramatic form. I wasn't interested in the conventional biography of the events but desirous of capturing the social/political dimensions and complexity of this unique revolution.

What you have here in this trilogy of plays is the final result of my effort.

-DTW

First published in the United States of America in 2020 by Boo-Hooray, LLC

160 Broadway, Suite 1110
New York, NY 10038
boo-hooray.com

All rights reserved under Pan American and International Copyright Conventions. No part of this publication may be reproduced,stored in a retrieval system, or transmitted in any form or by any means, electronic, mechanical, photocopying, recording, or otherwise, without prior consent of the publishers.

BOOK DESIGN: MARTHA ORMISTON, MRFA STUDIO

COPY EDITORS: CRAIG KELLER, DIANA WARD

Second printing

℗ 2024, The Estate of Douglas Turner Ward

ISBN: 978-0-578-57611-4

Library of Congress Control Number: 2019913778